Because of You

MATRIMONY! BOOK TWO

BY JO-ANN POWER
WRITING AS CERISE DELAND

DRAGONBLADE PUBLISHING, INC.

ARE YOU SIGNED UP FOR DRAGONBLADE'S BLOG?

You'll get the latest news and information on exclusive giveaways, exclusive excerpts, coming releases, sales, free books, cover reveals and more.

Check out our complete list of authors, too!

No spam, no junk. That's a promise!

Sign Up Here

www.dragonbladepublishing.com

Dearest Reader;

Thank you for your support of a small press. At Dragonblade Publishing, we strive to bring you the highest quality Historical Romance from some of the best authors in the business. Without your support, there is no 'us', so we sincerely hope you adore these stories and find some new favorite authors along the way.

Happy Reading!

CEO, Dragonblade Publishing

Additional Dragonblade Books by Author Cerise Deland

Matrimony! Series
If I Loved You (Book 1)
Because of You (Book 2)

Naughty Ladies Series
Lady, Be Wanton (Book 1)
Lady, Behave (Book 2)
Lady, No More (Book 3)
Lady, You're Mine (Book 4, Novella)

The Lyon's Den Series
The Lyon's Share

Fleet-of-Heart Chronicle
Serving London and environs

NUMBER 19—Volume I. Monday, January 9, 1815. Price~Sixpence Halfpenny
Published Mondays and Fridays

WANTED: Matrimony!

Adverts for Happily-ever-afters!

Frustrated in your search for domestic tranquility? Search no more!

Place your advert with the *Fleet-of-Heart Chronicle*!

News sheet now totally devoted to marital bliss.

Find happiness in a thrice!

Affordable!

Exclusive. Confidential.

The strictest honour observed!

A man in search of an educated wife of refined graces!

January 1, 1815

A man of distinction seeks a lady of grace, good humor, education, and fine character to wed. She would be a plump, fresh person, of pleasing countenance, vigor, and good health and have desire to bear children. The gentleman is of status and can give his wife comforts of home, hearth, and affection. Traveling often to Paris, the German states, and Vienna, he wishes an estimable companion who favors travel. Therefore, his wife should have an excellent command of the French language and culture to complement her husband in his social strata. If she should also display perfection in vocal and instrumental music, that would be ideal.

The gentleman has two charming young daughters who need and desire a loving new mama. The prospective lady should readily agree to rear stepchildren.

The lady need not bring any property with her to the union, only a charming person with feminine instincts to entertain in good spirits her husband's refined social circle.

~Mr. G.R. of London and Kent.

Direct responses to G. Hammond, Publisher, 140 Fleet St., London.

Spinster desires kind, respectful husband!

January 6, 1815

An honorable young lady, twenty-six years of age and a spinster, desires to marry a man who offers kindness and respect to his wife. She has resided for years in the English countryside, but is well educated and speaks excellent French. Her social graces are of the highest order.

Her prospective groom should be of agreeable countenance and established in his business, profession or income. His age should be between 30 and 50 years.

The most excellent references can be given as to character, temperament, and refinement.

Letters should be sent to G. Hammond, Publisher, 140 Fleet St., London with all due speed.

Chapter One

140 Fleet Street
City of London
February 21, 1815

DAISY MOLYNEAUX CHECKED the name on the new wooden shop sign banging against the red brick building and called to her driver that this indeed was her destination. She climbed down from the carriage and caught her leghorn hat from flying away in the gusts off the Thames. Her cerulean-blue woolen gown and matching hat were new, and her attitude trepidatious and resolved. She swallowed hard, plunked her pence into the cab driver's hand—and straightened her spine.

"Up, up, up!" Daisy heard her Aunt d'Harcourt's old injunction. "You get nothing by slouching, *Marguerite. Tu risques gros!* Never can you hide that height of yours. Win! Stand tall."

Indeed. This was where she would make a stand. This was the place. The time. Another fight she must win.

Either she walked into this shop and demanded what she required or she would live forever as she always had. And that, she would not endure.

She licked her lips and strode toward the door of the newspaper office. As she thrust it open, bells above the lintel jingled over her head and she startled at the joyous sound. She blinked. The notes jarred. She was so unused to happiness.

That too would change.

She collected her courage, pausing—and inhaling fragrances of newly cut paper and ink mixed with oils and lumber. The sight of the two large presses brought a smile to her lips. Printing shops were places of comfort, where words became stories and stories folded into books. And books told tales of daring, the triumph of ordinary women, and escapes from prisons of iron—and of the mind. If she'd known she'd be so at ease at once, she might have saved herself her sleeplessness last night in that ramshackle inn in Lambeth.

A woman hurried from the back room, a young child hooked on her hip. She was pretty, with sable-brown hair shot with red, inches shorter than Daisy, and the boy in her arms was no more than three or four, with an imp's grin and fingers covered in black ink. Most of that now marked the lady's plain pink muslin gown.

"Good afternoon!" she bade Daisy. "Please come in. I am Mrs. Hammond. Are you here about the advertisements?"

Daisy smiled, recalling the name of "G. Hammond" on the bottom of the advertisements, the person who was to receive all correspondence. "Yes, yes. I am."

"Forgive me. My son has found a new use for our supply of ink, and I must change. Are you in a hurry? I hate to assist you in this untidy state. Will you wait while I change my gown? Please?"

Oui, naturellement. "Of course." Daisy wasn't leaving until she had what she needed.

"Oh, I do thank you." Mrs. Hammond began to retrace her steps toward the back room, child in hand, then she whirled and said, "I won't be but a minute."

The bells ting-a-linged again.

Mrs. Hammond frowned and turned to welcome her newest visitor. "May I help you?" she asked the woman who rushed inside and pushed the door closed against the wind.

A silver-haired lady with a dove-gray gown and matching dour countenance nodded. "I hope so. I am here to place an advert."

"Wonderful," Mrs. Hammond said. "I will be with you in a minute." Then she disappeared.

The newest customer looked Daisy over as if she were an impediment. "Are you a customer?"

"Yes, madam."

"What sort?" She sashayed near, then sniffed in such a way that Daisy had the impression she was attempting to smell her person.

Très arrogant! Aunt d'Harcourt would have cowed her with her evil eye and shunned her with a rustle of her very fine, very rare Lyon silks. But the last gown in her aunt's famous court collection had gone to the dustbin last week, and Daisy had learned from Aunt d'Harcourt's acidic *hauteur* that one caught more flies with honey.

To the lady, Daisy smiled more in acknowledgement of her aunt's mistakes than at the woman's intrusive words, and said, "A good one."

"Happy?"

"*Pardon?*" She let slip her French pronunciation.

To which the woman examined Daisy with more disdain. Even though the most hated Frenchman of them all was still a resident of the island of Elba in the middle of the Mediterranean, every Englishman or -woman from age eight to eighty-two suspected anyone who sounded French to be Napoleon's collaborator. Daisy was the very opposite of a supporter of the usurper who had dared to crown himself Emperor of the French.

"Are you a happy customer?"

"Yes." *I'm not certain of that yet, but I will not discuss my business with you.*

"Hmmm." The woman mulled over Daisy's brief answer. In impolite inspection, she strolled around one large printing press in the center of the room. She fingered this and that, sighing in her boredom.

Mrs. Hammond, true to her word, appeared a few minutes

later in a bright—unmarked—green wool and greeted Daisy. "Now, I do believe you were first. Would you like to come into my office?"

"I wonder if I might have a word first, madam?"

Mrs. Hammond spun on her rude customer. "This lady arrived first."

"But I have a matter you can deal with quickly."

"Madam. This lady *was* first."

"I simply wish to know if—"

Mrs. Hammond extended a hand toward Daisy even as she stared at her second customer. "This way, if you will, ma'am."

Daisy followed, a smile curling her lips.

Mrs. Hammond offered Daisy a chair before her desk and took her own behind it. In a room that left off toward the rear of this one, Daisy heard an older woman cajoling the child.

"I am the publisher of the *Fleet-of-Heart Chronicle*. How may I help you, madam?"

Mrs. Hammond ran this newspaper. How thrilling. How unusual. Fantastic to think a woman in this city and in this year worked such an enterprise. Oh, to have the means to be in business and to make a living by working with words.

Daisy folded her hands over the top of her reticule. "I am Miss Margaret Molyneaux." She waited. But clearly the woman did not recognize her name. "I responded to one of your advertisements."

"Molyneaux…Molyneaux. Ah! You liked the advertisement placed by a gentleman of the name of… Hmmm… Oh my! It comes to me. Mister…"

"Mr. Ruxton of Kent and London. He opened his advertisement with the words, 'A man of distinction seeks a lady of grace.'"

"Of course. I do recall. Oh my," she said, and frowned. "You corresponded with each other for a while through us, then decided to complete your engagement between yourselves. You did seem well suited." When Daisy did not agree, Mrs. Hammond tipped her head, her hazel eyes much too cheerful—and her attitude increasingly on guard. "You were suited."

"We were." *We are. I thought. But now, I am not certain.*

Mrs. Hammond clasped her hands together. She swallowed hard on some emotion that forced her smile into sharp lines.

Alarm raced through Daisy's veins. "We also set a date. I now have a problem. Mr. Ruxton did not appear at that appointed day and time. In fact, it has been four days since he was to meet me, and I am at a loss as to the cause of his delay."

"I see."

But she didn't. "I need your help, Mrs. Hammond." The woman could not see what this failure to appear at Gunter's Tea Shop was costing Daisy. It wasn't just the money she'd spent to travel to London from Lyme Regis, but all her hope for a new life dying a slow death. "I must settle this. I must talk with Mr. Ruxton to learn if he is for or against the marriage. I cannot stay in London if he will not marry me."

"A problem. Definitely. You...you have come at some expense."

The woman thought Daisy required reimbursement? Nothing so mundane. "I am not in need of the man's money. But an agreement is an agreement."

"Certainly, it is."

Mrs. Hammond wished to avoid discussing something. What was wrong?

Daisy gathered her gumption. "I wish to settle this matter with Mr. Ruxton. You understand, I'm sure, that I've no intention to offend him. But I need an answer as to his desire to marry. You see, I do wish to secure my inheritance with the help of Mr. Ruxton. He promised me that when we wed he would accompany me to my former home and address that situation. I have done much on my own, but I need a man to assist me. One who is my husband. In this country"—she purposely did not state which one—"a woman always needs a man to put pressure upon the law."

"That I do know, Miss Molyneaux. I know it firsthand."

"Then help me, madam. Tell me Mr. Ruxton's address."

"Oh! I've never done that." Mrs. Hammond put one hand to her throat. "I could not break the confidentiality of a client."

"Mrs. Hammond, I ask so that I may go and get the answer I deserve. If Mr. Ruxton has changed his mind, it is only fair and proper that he tell me himself. If you cannot help me, I shall have to resort to some other means."

"I hate to think that you would be so upset as to—"

"I could go to the Bow Street Runners."

"Oh, don't do that!"

"Why?" Daisy had to press her advantage. Runners, she knew, were hired to chase criminals. Document illegal behavior. The English spoke of them with disdain and awe. One did not hire them willy-nilly.

"That…that is so unnecessary."

"Is it? How do I know that you run a legitimate business here? That you promote the connection of those interested in marriage? That you give as you promise? That you are not charging exorbitant prices as a…a trick to take money from unsuspecting strangers? That you are not running some gambling house here?"

"Oh, Miss Molyneaux!" The young lady sat back, fanning herself. "I assure you that we are legitimate."

"Prove it!"

"There is much…so much you do not know."

But you do. "Tell me."

"It is not my place. And I do not know the current news of what has happened. I would be rude, thoughtless, if I even attempted to reveal what little I do know."

Daisy sat back, her insides jumping, but calmly folding her hands over the top of her reticule. She had years of experience dealing with her intractable Aunt d'Harcourt. This lady publisher appeared more considerate than that termagant of her mother's family, but Daisy would always make use of the considerable stamina she'd built winning any argument with her aunt.

Including this important one. "Then give me Mr. Ruxton's address and I will learn the so-called 'current news.'"

Mrs. Hammond bit her lip, nodded, and stood. "I will look in my files for his address."

Daisy beamed. After all, it cost nothing to be gracious in victory.

Chapter Two

No. 3 Chesterfield Street
Mayfair, London

"Pardon me, sir, I know you wished not to be disturbed." Nuttley, the doddering butler, appeared on the carpet before Garrick and frowned. The man was usually jovial as well as obedient—and his lapses into grumpiness tended to be few, if well founded.

Irritated as Garrick was at this intrusion into this week's check of the company's Portuguese and French warehouse records, he could do naught but soothe the man's anxiety. He put down his pencil, closed the black leather portfolio, and removed his spectacles. "Very well, Nuttley. What is it?"

"Well, sir. We have a caller."

"*We?*"

"Most unusual, she is." Nuttley was always blatantly honest, too, about those who appeared at the front door.

"She. I see. Why is she unusual, Nuttley?"

"I do not recognize her name, sir." Nuttley, at the age of eighty-two, had most likely met and received every lord or lady in London since the First Coming. Within his superb brain, he held details about others that even *Debrett's* did not—or could not—publish. In short, he was better than a newspaper and functioned as the Ruxton family's faithful Cerberus at the Gate. "However, I will say, sir, she appears worthy."

Worthy was Nuttley's word that codified whom he approved to enter into the domain of the Eighth Baronet BeauClaire of Ashford. One of the ladies who had called the day before yesterday with her mama to express sympathy had been declared worthy of reception. Garrick had not agreed. The younger woman had once been the love of his life, but he had admitted them and tolerated their feigned concerns for ten minutes. If that.

"Worthy. Well then! We must see her." Garrick rubbed his tired eyes. He'd been at this bookkeeping business all morning. He'd finished the household records of the past two years only yesterday. He still had questions for his uncle about the person to whom large sums of one thousand pounds and more were occasionally paid. This distraction to receive a caller, while not conducive to his gaining any clarity on any of his new questions about goods stolen from his shipping company, was welcome. "Does our caller have a name?"

"She does, sir. Miss Margaret Molyneaux."

That rang no bells for him. "And her reason for calling?"

"She says, sir—" Nuttley, who suffered lately from a new palsy of the mouth, winced as he tried to explain. "She says, sir, she is to call upon Mr. G. Ruxton."

Garrick examined his uncle's infirm man. "And why does she wish to see…ah…Mr. G., eh?"

"Her words, sir. Mr. G. Of her purpose," Nuttley said as he shook his head, "she will not tell me. Though I did persist, and she tells me she has a letter which proves she was promised he would meet her four days ago."

"Meet him? Indeed!"

"Her words, sir."

"Four days ago?"

"Yes, sir. Shall I throw her out?"

Nuttley would like nothing better. If he did not recognize the caller's surname among the upper one hundred, he would deem it his duty to pitch the creature to the curb. Garrick was torn between laughing at the prospect or applauding his servant.

"Why do you think she merits a toss, Nuttley?"

The butler drew himself up into his dignity. A sign, then, the caller was a lunatic. "She insists, sir, she must speak with him. She says—I do quote, sir—'He owes me that courtesy.'"

"My, my." Garrick was flummoxed by that. What was this odd tale here? One to add to that of a London gaming hell taking advantage of the current tragedy for a quick quid? Although this would be the first woman who'd come claiming he himself was to have met her—the graver one was the mystery his friend in Whitehall had lately brought to Garrick's attention.

"Where is she, Nuttley?" The old man often showed the less respectable to the nightwatchman's cubicle off the foyer. Cooling their heels in that tight space, a few charlatans had gotten cold feet and fled before they formally asked for their due.

"The front parlor, sir."

So she was a good actress and merited the salon for her skills. "And you told her nothing about…hmmm… 'Mr. G. Ruxton'?"

"No, sir."

"Good." Garrick rolled down his shirt sleeves, buttoned his waistcoat, then reached for his frock coat. "I will see her."

DAISY FIDGETED. NOT her best action, considering the circumstances, but she could not contain herself. Her moment of truth—indeed, her moment of consequence—had arrived, and just to look around the pristine appointments of this home, she was impressed.

And you must not be. He is just a man who has a home of his own.

Exactly what she had hoped for.

A man worthy of her. One who afforded such luxury. The blue watermarked silk settees. The apple-green damask Rococo chairs at either side of the alabaster fireplace. The *trompe l'oeil* lilies and ivy climbing the far wall.

She could hope this man had the steady income to go with this display of wealth. That he had friends who had helped him achieve such success. That he still needed a wife to help him raise his two daughters. And that her own knowledge of history, flowers, watercolors, and French still recommended her to him.

Who was he? This man who lived amid this splendor? One who might still take one look at her, her height, her long French nose, and excuse himself from the offer he had made?

What was taking him so long?

Punctuality was the height of good manners. Had he any to accompany his wealth?

She wrung her hands. Her gloves were clammy with her perspiration. Not ladylike to be so anguished. How could she offer her hand in greeting?

She yanked off one glove, then the other.

Oh, where is he? I must finish this!

The doors clicked open, and she whirled toward her fate.

"Miss Molyneaux," said the creature who appeared upon the threshold. He filled the doorway. Framed, as if by a master portraitist, he was the perfect picture of a dark Apollo. Tall. Taller than she. Even at this distance, she could see he had inches on her. Broad of shoulder. A man of muscle and might. An angular face, straight, strong nose, and blunt, square jaw. And lips that showed humanity and humor. Such men were rare. Save the bold, handsome smithy in her village whose forearms inspired poetry in all the local girls. "Miss Molyneaux?"

"*Oui, monsieur.*"

That took him aback.

She had gone to French *again*! She bit her lower lip. Why could she not tame her tendency to fall back into her native tongue? Surprise always rattled her.

And he was a marvelous shock. Mr. G. Ruxton in the flesh was a mouth-watering mountain of a man. Delicious and—

Evidently, no less surprised than she.

He blinked, clearing his vision to find a finer definition of her. What was the better English word? *Study.* He studied her as he satisfied his curiosity with a long examination of her person. From her hair—white curls of which had infuriatingly escaped her chignon and hat—to her lips, her long walking coat and sturdy half-boots, then back up again, he absorbed her. She quivered under the inquiry of his iridescent gaze.

He strode two steps nearer. "You are French, *mademoiselle?*"

Had he noted in that perusal of his that she wore no wedding ring? Just so. She inhaled, applauding his powers of observation. "By blood, *oui, monsieur.* By circumstance, however, I am English. Or have been since I was six and fled to this country with my family."

He extended his hand toward one of the two luxurious blue silk settees. "Please. You've come to call on Mr. Ruxton?"

Was he not her man? "I have."

"Do sit," he invited her.

Confused, she took the settee and sank into plush comfort.

He stood before her, a tension to him that spoke of a façade of nonchalance. "I am Mr. Ruxton."

She swallowed at the odd rush of warm flutters in her stomach. This was the man who answered her advertisement? He must bear some impediment, hidden and rare, which drove women away. To look at him was a gift no female in her right mind would turn from without good reason. Whatever that was, it certainly escaped her.

"Mr. Garrick Ruxton."

"Oh." *Incroyable.* How did one imagine such a striking man as one's companion through life? One who advertised for a spouse, at that. Surely, with such looks, he could not possibly be wise or witty, educated, or even…honorable in his dealings. That would be too much to ask.

So near she could see that his eyes, large and curious, were the most beautiful sparkling color. That of foam upon waves of the sea off Étretat. He winced in confusion, his inky lashes fluttering at her. "Do you seek me, *mademoiselle?*"

"I do." She frowned, anger seeping into her awareness and straightening her spine. She, the afflicted, the deserted. He, the rich, the rude. Anger poured out of her. "Yes, sir, I do. You were to meet me four days ago at a tea shop. You chose it. Gunter's in Berkeley Square. At three o'clock, sir. And you did not appear. I waited, sir. I waited for more than two hours, but then left. I assumed I had, for some reason, gotten the days mixed. Or you had. I returned the following day at three. Again, you did not appear. I remained for one hour and departed. The next day was Sunday, but I returned, nonetheless. But, of course, you did not appear then, either. And now, unless you give me good apology and reason, I will return home, sir. I will pay my fees at the carriage inn where I have roomed these past few nights. I do have enough money to pay my way, so do not assume I come to beg money of you. Never would I do that.

"But I do need something else. I think it only fair. I called upon Mrs. Hammond at the *Chronicle*'s offices this morning and begged of her your address. I find it very discourteous of you, sir, to not have appeared. An explanation is most necessary. As you did promise to meet me. And after all you had written to me, sir, and asked of me, as well, I do require some salve to the wound of your rejection."

There, she'd confronted him. She straightened her spine and gave him the *hauteur* emulating her indomitable Aunt d'Harcourt. True, every word. Some of them bitter, yes, they were. But he deserved it, for he seemed of right mind and of good health. And if he performed these sorts of shenanigans on many ladies, he would know now that a woman should not be so abused.

He had sunk to the opposite settee as she spoke and had not moved a magnificent muscle as she berated him.

"I see," he said again, though it was clear by the look on his face that he understood little of her condition. "I agree that you do indeed deserve an explanation. A meeting, certainly, was not possible. A note to tell you of that impossibility was well deserved."

That irritated her. He took no responsibility for this? Absurd! He spoke in vague terms she knew all too well. It was the rhetoric of her Uncle d'Harcourt when he wished to elude accountability for his actions.

She had long since been done with such hypocrisy. It offered no explanations, no apologies, and worse, not even any excuses. Her uncle had died, blustering and incapable of any humility. So too his foolhardy sons, her two cousins. Even her father had used such rhetoric. Of all her family, only her aunt had survived to older age to demonstrate to Daisy the silliness of indirect discourse. The rage it inspired in her and the toll it took on her sanity had been enormous. She would not allow Mr. Ruxton to get away with that.

"Why, then, did you not come or send me a letter, sir? You were most rude."

"Miss Molyneaux." He put a hand to his forehead, then gazed sorrowfully at her as she shook his head. "There is a great mistake here."

Done by you. Oui. *Claim it!* "What?"

"I believe that you may have believed you were to meet my uncle."

"Believe? Sir, I… What? *Your uncle?*"

"You must have been meant to meet Mr. Daniel Ruxton. I must ask him, but it must be so. I see no other explanation."

That threw her off balance. "What do you mean?"

"Daniel Ruxton is my uncle."

"Why would I want to meet your uncle if his letters were signed as Mr. G. Ruxton?"

"My uncle is a prominent man in London. In politics and Society. He conducts much of his private business under assumed names. He's done it before. I do apologize, *mademoiselle.* This is very disturbing, I know. Allow me to introduce myself properly. I am Garrick Ruxton."

"But…Daniel. He is the one I was to meet?"

"It must be so, miss, for I have only just arrived in London five weeks ago, and I planned no such meeting with you or anyone. Furthermore, I know nothing of this *Chronicle*. A newspaper, is it?"

"It is. Yes. But...but why is Mr. Daniel Ruxton not here receiving me?"

"Miss Molyneaux, my uncle is indisposed. He has been for more than ten days."

"He's ill." Logical, then, that he'd failed to write and to appear. Logical too was Mrs. Hammond's reaction to her questions. "I hope his malady is not very serious. Is it?"

"Indeed, Miss Molyneaux. He is quite incapacitated. You see, he was on his way home from a meeting one afternoon when he was trampled by a runaway carriage."

"No!" She caught her breath. *Carriages. Runaway horses. Their cries. The worst.* She shook her head. "How terrible. How is he?"

"He has lost his left leg. Crushed in the melee. Our surgeon has amputated the limb. We question now if he will live."

"Oh, this is horrible. The loss of... What a tragedy. I...I wish to convey my sincere regards for his recovery. Oh my. Carriages...carriages are dangerous." Her throat closed. Tears burned her eyes. The cries of horses caught and flailing rose in her ears. *Oh, how they scream.*

She could not see. Her heart pounded. She reached over and fumbled inside her reticule for a handkerchief. But before her poor fingers could find her own, one was tucked into her hand. *"Merci. Merci."*

"Miss Molyneaux?"

She stared at... Who...who was he?

"You are not well!" He went to his knees before her. Pressing the back of one hand to her forehead, he regarded her with fright. His gaze—luminous seafoam green—delved into hers.

"No, I..." She shut her eyes to the vision of one gray Percheron, his legs pawing the air, and their coachman who fell upon him, torn by the sharp points of his hooves and the knives of the mob. She put her hands over her ears.

He caught her hands and clasped them to her lap. "Look at me. Look at me."

She shook her head.

"Me! Here. No, no, no. Don't swoon." He worked at her bonnet and tore the hat away. Then he was loosening the frog that held her coat closed. Her gown had two buttons, and he undid those. Her hair he brushed back over her shoulder. "Air. Breathe. Deeply. Yes. Yes. Again."

She grabbed huge gasps of good air. Following him in imitation, she closed her eyes and came back. She was in a salon. Of blue and green with ivy upon the walls. So like *Maman*'s gay citron breakfast room.

Why did she remember that room above all others in their chateau?

The color. The color of sun.

"Better?" asked this kind man on his knees before her.

"I… *Oui*. Yes, yes, I am." She straightened. Licked her lips.

He had threaded his fingers through her hair near her ear.

Why? Why was she anxious? Oh, *La Terreur. Oui.*

She shouldn't have her hair down in disarray in front of a strange man. What was wrong with her? And with him, to be so bold?

"We are in Mayfair," he crooned, and cupped her cheek. "Listen to me. We are in Mayfair. You are safe and here. Here… Just here."

"Yes, yes. I am with you," she whispered, finding herself in this glorious salon and in her right mind, discovering her embarrassment to have lapsed into the nightmare of the past. She'd rarely done that these past few years. Why now? *Why?* Of course, the talk of accidents with horses. "I—I do apologize, sir. I do not usually drop into such a… What do you call it here? A black study."

"Black. Brown. Matters not. It is a memory you recall with sight and sound and—"

"Smell. The odors of horses and men bleeding and... Oh!" She sat taller and pressed her lips together. "You think me fit for your Bethlehem."

"No, certainly not!" He took both her hands again, and the warmth of his tender touch soothed her. "You have had a shock."

"Years ago. Your...your story of your uncle and the carriages took me back."

"Clearly. Sit here. Do not move. I will have tea and brandy sent."

"Oh, no. I assure you that—"

"And I assure you, Miss Molyneaux, I would be the worst scoundrel in London if I allowed you to leave us here today without some refreshment after such an episode of anguish." He raised both palms in warning as he rose and backed away, then headed for the bellpull by the draperies.

For long moments, they regarded each other with tenuous smiles. Then the old butler appeared on the threshold. At once, Mr. Ruxton allowed his man entry to stand upon the sky-blue Aubusson. The rug, with its cerulean and cream scrolls rich with embellishments, gave the effect of the old man standing on a cloud.

"Nuttley," Mr. Garrick Ruxton said, "a tray for us. Tea, sandwiches, brandy. Anything else you wish, Miss Molyneaux?"

Nuttley—a little man whose hands and head shook with St. Vitus' dance—regarded her with a paternal smile and a question in his cloudy eyes. "Cook has a very good cake today, miss."

She adored cake. How could this little man know that? The perception of British butlers astonished her. "I would enjoy that."

He seemed to float on air at his successful guess and tried for another. "A nice white wine from Bony's favorite vineyard?"

"Champagne?" she asked with bubbles of hope in her heart. She'd had a glass last week at her friend Christine Duvalier's house in celebration of Daisy's coming nuptials.

"We do have a bottle of that," he told her, and of Mr. Ruxton, he asked, "Anything else, sir?"

"No, that's all for now, Nuttley."

"You are most kind," she told her host as the servant departed. "And I have intruded. I do beg your pardon. I had no idea Mr. Ruxton was injured."

"Sir Daniel," Garrick said with a tone of polite correction.

She tipped her head. "Excuse me?"

"My uncle is Sir Daniel Ruxton, Baronet Ruxton. Eighth of his line."

"Forgive me. I had no idea."

He walked toward her and took the settee opposite. An arm flung across the back, crossing one leg over the other, he regarded her. His perusal this time was friendlier than before, but inquisitive. "You truly have no idea who my uncle is?"

She knew not what his phrasing implied. She told him what she could. "I do know that he wrote to me for weeks. That he is a widower with two young daughters whom he loves dearly. That he wishes for himself to have a normal life again, which, since the death of his wife, he has not enjoyed."

With knitted brows, he took that in as if he weighed it in his heart. "My uncle is a kind man, a good one, Miss Molyneaux. He does suffer with this injury. I will tell you that. We do pray for his recovery."

"As do I, sir. As do I. Oh, not…not because I wish an apology. Not now. But because one should not suffer so dearly. Life is difficult enough without…without chaos." And now chaos was hers. If Sir Daniel did not marry her, chaos was once again hers.

"Just so." Mr. Ruxton pressed his hands together. "I gather you understand that well."

She stared at him. "I do."

He inclined his head toward her. "The chaos of your particular memories."

She flinched. Her particular memories. She successfully hid them most of the time.

"The Terror?"

"*Oui.*" Would she never escape it? "The Great Terror."

"I must ask, miss, why precisely were my uncle and you to meet at Gunter's?"

"He was to bring me home and—"

"Pardon me." The man blinked. "You would come...*here* with him?"

"That's normal. I mean—"

The man's angelic eyes turned a shocking green. "To live?"

"Well, yes. That is the way."

"You were to be his..." He gazed around the room, looking for a word.

"Wife."

Chapter Three

H E FOUND HIS voice. Of all the surprises of the past months that he could not explain, this staggered him the most. "Tell me that again."

She met his gaze squarely. "Your uncle was to marry me."

Shock froze him. Jealousy inflamed him. Desire for this woman ate away both. What was wrong with him? "Explain that to me, please."

"I know it sounds odd. Even to me, it—"

"Odd?" Where was his logic? "My dear Miss Molyneaux, it is quite ridiculous."

"Not so, sir." She sniffed and patted her reticule in her lap. "I have letters from him. Our complete correspondence."

"Corres—" He fought with himself not to drown in those big brown eyes of hers. She was a contradiction. Dark, fathomless eyes, platinum curls, elegant as a princess, vulnerable as a waif, yet gritty as a Society dragon to claim his uncle would marry her. *No frivolous chit here, but a woman of mettle.* "Correspondence? So he did not know you."

"Nor I him. *C'est vrai.* But we grew to know each other over time in numerous letters. Oh, I don't know much about his current life." Her gaze embraced the décor of the room with a palpable yearning. The lilies and ivy and plaster acanthus leaves that curved around the doorframe. The roaring fireplace. The carpet beneath her dainty boots. "But I grew to like him. He told me of his hope to enliven his daughters' days. How they miss their mother. How he does. How he wishes for a wife to create for his girls the affection and joy his wife did."

"He did love my aunt with all his heart." Their love affair had broken all the rules. They'd fallen in love at first sight. Defied everyone. Ignored the practice to marry for land and money. Though it cost them dearly to run away and wed, they had weathered their families' scorn over the past twelve years and reestablished their standing in the *ton*. Notoriety did not stick to them as they proved over and over that they contributed much to the good of the country. How could Garrick's uncle think to want another?

But I want this one. Mad as it is. Character unknown. Beauty in every line of her exquisite visage. Fortitude in every line of her elegant body.

He ran a hand through his hair. All of this was absurd.

Did desire come so easily? Love so quickly to some? And not at all to others?

Like my parents and brother.

He closed his mind to the past and concentrated on what she'd said. An explanation of how and why she could wed a man she did not know.

"They were quite a match, your uncle and his wife, he told me that. Yes. Wrote of it in eloquent prose, he did. I told him I hoped I might fulfill part of his aspirations for a loving spouse. A helpmate."

Garrick did not believe a word of it. Uncle Daniel was a rational man, apart from the passion with which he adored his wife. How could he suddenly think to marry a woman he did not know? This one—ethereal in beauty and determined in her quest—must have hoodwinked him. Had to. "How did you meet?"

"By letter, of course." She patted her reticule again.

"And when?"

"In January."

"No, no. *Where* did you meet?"

"On the page."

"*What?*"

"Through our words, sir."

He scoffed. Anger at himself had him ready to argue with her. "That is the silliest thing I've ever heard."

She drew back, her large doe eyes wide in affront. "Not so. How one expresses oneself on paper is the essence of the soul."

He scowled at her. *Push the need away, man. She gives too much, too easily.* Pretty words. Pretty diversions. "Why would he do such a thing?"

She rolled both shoulders. "You must ask him."

"I can't."

She glanced toward the hall. "He…is not here?"

"He has difficulty speaking, Miss Molyneaux." He leaned forward to fix her with all the torture he'd endured from the revelations of the past few weeks. Lovely and distractingly stunning as she was, she was a charlatan. *Must be. Then I cannot want to taste her lips, make her laugh, make her sigh in my arms alone. Focus on her words, not her mouth or her lovely eyes or her… No. No!* "My uncle is in agony."

"Oh! Oh, of course. In his condition, yes. I am so very sorry, sir."

Her despair seemed so real. But was she acting? Had he missed something that her beauty and her sweet demeanor had concealed? He mocked his folly. If he became any more aware of her, he'd marry her himself! No, by God. He'd become enamored of a woman within minutes of meeting her once before, and that had been a catastrophe. *This woman is different. So much so. She is here with this ridiculous tale, making this situation worse. Why?*

"Did someone put you up to this?"

She stilled, insulted. "*Absurde!* How dare you!"

He'd angered her. *Good.* He'd push farther. She'd break. "I must know. You have come here with a rare story. Sporting your claims that my Uncle Daniel would marry you."

"They are not, as you call them, 'my claims'! They are the truth!"

He nodded to her reticule. His anger, an emotion he had learned to take the utmost care to control, burned hot in his head. "Prove it."

She clutched her reticule to her chest. "I would be a fool to give them to you."

"Show me one. Just one."

She shot backward, fright undoing her.

The gentleman inside him flinched at his attack. "I apologize. Will you please…please show me one of his letters?"

She cocked a long blonde brow. "Otherwise?"

He sighed. "Otherwise, I shall have Nuttley show you to the door."

"Why?" She arched her back in such a way that she pulled around her an invisible, but impenetrable, shield. "Are you too weak to do it yourself?"

Very well. He deserved that. But he had seen her measure his shoulders with her gaze. She had sized him up in many ways, hadn't she? That came from years of analyzing others. Probably as a matter of survival, too. Acceptance conquered his pique. Humor arrived and curved his lips. "I apologize. Years ago I learned anger gets me nowhere. You try me."

"No less than you do me, sir."

He put out his hand. "Show me one letter. One. Please."

Nuttley appeared at the open door. He carried a silver tray laden with food and drinks in hand. His little bald head wobbled back and forth as he examined the two in the room. "S-sir? Shall I?"

"Come forth, Nuttley. The lady will have champagne. I shall have a brandy. A large pour."

"Y-yes, sir." The man went about his duties with haste. He gave Miss Molyneaux a plate with a selection of sandwiches and tarts, plus her bubbly white wine. Only after he finished by serving Garrick a tumbler filled to the rim did he bow briefly and head for the door. There, he paused and tipped his head at Garrick in question.

"Do leave us in privacy, Nuttley." Garrick took a long, satisfying slug of his drink as the little man closed both doors upon them.

She put down her plate and his handkerchief beside it on the deal table. Then she dusted her hands on a small serviette and dug in her leather reticule. He heard the thud of this and the slide of that. Finally, there was a crinkle of paper.

He watched her hands, her long fingers sorting all that she extracted from her case and set to the cushions. Why should he appreciate her fingers at work? And wonder how they would feel on his…

Hell. He took another sip. The brandy gave him a rush that washed away the fascination with her fingers. *Dear God.* He was going crazy with all the mysteries thrown at him! *Concentrate, man!*

What she finally dug from her case shocked him. Letters, bound in red ribbons. Dozens and dozens of letters.

She pulled the first one and handed it over. "You can see by his date that it was sent in January."

He unfolded the parchment. Good stuff. And to his shock, it was a missive on his uncle's formal stationery and in his handwriting. Bold scrawling and slanted upward to the right. As Uncle Daniel wrote, always. Even curving the letter "s" poorly so that recognizing a word with it was difficult.

Garrick took the chair near her once more and stared at her. "It is his."

She nodded.

He handed it back to her. "Put it away. Please give me another." He pointed toward the end of her stack. "One that talks of wedding plans."

She regarded him with a wary eye.

"I promise to return it." He put out his hand.

She thought it over for a good, long minute, then fished from her pile another.

He sat back to read it. Written on the first of February. Daniel told her of his wife, Emily. How he had adored her. How he wished he might offer her half the love he had borne for his wife. But he would be realistic and not promise what he might never give her. He wanted to know, however, that as his new wife, she could devote herself to his two daughters. Ages eight and six, the girls were at a tender age, and they pined for their lost mother.

One passage struck Garrick for its poignancy, and he had to reread it to get the tears from his eyes.

Tell me of your capacity to love, mademoiselle. You have suffered so much at the loss of your home and the terrible way you lost your family. Rioters and mobs can be hard to forget, especially if they have hurt your loved ones. Can I be assured that you can shower my daughters with the peace and serenity and the joy of love which you may not have enjoyed yourself?

Garrick let the letter drop to his lap. He regarded before him this woman, this stranger, this *émigré* who as a child had escaped the horrors of mobs armed with picks and knives. Compassion for her that was new and ripe with sorrow swept through him. She was a young woman made of courage, fired in tragedy, fortified and ennobled by it.

"What do you read, Mr. Ruxton, that brings such sadness to your countenance?" She met his gaze with the same sympathy he bore her.

"You must have been able to convince him of your ability to rear his daughters with the love and grace they missed."

"I did not think of it as convincing him."

"I am at a loss, *mademoiselle.*" He lifted both hands then let them drop to his lap. "My uncle is in severe distress. He should not marry. I doubt he would even be aware of what he did if he were to affirm his desire to do so. I doubt any clergyman would permit it. Not in his condition."

She lowered her head, her body still. Then, as a flood breaks a dam little by little until a torrent overflows all before it, she shook and sobbed her heart out.

"Oh, my dear Miss Molyneaux." God, what was he to do with her so bereft? Her anguish sank into him and melted every reserve away. He went to her side and gathered her to him. In the shelter of his arms, she let herself go even more and met his embrace with her own. There she sat, with her head against his chest as she cried out her sorrow and he stroked her unbound hair down her back. She was slim, but strong, her breasts large and warm, and as he came to his senses, he felt the obvious male attraction he had for her grow. Significantly. And embarrassingly so.

Shocked, stricken by his forwardness, he gradually held her away from him. But by heavens, he was loath to let her go.

"*Je suis désolé, monsieur,*" she whispered as she shrank from his touch, nervous and shy at her raw emotions. She swiped furiously at her tears with her fingers. "I appreciate your aid."

He picked up his handkerchief near her plate and handed it over.

"*Merci.*" She took it and sat back to regard him with sweet, sad eyes. "I must leave. I do thank you for your time and your explanation. Please…please convey to Mr. Ruxton—excuse me, Sir Daniel—my best wishes for his recovery."

She tried to say more, but her lovely lips shook with her despair.

He grasped her hands in his. "Allow me to have our carriage take you to your lodgings."

She swallowed hard to keep her tears from falling once more. "I cannot allow you to do that."

"Why not? A small courtesy from us to you. Allow it, Mademoiselle Molyneaux. Please."

She bit her lip and nodded. "I would like that. Greatly."

"Good. I will get Nuttley to notify our groom. May I offer you more champagne while we wait?"

She smiled through her misery, her lovely mouth quivering in the attempt.

"Have you had luncheon?"

Her chocolate eyes went wide with affront.

"I meant nothing by it. Only help. You liked Cook's cake, and so I thought…"

"I see. Yes. Kind of you. So, perhaps, another slice? While we wait?" she asked with a laugh that brought only a cascade of tears.

He was beside himself with misery. He had hurt her, insulted her, cajoled her, and now there was this immense suffering that she seemed unable to control. Or escape.

Damn. He hated it when he could not help a woman.

"Perhaps you'd like to refresh yourself upstairs. In one of the bedrooms?" He indicated her hair on her shoulders and her hat on the floor. He rushed to bend and pick it up. God, he'd not only undressed her today, he'd embraced her like a lover. What was wrong with him? "Forgive me. Here you are."

She took it from him. "Thank you. Yes. I would like to do that. Before…before the cake, *oui*?"

"*Oui.* You will feel better after you do that."

"Will I?" she challenged him on a little laugh.

"I do hope so."

She shot to her feet, and, for the first time so near, he saw her in her statuesque glory.

He rose, and yes, oh, yes. She was but three or four inches shorter than he. He was so very tired of bending over and breaking his back to speak to these tiny English girls. This one, this exquisite French one, would fit so well against his body. Had done already. A symmetry not to be duplicated.

Was he quite mad? Desiring a woman, manhandling a lady minutes after meeting her? He was quite undone with so many problems that he'd thrown his manners to the wind.

He stepped toward the foyer. "Allow me to show you which room."

"Tell me where. I can find it."

Off she went up the central stairs, to return minutes later. She stood before him, her gorgeous pale hair caught up beneath her big leghorn hat. She carried her pretty wool coat, and in her complementary cool blue day gown, she had the figure of a lush creature.

His mouth watered, and he forced down his unruly interest.

"Do come. Have your cake."

She sat. Her tears were gone but her eyes were limpid with her heartbreak. He'd been terrible to make her cry, but she seemed ready to smile and forgive him. For the few minutes, the two of them ate and drank in silence. Indeed, the time cast a pall over them that Garrick wished to dispel and knew not how. If only he could do something more for her. But the only thing he wanted for himself was to keep her. Make her smile. Make her laugh. Here with him.

And that was so very wrong of him.

She finished her cake, used her serviette to pat her plush lips, and rose to her feet.

"Thank you for sharing my uncle's letters with me." His words were a poor excuse for the torment it was to send her away into the harsh world.

She attempted a congenial demeanor, but she struggled to summon the charm of it. She nodded, and he led her down the stairs to the foyer, her coat over his arm. Nuttley awaited them and took her mantle from Garrick. She shrugged into it with her thanks and a firm little smile. Then she bid him *adieu*.

But he could not bear to part from her, and walked out behind her to the street and the open door of his uncle's town carriage.

He shooed away the footman. The man was new, one of three whom Garrick himself had hired after Daniel's accident. All three were from the docks, men whom he'd hired on recommendation from Lord Bellamy, one of his good friends who had hired six a few months ago to protect his wife from thugs.

Garrick assisted her up into the carriage himself, at war with himself about letting her go into the world alone. To an inn, of all places. Her hand was ice cold and stiff, an affirmation of her own apprehensiveness. He did not let her go and tugged at her to look at him. "Tell me one thing."

She examined him slowly as if she were memorizing his features.

"Why would you search for a husband by posting an advertisement in a newspaper?"

"Because the last person in my family had died, and I could remake my life. Your uncle sounded like a man who had given love and received it. Nothing finer could any man or woman wish for than to give and receive love. And I, for once in my life, wished it for myself."

Chapter Four

H E STOOD LIKE a statue watching his carriage roll away with her—and her sentiment echoed in his head like a melody he had forgotten.

He scrubbed a hand down his face. *Not forgotten. Buried.*

How did a young woman who had seen such horrors still have hope that love might transform her days?

I do not. He stepped to the front door, but paused to watch the carriage turn the corner. *Someone loved you. The memory lingers.*

I should have kept you here. Asked you to stay and…

Foolish.

He opened the door and closed it against his remembrances of the only one he knew had truly cared for him. He had this marriage business to discuss with Daniel, and his own regrets of not saving Mademoiselle Molyneaux from her disappointment served only him.

Not lovely, resolute her.

He took the stairs to his uncle's suite two at a time. Since the fellows who rescued Daniel had brought him home from the accident near Whitehall, the household footmen had cleared much of the furniture and the bigger rugs from the bedroom. One chair near a small deal table remained near the far wall. Another, larger chair stood beside the head of the bed. Commanding the center was a huge, draped four-poster reminiscent of the last century. Lying there, buried in covers, was the still figure of his uncle.

Eyes open, Sir Daniel Ruxton watched Garrick approach. He lifted one hand and beckoned to him with two fingers. He was a big man. All the Ruxtons were. Even back to the eleventh century, they were renowned for their size. Normans all. Tall, broad, wielding battle-axes for their masters since before William conquered the Saxons. Before Rollo controlled Normandy. Even as Daniel lay there now, minus one of his long limbs, he was a creature to behold.

Garrick went to press his hand to his uncle's in greeting. Then, as was his wont since the accident ten days ago, he sat in the large wing chair so near the bed that he could talk to his uncle, and Daniel might, with will and strength, whisper back.

"I heard voices," Daniel rasped after the two men looked each other over and Garrick fixed the coverlet over his uncle's chest.

"A lady came to call."

In reply, Daniel only cocked a long, pale brow.

"Her name is Margaret Molyneaux."

"Ah," said Daniel without sound. "Daisy," he murmured with a smile.

Daisy was her name. So appropriate. An elegant flower of a woman. *Daisy.* The name suited her. The pale petals of white-blonde hair and the dark brown velvet eyes. Daisy. Margaret. From the French, Marguerite.

"Bring her up," he said.

"What?" Garrick could not believe his uncle wished that. "I told her. Told her what has happened."

"Not all of it, I hope." Daniel glared at him, and the agitation of it cost him dearly, for he began to sputter and cough.

Garrick shot up and reached for the pitcher of water servants kept at the bedside. He poured and then lifted his uncle beneath his shoulders. "Don't be distressed. Please. Take a drink."

Licking his lips, his uncle lay back with a sigh. His pale blue eyes were riveted to Garrick's. "All of it. Must know."

Garrick took his time. "I did not tell her all. No. Not more than she needed to know. But then, I did not know who she was or if she was truthful. I had a devil of a time making sense of it all."

"Should have told you." Daniel shook his head. "Sorry. Bring her to me."

Garrick had expected his uncle might want that. But he doubted the man had the strength to deal with the issue. Nor did Mademoiselle Molyneaux. Daisy. "She's gone."

"Gone?"

"Yes. I told her about your accident. I had to, Daniel. I needed to make sense to her. I barely made sense of it myself, to be honest."

"I forgot…so much about her. The pain and the morphine…"

"Understandable. Do not distress yourself."

His uncle ran a shaking hand over his brow. "She does not deserve…"

Garrick sighed. "I agree. She seems…a fine woman."

"Tell me." Daniel moved a finger in the air. "Hair. Eyes…all."

Where to begin? "She is…extraordinary."

Daniel closed his eyes and inhaled. "Knew she'd be. How so?"

"Hair the color of fine white wine. A heart-shaped face. Eyes that meet yours with light and the brown of…" Garrick was sounding deranged.

"She's beautiful?"

"Very. More than a daisy. A lily. Rather exotic looking." And, as an afterthought, he added, "Regal."

"She is."

Garrick examined his uncle with sharp regard.

"She is the great-granddaughter of Louis XV."

What? Impossible. "She told you this? I thought the mobs had chased them all down."

His uncle nodded and started to speak but coughed. "Fled. Many ran. Came here or to Scotland."

Many had fled to the German principalities or north to the

Dutch. Garrick sobered at a picture of her as a beautiful child, fleeing, scared, crying. "When they fled, she must have been very young."

Daniel held up six fingers.

"Yes, six years old." Garrick recalled she had said that.

"Get her, Garrick. Bring her." Daniel pointed to his side.

"Why?" That would be cruel. To ask her to return to the sickbed of the man who had raised her hopes of…of what? *To give love and receive it.* "I told her you were in pain. That you are not well."

"You didn't tell her I'd die?"

Half the challenge to staying alive after such an amputation was to believe it possible. "No. The incision is clean. The surgeon says you have no infection. You have a good chance to recover."

"But you know, Garrick, the chances…" His uncle was proud, self-interested, a dedicated businessman, but a realist.

"They are great, Daniel. Great! You have Elizabeth and Susana to live for."

"My girls need…" He coughed then waved away more water. "Those who arranged this accident in the street want me dead, Garrick. You know it." He started to cough again.

This time, Garrick poured more from the pitcher. The talk of an attempt on his uncle's life was the greatest investigation Garrick now faced. Certainly, the missing shipments to the army on the Continent were no daydream. Garrick's friend, Lord Courtenay, who advised the Army Commissariat in Whitehall, had not made that up. Nor the new evidence of his own innocence in the death of Adam Foley that had come to light with the deathbed confession of Viscount Gordonston one month ago. He was besieged with mysteries to solve. He did not need to add to the mix a new wife for his uncle. A wife who might become a widow all too soon. A wife who was a stranger, an exquisitely beautiful stranger.

Daniel grabbed his arm. "Get her. Bring her back."

"That is not fair to her, Daniel. She is already devastated by the news of your health. Let her return to her home in peace."

"No!"

Garrick stared at his uncle. "Why would I do that and torture her more?"

"She needs me. Me! I made her a promise, Garrick. She has suffered. A child of *émigrés*. She's lived here and everyone has left her. She is alone. Get her. Here. Bring her here."

So Daniel knew of her childhood miseries. No wonder he wished to marry her, sight unseen. For all his pride and arrogance, he had a good heart and compassion for others. Especially women who had suffered hardships. "I cannot do that and hurt her more. She was sobbing for you, for herself, for her future. How can I bring her back to let her suffer more?"

"I will marry her."

Garrick's guts twisted at the idea of Daniel touching her. "No! You are in no condition to marry anyone, and you know it."

"She needs protection."

"She lives here in England." Though that was no guarantee of safety.

"No matter. You know it."

He did. Two years ago, four Frenchmen had sailed across the Channel to Bournemouth and found the family of a French viscount in the country. They invaded the house at night, tied all the family, including four children, to chairs, then burned the house down. So Garrick would not argue that point.

Daniel glared at him. "The French hunt…every day."

He was right. Bony was gone to Elba. The Allies controlled the city of Paris and the countryside, but the French had not found peace with each other. They roamed in gangs, pillaged each other's villages, assaulted and killed returning nobles and their families—even now the new French king, Louis XVIII, had promised safety to his many of former courtiers, bestowed their aged titles on them, and returned their lands. But he had no control over his citizens. Twenty years of murdering their own had not sated their revolutionary zeal. Many still paid with their lives.

"Garrick," Daniel whispered, "I promised her."

Garrick stared at his uncle—and suddenly saw the rationale of the man in bed. "And she was to help you."

Daniel closed his eyes.

He did not wish to explain? Garrick set his teeth. He'd have the truth.

"How?" He should not be pushing Daniel to such extremes. His uncle was weak, exhausted, in pain. But Garrick had to hear it in his uncle's own words.

"To be my eyes and ears. To be my new lady in Society. To be mother to my girls."

To be his wife to aid him in becoming the next prime minister. Oh, that Garrick could see. That he could understand. Because for all his uncle's success in business, all his charity, all his recognition in social circles, Sir Daniel Ruxton had one flaming desire—he wanted to be the only man in power. And one could do anything, gain wealth, friends, happiness—his grandfather had taught them all so well—if one had in one's bed an adoring spouse and an eager, inventive lover.

Of the four men in the Ruxton family, only Daniel had been successful in getting a wife who filled those criteria. Garrick's father, Robert, had married for love but soured that marriage with his scandalous liaisons. Garrick's brother John had married a childhood sweetheart and discovered she adored the act of sex so well that she indulged herself with any man she fancied. And as for Garrick himself? Ah, yes, he had cared too quickly and too frivolously. Maribelle had renounced him at the first sign he was to be not so well noted as notorious. It was what a suspicion of murdering a man had done to Garrick's reputation and future prospects.

He shook his head at the probability of Daniel marrying Daisy. "That's noble of you, Uncle, to want to help her, but you must recover first."

"She deserves a husband. You say she's beautiful, kind, and

caring. All to the good."

Garrick could not believe the sacrifice this man so blithely asked of another. This family belief that love was a feeling to be followed at all costs had caused more problems than it solved. And it had all begun when Daniel had run off with a duke's daughter so far above his touch that it had taken years of bowing and scraping to their betters and a small fortune to gain back their *entrée* to polite Society.

Garrick's father's bankruptcy, his brother John's attempt at divorce, and the accusation against Garrick of killing a man six years ago had been disasters to overcome. His uncle had worked tirelessly to burnish the family name, to heal all blemishes the others had caused, but now he might not live to see it shine.

"Why would any woman want to join this family?"

Daniel licked his lips. "My reputation is spotless. Spotless!"

Then why did someone push you into the street ten days ago? No accident, that. How spotless can you be if someone wants you dead? "You have a good reputation with your devotion to your wife. Not the rest of us."

"Your father and brother chose badly. And your choice? Ah. She had no spine."

No wish to flee with me to Portugal as an outcast.

"But this young woman is an *émigré*, Daniel. From the countryside. She may know nothing about our family and our misadventures in love."

"And if she does, she may discount it." Daniel raised his brows. "She has faced more than you and me."

"That may be so, but it is no reason to demand she join a fight she did not anticipate."

"My being a cripple, you mean."

"Your becoming the prime minister, I mean."

"Summon her. I will ask her."

"No."

"Fine," Daniel sputtered with impatience. "Where's my bell? Shit. Get Nuttley."

"No!"

"I will have him do it, boy!"

The insult of a tyrant. Garrick swallowed a retort, put his hands on his hips, and glared at the ceiling. "This is madness."

"Get her." Daniel sank to the pillows, his complexion even more bloodless than before.

"I will. You'll see she will not agree to this." *What person in their right mind would do that?*

"She will. She is mine, Garrick!"

Like hell. She'll marry me! Me! A man who truly wants her for herself is who she deserves. Garrick shot taller, shocked at his own private declaration.

But…that's ridiculous.

He stared at his uncle and cursed, then turned on his heel. Heading for his rooms, he stomped through the hall, slammed his door, and rang for his valet.

Where was his greatcoat?

And where was his sanity?

⇛⇛⇚⇚

THE CARRIAGE, LIKE the house, was a sumptuous vehicle. All damask pillows, thick carpet on the floor, and hefty silk straps to hold as the horses picked up speed.

Daisy sat back, breathing deeply, attempting to quiet her jittery body and disquieted soul. She searched the faces of strangers in the streets. Where was her serenity?

She must find it in her solitude.

To be mine forevermore. No husband. No daughters to care for and rear. No house to administer. No one. No one.

The sun was setting, the gas lamps not yet lit, and in the twilight, the fog lent a hazy aura to the change of day. The wind had turned nasty, buffeting the carriage and howling. Tonight outside it would be freezing, but she hoped the innkeeper might light the fires higher and provide more warmth than last night.

Tomorrow, she would leave early on the first post south. Back to Lyme Regis.

She sagged at her failure here. She did not want to return to that tiny cottage, so full of the ghosts of her bitter family. Her only friend in the small town of Lyme Regis was a happier soul. Christine Duvalier was also an *émigré*, two years older than she but set in her existence as a tutor of French language to many English families' children. Daisy could prevail upon Christine to allow her to be a guest in her little house until she could find a cottage of her own.

But she did not wish to do any of that.

She had planned to go to Molyneaux. Home to the ancient chateau. Home to the stables and kennels. Home to the century-old garden parterre where she'd danced the minuet with her sisters in the fountain and hunted in the lush forests for wildflowers.

Why did she have to go to Lyme Regis?

She sat taller at the rebellious thought. She had her aunt's inheritance. "Yours, girl. Such as it is."

Not much—one hundred and two pounds and a few old jewelry pieces—given what the world had taken from her entire family. But she knew if she took the jewelry to those who traded fine French pieces for cash, she would realize enough to eat well for two or three years.

"A parure of rubies and diamonds is rare, Marguerite. Waste it not on other baubles," her aunt had warned.

Daisy huffed and crossed her arms. "I would buy respect from a husband. But without a man, I could..." *Do what?* Use the money as frugally or foolishly as she wished. She had meant to tell her husband about it. Share it. Use it for her new life.

She still could. Only use it for her own life, alone. *I am capable of that. I am used to...loneliness.*

Until what?

Until I find a position. As governess. For a pittance. Or teach in one of those girls' schools where the only French they wanted their students to learn was court language. As if that would benefit any woman when those outside banging on the doors were men who wished to rape them and carry them off to...

She put a hand over her eyes.

Stop this.

Find a new way. It was best. *A new way. But how? And where?* She could go to the New World. Boston or Baltimore. Except she hated the sea. She clutched at her memory of crossing the Channel so long ago, unable to eat for the waves that churned her stomach and made her gag.

No. She'd not go to the New World. But keep this old one. This very old one would have to do.

Oh, but this was the same argument she'd had with herself before Christmas just after Aunt d'Harcourt died.

The carriage turned a corner and picked up speed.

She inhaled deeply and forced her mind to go blank. This way was best to recover. Best to breathe. *One, two, three, four, five, up to my crown and exhale, one over my forehead, two down my nose, three over my lips...*

Alone now, she no longer fought the blindness. She let it fall over her. The sooner she sat and flowed into it, the sooner reason would return.

She'd been grateful for the champagne. The bubbles were more than inebriating. They helped her to capture the surprise of Mr.—*Sir Daniel's* accident and the results. The horrid results.

That left me alone. Again.

She pressed her lips together. Embarrassed she had cried in front of Mr. Garrick Ruxton, she shook her head and fought the old visions of herself crying when others had died. Her mother on the guillotine. Her father of the ague. Her sister of disappointment. Her aunt of bitterness that wizened her and made her fifty years look like seventy. Grief was a journey. This was another one for her. New for the person she lost, old for the emptiness that dropped over her like a shroud. There had been so many. So very many. And she had survived them all.

Time to go on, Daisy. Time.

In her method that she had devised at age six, she sat and counted the dead in her family on her fingers. One loved one for each finger. Ten. Ten. Gone.

Only I remain.

Only I.

The carriage took a turn, sharp, sharper than it should.

She grabbed the pull.

The carriage swayed. Another approached. She heard their horses wheezing, dragging air into their lungs. One groom at the rear yelled to her coachman. The lashes of reins of horses smarted so loudly that she winced.

A man hollered out to "Move, move!"

That was not her coachman but another.

The carriage swerved left, and the jangle of tack from another coach grew louder.

Daisy leaned forward to look out her window toward the lane and glimpsed an old black hack pulling abreast of her own coach. But it was much too near.

"Over!" yelled the driver of the hack. "Over!"

Her coachman veered even more to the left, to the side of the road. Two ladies in the street yelped and jumped toward the shop windows.

Another hack behind the first approached. As it came even with her, she saw the driver, his florid face fierce as he whipped his horse to run faster and skew his carriage near her coach. Nearer than the first hack.

What were they doing?

Her coachman roared to the hackney to "Move over! Over!"

But they careened down the street, pedestrians shouting and running away from the brace of them, headed for the safety of houses and shops.

"On! On!" her own coachman yelled as he tried to control his horses…but they picked up speed as the second hack kept pace with them and rammed them once and then again.

Her coachman roared at the top of his lungs as the carriage took a sharp turn to the right, and Daisy clutched the handle pull and flew against the wall. In an old recurring dream, she hugged the silken wall as the conveyance slowly, slowly turned on its side. She braced herself, feet and arms out against the fall.

The horses screamed.

The coachman roared his anger.

She tried to sit up. But she was turning, turning, face-first and...

The coach righted with a jolt.

Her teeth clacked together.

A gun fired. A loud, cracking shot. A pistol?

She ducked.

Men shouted—and her coach rumbled to a stop.

She reached for the door latch.

Behind her, someone wrestled with the footman. The coach bounced with the force of their blows.

Her carriage door jiggled. A face appeared at her window. Craggy, dirty, and dark. The man hung on her door, a stranger, flinching in his efforts to pull it open.

"Get him!" yelled someone.

And the man who leered at her through the window was hauled backward. She heard him cry as he hit the cobbles.

She thrust open the door herself and jumped down. One of her footmen pulled her from the carriage and shoved her toward a bake shop window filled with cakes and breads and...

She whirled toward the sound of men grunting, punching each other. Her coachman was dragged from his perch by another assailant. Giving as good as he got, the Ruxton man had a bloody nose, but his attacker sneered and pulled from his boot a knife.

A long, fat, shiny blade.

She set her teeth. A weapon...anything would do. She scanned the street. In the crossroad stood a boy, frozen, peering at the melee, with his broom in his hands.

She ran to him and seized his broom. "A pound for this!" she yelled at him, and ran toward the fellow who had her coachman beneath him, flat to the walk, his knife...his knife...oh, *Mon Dieu*...to his throat. And there, above him, she whacked him on his back and on his head.

He sagged, collapsing on top of her man.

"Good, miss!" He scrambled to his knees and seized her broom. "I'll finish 'im!"

Her two footmen had their two attackers on the ground. Her coachman stood, his broom at the ready, but he had no need. The two were unconscious.

Pedestrians huddled together, murmuring to others, staring at Daisy and her Ruxton servants.

She whirled and stared at the coach. It was scarred, scraped, hooked side by side to an old hack by its wheels.

One of the Ruxton footmen trotted up to her and put his hands to her wrists. "Are you hurt?"

No. She shook her head.

He called to his friend, "Hail another hack, Fred. Miss, are you well?"

She tried to speak around the lump in her throat, but only shook her head and pointed to their coachman.

He was seated on the walk against the window with the pretty iced cakes and shiny brown bread. He had his legs out in front of him, head hanging.

"Oh, hell," yelled the footman. "Roger?" He ran to him.

She stood, weaving a hand through her hair, her gaze on the knife. On the walk. And the coachman... *Is his name Roger?* He moaned, his hand to his forearm, and he bled... *Mon Dieu,* he bled a bright red.

She gagged.

Then staggered toward the coach.

"Oh, miss," moaned the Ruxton man. "Don't—"

She clamped a hand to her mouth.

The fellow caught her up in his arms and set her into their

ruined coach. "We'll return, miss. Soon as we can hail a cab."

She agreed. Of course they should return. Go home. Call the *gendarme*. Get away from these men. Their knives.

"Our man, bleeding, 'e is," he told the other footman as they carried the coachman toward her and put him gently to the floor of the carriage.

She tore off a part of her petticoat. Damn the strong cotton! It came. It ripped, and she bent to bind up the poor man's arm. He'd fainted. All the good. His blood was bright. All down his arm.

She swallowed her need to vomit. His blood…so much of it. Everywhere. Everywhere.

One of the men ran to her, yelling, then stood in the open door and spoke to her. Felt her head. Took her cold hand.

She stared him. *What did he say?* She shook her head and…

Chapter Five

"S IR!" NUTTLEY RAPPED on Garrick's bedroom suite door with an alarming urgency.

"Come in!" Garrick put off his valet's attempt to help him don his greatcoat.

The butler strode through to the bedroom and stood frozen on the threshold, his face white as parchment.

"What's wrong?"

"Sir! An accident. The coach. Gilbert's bleeding. Knifed. Miss Molyneaux, too—"

Daisy? "She's been stabbed?"

"Not certain, sir. But injured. All of them are in the foyer."

Garrick rushed out, motioning for Nuttley to follow. "What happened? Do we know?" he asked as he ran down the stairs.

"No, sir."

Garrick halted at the sight of the bedraggled party. The footman Landry, his blue livery greatcoat ripped, was bent over Gilbert the coachman, who was splayed out on the black and white tile floor. Miller moved toward him with Daisy in his arms. She lay there, dazed, her cheek bloodied, her lips parted, her pale blonde hair hanging in loose waves about her shoulders.

Gilbert blinked up at him, awake, clutching his left arm. A bloody strip of cloth bound his upper arm. "Fine, sir," he kept repeating like a puppet. "Fine."

"The parlor at once for both of them! Nuttley, send a footman for that physician around the corner." Garrick wanted to take Daisy into his own embrace, but she appeared bewildered. Lest she have some internal injury, he dare not jostle her more than necessary. His heart pounding, his thoughts whirling as to the cause of her state, he pointed upward.

Miller followed. Behind him came Landry. They climbed the steps in a column and strode into the sitting room.

"This settee for our lady." Garrick told them. "Gilbert on that one!

Miller arranged his burden carefully on her back. Landry, the other footman, fixed Daisy's skirts properly around her long legs.

Garrick sank to her side, a hand to her cheek. "Nuttley. Ammonia. Smelling salts. Cotton cloths and a salve. Hot tea and biscuits. Get that man here fast. Miller? Landry? Are you harmed?"

Both answered they were well.

Miller talked, but Garrick focused on Daisy. His heart pounding, his mind frozen, he had to see for himself as much as possible that she had not broken any bones, or worse, had bleeding they could not see.

He undid the buttons on Daisy's walking coat and pushed back her soft curls, wild around her face. Her left cheek was grazed and bloodied, but he saw no other wounds. He ran his palms down her arms. They seemed intact. She simply stared at him during his pursuit of the details.

"You'll pardon me for this," he told her and those in the room who'd take surprise at the impropriety, "but I must." She might not understand him, but he did need to learn her condition. Shoving her skirts to her knees, he examined her long legs. She had no broken bones. He turned her hands to and fro and found both badly abraded. Her coat was dirty, and the skirts of her gown, too. But her half-boots were on. New, they were, unscuffed.

So then he cupped her chin and smiled at her. "You are

shocked. Understandable." Recovering his own senses, he asked of Landry, "Tell me how badly Gilbert is hurt."

"He's got the wind knocked out of 'im. Stabbed, he is. But the lady saved him, she did."

What? "And got attacked herself?"

"She went for the bloke, she did, sir. Then swooned. Soon as she clobbered him, sir."

Confused, frightened for her, for his men, Garrick set his jaw and cleared his head. "Tell me all."

Miller, who stood beside him, shuffled his feet and inhaled deeply. "We left 'ere, headed south for the Strand. Traffic was thin. Most were at home for tea or dressing for dinner. The wind picked up and howled at us. Cold, it was, sure. We'd turned to enter the lane to cross the Thames at Westminster Bridge when a hackney ran up so close that our Gilbert had to charge left to avoid him. Close behind came another hack up on us fast. Too fast. Twice our speed, or more. Gilbert shouted at him to move over, but the damn bastard's wheels... Sorry, sir, for the—"

"No, no, go on!"

"Their wheels and ours locked. You could 'ear them grinding round 'n' round together. Gilbert tried to pull away. The other bloke didn't care. Didn't move. Sneered, he did. But we had to turn the corner and nearly went over on our side. Maybe it was then our lady was thrown inside and knocked her head. Don't know. But she's got a lump, sir."

Garrick saw it, a red lump on her forehead swelling as they spoke. "And you? Gilbert? Landry?"

"Gilbert was thrown from the box. I held on to the back for dear life. Landry held on, too. But our lead horse spooked. Reared, 'e did. Took a sudden spring and drew the other horse with him, quick like. Then two men jumped out of the hacks. Came out like snakes and ran at us. One to the coach door."

"To get at Daisy?" *As if they were hiding until they could attack?*

Miller frowned at him. "Aye."

Could they know her? Or is this another attack on us? "Then what happened?"

"We saw our Gilbert were thrown, and Landry and me, we jumped off the back. Our two horses stopped, don't know why, or how, but they did. Stopped at the foot of the bridge. Had nowhere to go with the shafts of the wheels gone and the coach so 'eavy. Landry and me we were fighting with two o' the bully boys and didn't see everything. But one attacked Gilbert and 'ad him down, awful.

"Then our lady? She jumped out! I didn't see all, but she was a witch, I tell ye. Me, I only saw the end of it. But she grabbed a broom from a sweep. Ran back to Gilbert and the fiend who tried to get at her in the carriage. They were punching each other, right smart, on the street, but she stood over 'em and waited, just so, then when the cur rolled on top o' Gilbert, she bashed him on the head. He might be dead. Dunno. He was still down when we left."

"And the others?"

"Me and Landry, we got two o' the four down. The fourth ran. And at the end, the lady, she told me to give the urchin a pound." Miller grinned like a fiend. "Aye, a full pound that boy got! Then, sir, she just stared at me, blank, she was, and poof! She just faded away. I was near 'er when she went down and caught her afore she hit the cobbles. Landry waved down another jarvey, and we all climbed in."

"A miracle you all fit in the cab. Tell me about Gilbert's condition?" Garrick's coachman had been with them for seventeen years. They'd not lose him.

"We got Gilbert in with us, don' know how. He's bleeding, sir. His arm. His head was, too."

Landry looked up at Garrick. "Head wound's stopped now. He's bad, but not to death."

Gilbert mumbled, "Not dead."

"Right you are, man," Landry said with a grin.

Miller chimed in. "No, not to death, thanks to our lady. And Landry got the urchin to stay with the horses and coach. Said he'd pay him two pounds. Ha! The boy wanted to do a jig. Calm, the horses were, when we left."

"And the wreck? The coach? What of it?"

"She's a right mess, sir."

"Does it block the road?"

"No, sir. Two lorry drivers volunteered to hook our coach to their tethers and pull 'er to the side o' the lane. You'll 'ave to decide what to do with 'er. I don' know if she can be saved. Maybe scrapped."

Garrick eyed his man. Breathing heavily, his face scratched, his knuckles bleeding, Miller seemed healthy. But Garrick had seen men keel over minutes or hours after a fall, a fight, or a shock. "And both of you? Landry? Your coat's torn. Miller, what of you, really?"

"Ah, me, sir. Could not kill me with an axe." Miller peered at Daisy on the settee and twirled his hat in his hands. "What do you think of our lady, sir?"

Garrick put his hand to Daisy's right cheek. "We shall see."

Miller, a dark hulk of a man, chewed on his lips. "She acted like a wild woman. Did what she had to to knock out that louse, sir. But she took one look at Gilbert bleedin' and 'er knees gave out."

"How long was she out?" Garrick asked, but knew that anyone who had been out a long time must have hit their head badly.

"A minute. Two. Not long. But she's foggy, sir. Shouldn't let her go ta sleep again. 'Ave to see 'ow she thinks. 'ow her eyes track." He put two fingers near his own eyes and circled them round and round. "I know from fights."

"Of course."

"Otherwise..."

"She may be hurt so badly she may not be able to think clearly."

The horror of it hit Garrick. She was hurt and alone. She had no one, no loved ones to notify. Not in town. Perhaps not in Lyme Regis. *We. We are her only support. And we are responsible for her injuries.*

The wretchedness of that undid him. For many years, he had lived without family close to him. His father and brother had never been stout-hearted supporters of each other or him. Garrick had grown up alone, relying on himself. Without anyone to call upon in times of trouble or sickness, he had coped but not fared well. Those years abroad in Portugal had bled him dry of any haughty desire to live alone, independent, far from England. At twenty-nine, now, he recognized and accepted a yearning to marry and create a family for himself. One that was loving and affectionate, one that would sustain all within it through sickness and health, unto anyone's darkest hour.

He flinched with the wretchedness of such a similar hollow life for this young woman. He had applauded her spirit, and acclaimed however she'd fought to acquire it, but he sorrowed for her as well that she had to endure amid solitude.

Meanwhile, he had to plan how to best care for his servants and clear the carriage from Westminster Bridge.

"Miller, do me a favor and get the other head groom, O'Shea. Have him take the brougham down to the bridge. Tell him to lead another horse and take another groom. O'Shea should decide what to do about the horses and the remains of the carriage."

"Aye, sir. I'll see to it."

"After you send O'Shea on his way, you and Landry sit and have a bite to eat. Ale, too, if you like. And we'll see if Gilbert wants to eat, too. After the physician sees him, though. And that fellow needs to see both of you after he's seen to Miss Molyneaux and Gilbert."

Miller winced. "Oh, no, sir. I don't like them bogeymen pokin' at me!"

"I'd say it's best, Miller. Allow him to examine you. Trained in Scotland, he says. Do it. A favor for me, eh?"

Miller pressed his lips together. "I can, sir. I will. But can I say, sir…?"

Garrick glanced up at him. The man gave the appearance of a rough-and-tumble sort. One who acted first and thought later. "Anything, Miller."

"This was not an accident, sir. Those two hacks knew what they was doing. Together they planned it, I'd make bet on it, Mr. Ruxton."

Miller spoke the very words that had rung in Garrick's mind since he first saw him standing in the foyer with Daisy in his arms.

"I agree, Miller." The idea that someone would plan to kill someone who visited this house and loyal servants was anathema for Garrick. But then, he'd run across ne'er-do-wells in Calais and Porto, those who would slit another man's throat for a flask of wine. "Go, please. And thank you, both of you."

The two men hastened away just as Nuttley reappeared in the sitting room.

The butler carried a tray, cotton cloths piled high, a vial of smelling salts, and a glass bottle of ammonia. "One of the maids arrives shortly, sir, with tea and soup. Biscuits, too."

"That's excellent, Nuttley. Put it all there."

"Sir Daniel heard the ruckus, sir. He asks about it."

"I will go to him when I finish. In the meantime, have a room prepared for Gilbert in the servants' quarters, third floor. And for Miss Molyneaux on the second."

Her sweet brown gaze riveted to his, her lips opening now and then as if to comment on it all, she listened to him. Placing her long, cool fingers on his forearm, she murmured, "Not necessary."

"It is." She'd have the finest they could give her. The family residence would be a start. "Of course she will be most comfortable there. We can best take care of her there, too." Bigger rooms than the servants' top floor. *Nearer me on the second.*

"As you wish, sir. I will inform the maids to freshen the rooms. Is there anything else before I go?"

Garrick rubbed a hand over his forehead. "Take good care of Miller and Landry. See that they eat. Miller is to summon O'Shea and give him my orders, but afterward, he must rest. Landry too. Catch O'Shea before he goes to Westminster Bridge and give him ten…no, twenty pounds. He should pay the two lorry drivers who cleared our coach from the road. And see that the boy, the street sweeper whose broom Miss Molyneaux appropriated, gets a hearty meal. And I hope you paid well the driver of the hired hack."

"Yes, sir. Handsomely."

"Good man."

Garrick unstoppered the vial of smelling salts, took a whiff, and shook his head.

"Anything else, sir?"

"Yes." He cupped Daisy's cheek, his blood boiling that someone had tried to kill her. The lump on her forehead was turning an ugly blue. He'd have them all thrown in gaol for assault, at the very least. "One more errand. Send our footman, Collins, round to Bow Street."

Nuttley drew back, appalled, as if Garrick had just uttered the worst words in the English language. "Sir?"

Daisy reached for his hand, her eyes wide and dark with fright.

"Yes, I know," he said in a consoling tone to her, and gave her an apologetic look.

But to his butler, he said, "Not done to hire a Runner." But after this incident, he needed assistance in his investigation. The financial records of the Ruxton family ships' cargos he did himself. With those, he progressed without help from anyone. He took his time, familiar with expenses and income items, orders and lading bills. So far, he'd found no extreme dip in any cargos. All missing items were a little of this, a trickle of that. Even the more complete records of the business near the St. Katherine's dock offices on the Thames showed nothing unusual. Yet goods went missing along the chain into France, and he hadn't found a wrinkle to reveal the source or rationale for the crime yet.

But the work he'd done investigating Daniel's accident was at an impasse. Daniel remembered nothing of the incident. Garrick had talked to the two witnesses to the scene, and neither man gave him much useful information about the assailant. One said that the man who had bumped into Daniel had a long, skinny face, was of middling height and weight, wore dark clothes, and carried an ivory-handled walking stick. His most unique characteristic, it seemed, was that he had turned to watch Daniel fall to the cobbles, and then run away like the winds of hell were after him.

But this attack on Daisy unnerved Garrick for its audacity. He knew not if Daniel's accident were simply that. And now, if Daisy's were the same. Or if the two were connected. Or why. One thing was clear—for both, he needed help to decipher the events. Bow Street Runners could be hired. He had the money. He certainly had cause. And he knew one of them who was as tenacious as a dog on the scent.

"Nuttley, do not despair. Get me Mr. Thynne."

"The Runner we had when our Mr. Foley died?"

"Thynne is the best there is. I will have him, and rest assured, with good reason. Our man Miller implies this accident was planned. We need a Runner to help us find these scoundrels and bring them to justice. They've run down four people, injured Miss Molyneaux and perhaps more bystanders. They've driven on public roads like madmen in broad daylight. They've destroyed valuable property, frightened and mayhap injured our horses, as well as acted like madmen and scared all of us. I must discover who they are."

And who put them up to this.

DAISY STRUGGLED TO make sense of things. Bow Street. Bow Street. Accident. Words clanged round and round in her head. She snuggled into the tender warmth of a hand. Someone stroked her cheek. Over and over...

Maman?

No. Definitely no. She blinked and viewed the expanse of a white plaster ceiling and, beside her, a ministering angel. Her perfect man with the dark hair and stark, masculine face.

Daring, darling Mr. Ruxton.

"Do not be alarmed! You're safe. Well, too!"

She stared at him. Mr. Ruxton. The one who was so perfect to gaze upon that one could imagine he had just descended from the skies and folded his wings as he took up mortal form. He even made her feel heavenly. She pressed a hand to his to stop him from caressing her face. "Why do this?"

"You're hurt. In the carriage?" he prompted. "On the bridge. Earlier."

She squeezed her eyes shut and thought about a carriage and a…bridge?

"Don't close your eyes." He sounded anxious.

"What? I…I don't remember a bridge." She caught his big, warm hand again. "Stop. Please."

He sat back on his haunches, shaking his head.

"Are you on your knees again?" She could not help but smile at him. Except her head hurt and she winced.

He gave her an answering smile that was as much sympathy as levity. "I am. It seems I find myself often at your service."

"Or…" She glanced at the cloth in his hand and the tray of vials and bottles on the nearby table. "My knight in shining armor."

"I would say that today Mr. Miller is."

Who is Miller? "I like you better."

His unusual eyes struck subtle flame. But he shook his head and hid his appreciation, then raised his cloth, at once somber. "You were struck on the head in our coach when two hackneys ran ours off the road. Then I understand you did yourself and all of us proud by seizing a broom from a street sweeper and pummeling one assailant until he collapsed."

She squinted, trying to fully understand that. "I attacked a man!"

"You did. Felled him, too." He waggled his brows, pride shining in his incomparable green eyes.

"I had...a stick." *Mais oui*, she was proud of herself.

"A broom."

"Yesss! And oh! Did...did your man pay him? That little boy needed money and a meal and perhaps, too, a caring mama."

"Never fear. The boy received your promised pound and even earned two more!"

She frowned, alarmed. "Why? Did he kill one of those fellows who—"

"No. He watches our horses and carriage while two of our men brought you and our coachman home."

Licking her lips, she took her time trying to envision a carriage and two hackneys. She met his gaze, and as her memory cleared, she said, "The coachman?"

"He's upstairs. Being cared for. We will soon have a physician here to examine you and Gilbert and care for you both."

"Oh, he's alive!" She was so happy, she tried to sit up, but her head spun and she groaned.

With two hands to her shoulders, he pressed her down to the settee. Indeed, she was back where she started. In this glorious room so fragrant, so springlike. A memory or a fantasy. Nothing really but happiness she could never reclaim. Not now. Because...*why?*

"Our coachman is indeed alive, and thanks to you. But I caution you not to try to move or exert yourself. Would you like tea or brandy?"

She shook her head. "I...I'm not injured."

"We're not certain. But you feel well, eh?"

She gulped, mentally taking inventory of her body, flexing her fingers and wiggling her toes. "I...I don't hurt anywhere...except my knee. My head, too." She touched her forehead and shrank from it in pain. "My neck hurts."

"Rest, then. Do not move." He touched her cheek when she

closed her eyes. "Keep your eyes open. Look at me."

"Easy to do," she said on a sigh that someone cared about her—and it was he. "A handsome angel come to save me."

He gave a short laugh. "Far from it."

"No one else here," she murmured, and let her eyes linger on his until the light faded and…

"Open them," he urged. "Come now. Be good. Best that way, *mademoiselle*. We need you to stay awake to fight any tendency to go into unconsciousness."

"Oh," she said, and pressed the heel of her hand to her forehead. "Daisy. I am just…Daisy. *Mademoiselle* instead of *princesse*."

"Why?"

"She does not exist." *Not without the deeds.* "Never without the deeds."

He put a hand to her cheek once more, and she covered his hand. His flesh was warm and tender, sweet too. No one had shown her affection in so long. "Who does not exist?"

"*Princesse de Molyneaux.*"

"And who is she?" he asked as if he cajoled a young child.

"Me. Used to be *Maman* before they killed her… I…I have a headache."

He narrowed his gaze on her as if he would carry her away to paradise. "Understandable. Are you hungry?"

"Yes. Thirsty, too."

"Well, you can drink. But we don't want you to move your head if it hurts."

"If…if there was an accident, why am I here? With you?"

"Our man brought you home to us. He thought we could take better care of you than those who run the inn in Lambeth."

She frowned at that logic. *Who was in Lambeth?* It all was so complicated. "Is that true?"

He smiled at her—and oh, how she liked the way his lips curved up in gentle regard of her. "I know so."

"Oh." She closed her eyes again, and he tsked at her to open them. "*Oui, oui!* I am awake. Aware! See?"

"Testy! Here!" he said with humor in his order. "Put this warm cloth on your forehead while we talk."

She took his folded toweling and did as he asked. "Why are you better than… *Qu'est-ce que c'est?* Lambeth?"

"At the inn, they don't know you. I doubt they would have called anyone to see to you. They might've simply put you in your room and left you there alone."

"To die?" Her heart pounded in sudden fright. "Am I going to die?"

"No, no. If you were to do that, it would've happened when the coach overturned."

"Oh my," she breathed, and at once what happened flooded back to her. "It overturned." *Did he say that before?* "And you called for Bow Street? Why?" She'd been pursued in carriages before. Along the river road of the Seine to the coast. To the quay. To the ship. Could it happen to her again? Why? Here and now? "Tell me."

"They come at my request. You must've heard me ask the butler to summon them. The accident you were in was on the road to the Westminster Bridge." He told all his story in clipped sentences.

But this time, she did understand it. Her mind flew to the damaged coach. So sumptuous and lovely. Now ruined. And people running, fleeing them, crying in fright. "My valise. My trunk?"

"At the inn," he said as if just realizing. "Your clothes are at the inn in Lambeth. I had not thought of that."

She nodded, confused again and frowning.

"I'll have someone go round to get them. If you can pen a note? Do you think you are able?"

"Yes, thank you."

"I'll get quill and paper. For now…" He waved before her eyes a little iced roll. "Want a bite of this?"

Her mouth watered. "I do indeed."

He held it close, and she took a satisfying bite.

She licked the crumbs from her lips and noticed how he watched her. Intently. Was she untidy? In her state of injury, was she quite unladylike? Her hand flew to the corner of her mouth. "Am I indelicate?"

"No." He cleared his throat. "Not at all." Then he raised the half-eaten roll before her hungry eyes. "More?"

"Yes, please." And she bit into it, her lips grazing his fingers as she took it all. "Oh, that…" She chewed and swallowed in glee. "*That* is heavenly."

He examined her mouth as though he made to sketch it. Then he flinched and said, "Glad to hear it. More?"

"Another?"

"There is another, yes."

"I am very hungry."

"I think it best," he told her as she munched the remainder of the crunchy pastry with sugary icing, "that you stay here with us. The physician comes soon. He can tell us what you may need to properly recover. And I have one of our footmen and a maid to retrieve your possessions from the Lambeth inn."

"I impose on you," she told him.

"I'd like to do this for you. After all, you suffered from an accident while in our coach. I cannot countenance your recovering in an inn when you will be more comfortable here."

Etiquette demanded she refuse. "I'm supposed to object to your collecting my clothes, Mr. Ruxton. But for the life of me, I don't want to."

He smiled again, and she had that glorious impression of him as an angel, her ministering spirit, come to earth to nurse her and care for her and tease her. "It's probably your training that says no stranger should collect your possessions. But I've explained why we are, and we should, and I will brook no argument."

"Oh." She thought that sounded perfectly reasonable.

"So you are not arguing, are you?"

"No."

"Good. I like a woman who agrees with me." He sent her a

teasing look.

"You are trying to make me laugh."

"I am indeed."

"Why?" She truly was curious.

"I think you are a person who has had too little laughter in her life."

"Ah." *How could he know that?*

"And one who has had too many people to argue with."

She pointed at him. "True."

"So you won't."

"Won't what?" she asked.

"Argue with me."

"No, sir. Not as long as you…"

"What?"

He could gaze at her again as if she were his most prized companion. "As long as you laugh with me."

"That, I am delighted to do, Mademoiselle Molyneaux."

She shook her head. "Daisy," she corrected him. "Merely Daisy."

SHE WAS MORE than "merely Daisy." She was more than their guest. Her uncle's promised bride. She was their responsibility. Hurt because their enemies, whoever they were, had orchestrated an attack. Whether or not they intended to hurt her simply because she was connected with the family was immaterial. They had been vicious. He would, in turn, be ruthless.

He could not let her go to be attacked again. Not by the lunatics who had no compunction about accosting all within the realm of Daniel Ruxton. Not by anyone.

Garrick had to press his uncle for more information about the attack on him and about any enemies he had. He'd avoided it because of Daniel's grave injury. But now, he must add more to his knowledge to investigate and find these culprits and put them down like the rabid beasts they were.

He knocked lightly on the sitting room door and walked through to his uncle's bedroom. The footman in attendance at this hour looked up from his post by the head of the bed and, at Garrick's signal, made to leave.

"Have supper and a rest, Williams. Send the next man up for his watch."

The footman nodded and disappeared.

His uncle had opened his eyes as the young man left.

"How are you?" Garrick asked, and picked up his uncle's wrist to count his pulse. It was faint, but nonetheless steady. A positive sign.

Daniel blinked. "What's the matter? All the noise, running up and down."

Garrick summarized the accident as thoroughly as he could.

Daniel's face lit toward the end of Garrick's tale. "And she hit the bugger with a broom?"

"Saved the day." Garrick beamed at the vision of it. "Hit her head. Maybe bumped her knee. But she fainted afterward. We have that physician here who sees to you and the girls now and then. He'll tell us more."

"Do not let her go."

Garrick inhaled and examined the man who had intended to marry a stranger. Even if they had exchanged letters and sentiments, even if they had been open and honest with each other, Daniel had never been a foolish man. Never cited in gossip sheets. Never hot to gamble. Never wild to lust after women. Never hasty to speculate on investments. Always measured, methodical, and logical. Save for his one rule-breaking elopement with a woman.

Could that be the cause of these mysteries? But how? There was no logical connection from that in Daniel's past to Daisy. Save another thought to marry. And no one knew that, except the two of them. And Daisy, by her own admission, had no living relatives. Had no fortune. Had only a desire to marry and change her life.

If Daniel's so-called accident was planned, who did it? Why? Was that connected to the missing shipments? Revenge? Envy? No connection whatsoever?

Garrick shook his head. How absurd was it all? Garrick had to know. Had to dig.

He sat in the chair the footman had vacated and crossed one leg over the other. "I hope to convince her to stay here, nurse her back to health, and keep her here to protect her."

"Right you are." Daniel lifted a forefinger. "Introduce her to the girls. Get that modiste in Half Moon Street to come and measure and make her a wedding gown. A wardrobe, fit for the lady of the house. Fetch the vicar from St. George's here and tell him we're to have the wedding I planned. Here. Day after tomorrow."

Garrick scoffed. "Surely, you must give up this idea to marry her."

"To protect her, she needs my name."

"Or perhaps that is the very last thing she requires."

"I want her. She is useful. French! She is the best of all who applied. I will have a French wife!"

How is a French wife useful to you? Garrick scowled.

Daniel raised a finger to the air. "I will have her."

No. She is mine. "I won't allow it."

His uncle glared at him. "Don't be ridiculous."

"Far from it."

Daniel set his teeth. "I *will* marry her."

"You need a license for that. Her consent. The clergyman's agreement to officiate at a ceremony for a man so severely injured."

His uncle narrowed his eyes. "You'd deny me this? Why? If I live, and I intend to, I will have her to wife. The best, I tell you, the best for me! If I die? Ahh. You'll inherit the title, the land, the business. What more could you want?"

"The reason…an indication of the cause of the attack on you and now her." Wild thoughts ran through Garrick. Why would Daniel need a French wife? For his politics? That was mad. And why all the mysteries? Beginning with the one of six years ago. "And if there is any connection for those disasters to what I endured with the death of Adam Foley."

"Ba!" His uncle went red with anger, spittle on his lips as he said, "A mess! You did that. You killed him."

Those three words riveted Garrick to his chair. Had Daniel always blamed Garrick for the tragic death of the shipping clerk and neatly covered it up with his suggestion that Garrick go abroad to avoid prosecution? And what of the other startling fact? The deathbed confession of Viscount Gordonston just before Daniel's accident, that he had lied about seeing Garrick push Adam Foley to his death? Who was lying here? Who was doing the manipulating? Was Daniel part of it? Or was Daniel simply now in too much pain and too deeply medicated to know fact from fiction?

But Garrick could not let the moment disappear without comment. He stared at his uncle and into the past that had been years of exile and hell for him. "So…you believed all along that I killed Foley?"

His uncle blinked. "What? What? No. Of course not!"

No?

"I misspoke. Give over, Garrick." He chewed his caked lips. "I'm incapacitated. You have me to your advantage."

You have had me at yours. For how long? Anger climbed into Garrick's head, and he could do little to shake it away. "I never expected nor hoped to inherit your business or your title. That was all to go to any son you sired or to my father or brother. Never me. But there is a reason for this heinous attack on you, Daniel. They wanted to murder you. Look at you! Minus a limb, for Christ's sake! Fighting for your very life! You need to be honest with me. Tell me whom you suspect and why. I cannot search in the dark for every little detail while someone continues to try to destroy us all!"

The haggard man in the bed turned slowly away, his face to the wall. He stayed that way for so long that Garrick thought he may have fallen asleep.

"You are right," his uncle said at long last when he had faced him. "I will list them for you."

A list? More than one person had reason to attack them?

"Lord Kirby."

"The MP for Folkestone? I thought he was your friend. Why would he turn on you?"

"Selfish bugger." Daniel struggled to sit up, and, failing, he cursed. "Long story. But take it as truth—he betrays all his friends. Too much ambition, that fast little boy."

Kirby also wanted to be prime minister? "Politics? He'd kill you for that?"

"People do, you know."

Garrick sighed. There was more to Kirby's enmity than desire for power. Money always was a good motivator. Was it with him? "Who else?"

"Richardson."

"Another MP. Come now! This is supposed to be a civil government."

"He's always had it in for me. Wanted Emily, he did. I took her from him."

A personal grievance about a woman marrying another? Possible, but why now, years after Emily's death and Richardson's own successful marriage? No, it did not calculate.

Why did Garrick not believe the culpability of these two otherwise respectable men?

"Then there is your friend, Courtenay."

This was more preposterous. "Why?"

"His cousin, the Frenchman Durand. His business suffers because of our success."

Durand's business had been smuggling, bringing French goods to England and to the Americas during the wars against

Napoleon. Because of it, he was rich. But few knew Durand was also a spy for Whitehall. "I have known Jacques Durand for years. He's in Calais now, and I hear no news from my men in France he would sabotage Ruxton & Company."

"Beware of him. Look at him. He is not honest. Courtenay would not tell you. If he even knows."

Garrick doubted Courtenay was in the dark about Durand's activities and value to the British war effort. But Garrick would investigate them all. The prices of failure were life or death now. He'd have to work fast. Share this list of three with the Runner he'd hired. Pick up his exam of the company records from the East End docks and new records from recent shipments to and from France. Hire more men to protect the house.

And protect Daisy. Do it myself.

Marry her.

It was what he wanted. *Her.* To be his. Not Daniel's, not now, not ever. To save her from any harm—from the challenges Daniel faced—that was what he wanted.

The promise of it froze him to the chair. But the rightness of it flowed through him like honey.

Daniel glared at him. "I've given you suspects. But I demand a favor in return."

A price. But not Daisy. You cannot have her. Garrick saw clearly now that for everything Daniel had asked of him or given him, he had always extracted a price. Now, to add to the worst of it, he did not trust Daniel at all. "What do you want?"

"You must marry Daisy."

Chapter Six

"SHHH!"

"She's pretty."

"Told you so," declared the child with the deeper voice.

"Yes, but you lie," whispered the younger.

"Do not."

"Do too. Papa said."

"Na-unnh."

Daisy bit her lip to keep from laughing.

"She's waking up," screeched the older.

"No. Oh! Eliza, she's dying."

Daisy did know that was not true. She'd eaten a very good dinner from a tray. Every bit of it, in fact. Drank red wine, too. That was long ago, she knew, because her stomach was growling and she was hungry again. Ever so slowly, she opened one eye.

Two little girls, golden hair in braids, peered at Daisy from the foot of her very large, very elaborate bed.

"Seeeee. Told you. Told you!" The younger one ran for the bedroom door.

"Ooooh," cried the other as she scrambled behind her sister.

"Come back!" Daisy called to them. "Please! Don't go!"

The two—exact duplicates of each other in hair, muslin dresses, and pink pinafores, save for their height—regarded her with wide blue eyes.

"Do come talk to me," she implored them, and patted the empty space on the mattress beside her. "I'm in need of good company, and you two, I wager, are the very best in the house."

"Uncle Garrick says you're his friend," the older one cautiously shared. "Are you? He says that's why he had the sawbones for you."

Daisy grinned. The physician was not a surgeon, but the girl had the right idea about the man's calling. He would have come to see to the coachman, too. That man was recovering nicely, so said that physician, from the beating and knifing he'd taken from the hooligan near the bridge.

"Papa said a lady came to be our new mommy," announced the younger with her back and her palms flat to the door, like some butterfly pinned to a flannel board. "Are you her?"

Daisy sympathized. While the men of the house had been discussing her, these children had gotten their meanings mixed. "I am your guest. For today."

"Not our new mother?" The youngest sounded as though she dearly wished for one.

"I was to be. But now, no. Simply a guest. My name is Daisy. Won't you come and tell me your names?" *Tell me what else the men have said about me.*

"I'm Elizabeth," the older one said with some sass, and stepped toward the bed, fearless. "This is—"

"Susana," offered the younger with a quelling look at her sister. "Susana Alice Ruxton."

"How do you do, Miss Susana Alice Ruxton? And Miss Elizabeth Ruxton. I am Marguerite Adrienne Victoire Molyneaux. But friends call me Daisy. I hope you will too. I am very happy to meet you. Forgive me—I would curtsy, but the physician told me not to get out of bed. I have hurt my knee and my head."

"You have a big bump," said Susana as she pointed to her own forehead.

Daisy nodded. "I have a big headache to match it, too."

"Do you want your breakfast?" Elizabeth offered, coming so

close that Daisy saw she would one day be a beauty. Diamonds, Society here called them. Elizabeth would blind all with her brilliance.

"I would."

"I can tell Nuttley." Elizabeth pointed her thumb toward the hall. "Shall I?"

"Please. What is on offer this morning?"

Susana drifted near with a beatific look on her sweet face. "Sausages. Fried potatoes. Do you like hot chocolate?"

"I do. Is that on this morning's menu?"

"Oh, yes. And for you, Nuttley will bring a pot! A big one!" she announced with the authority of one decades older. "Just say you don't like tea or coffee."

"Susana!" her sister scolded her.

The little girl ignored her sibling. "Will you?"

"Only if both of you drink with me. What do you say?"

Susana clapped in delight.

"Elizabeth?" Daisy asked the reluctant girl.

Disbelief disappeared from the older one's oval face. "Yes. I do like chocolate."

"Wonderful. It's settled, then. Do summon Mr. Nuttley for me, Susana, and we shall have a party. A hot chocolate party, eh?"

Minutes later, Nuttley had come and gone with their requests, returned with the specifically defined breakfast plus three cups and saucers, then left the three young ladies to enjoy Daisy's repast. Just then, another person knocked upon the outside sitting room door.

"That's most likely your Uncle Garrick," Daisy told them as she put down her fork and tugged the bed covers up to her shoulders. *He's come to check on me, just as he did twice in the middle of the night.* "Do let him in."

Susana disappeared to do her bidding and returned, leading into her chamber a man who could not contain his amusement.

"Good morning, Daisy." He bowed elaborately, his rich, dark hair combed slick and wet from his bath, his waistcoat a royal-blue damask and his frock coat a smashing bottle green. He wore buff trousers that fit his form much too well. For the precise fit of his clothes to the span of his shoulders to the definition of his hips and long legs in his pants, she praised the skills of his tailor and the wisdom of heaven to bestow *joie de vivre* on this man. Add to it all, the humor shining in his opalescent eyes brought a smile to her own lips.

In her old, plain muslin nightgown, she wished she looked half as delicious as he. "Good morning to you, sir."

"Garrick." He held up a hand. "If you are Daisy, I am Garrick."

Susana frowned at him, then her, then screwed up her face in question at Elizabeth.

Who shrugged.

"You have a healthy serving of everything, I see." He surveyed the remainder of her eggs, sausage, and bread. To say nothing of her large pot of chocolate.

"I do, thank you. I am ever cheerful when I am afforded good food, excellent accommodations, and delightful company. All treasures, too scarce and too rarely acclaimed by so many who have it in abundance. The girls are ensuring I do it all justice."

"Which they are very good at doing."

Daisy regarded each charming child in turn. "I make use of their expertise."

He barked in laughter. "But now, girls, if you will excuse yourselves, I must speak with Daisy in private."

"She says she's our guest, not our mama," Susana complained. "Why not? Papa said—"

"She is our guest, Susana, yes. Now do run along. I believe you have your lessons to attend to."

"Miss Pearson," said Susana as she sidled over to Garrick and gazed up at him with blue eyes that would one day bewitch a fellow, "is a lemon."

"She is a very good governess," he said in such a manner that Daisy had the distinct impression he and Susana had had this conversation before.

"She's mean, Uncle Garrick." The child knew how to needle. "And one eye wobbles—"

"Now, Susana—"

"But if Papa marries Daisy, *she* can be our governess."

"Susana!" said Elizabeth, and tugged her sister's arm. "Come on. Leave them be."

"No, I want to—"

"Go along, Susana, please." Daisy grinned at her new little friend. "Your uncle and I must talk."

Susana stood, wrinkling up her little nose. "Will you play cards?"

Elizabeth rolled her eyes. "Don't, Daisy. Susana cheats."

Her sister grumbled and crossed her arms. "Do not, Miss Piss."

"Susana!" Garrick gave his niece the evil eye. "Leave."

"I'll come back," said the little mischief maker with a firm nod at Daisy.

"Good, but for now"—Daisy shooed her away—"off you go."

When the door had closed upon them both, Garrick turned toward Daisy with concern lining the edges of his mouth. "You plan to play cards. Fine entertainment. Perhaps you could persuade Susana not to cheat."

"She really does?"

"Indeed. We are constantly buying new decks. Heaven knows what she does with the ones she removes from her hand. Now. How do you feel this morning?"

She inhaled. "Better. Rested, even though I had a visitor at least twice in the middle of the night."

His brows darted high and his eyes twinkled. "I do apologize."

"No need. I enjoyed looking at you in the moonlight."

He blushed.

She laughed. "You are so handsome at every time of day."

"Hmmm. And you have hit your head."

"Whereas you don't like to be complimented."

"Men do not take it well. No. We want to be praised for our wisdom, our power, our strength."

"Whereas women want it always. A man who is blessed with good looks should be told how he affects others. Especially by women."

"A man wants to know he pleases a woman with something more than his looks."

She pointed a finger at him. "Your wisdom, your power, and your strength."

He chuckled. "Exactly. I do apologize for intruding on your rest."

"I knew you were here last night. A presence, benevolent and wise, come to me in the still of the night."

He stared at her, as if he could not have enough of the compliments she spun, but then he caught a breath. "I am concerned about your health. I did not mean to wake you."

"You didn't. Not really," she said in a flight of whimsy. "Each time you appeared, for a moment, I thought I dreamt you."

As if she drew him by invisible cords, he came near. "And I thought you were asleep."

"I played twenty winks."

His eyes danced over her. "Quite well, too."

She made a semblance of a bow. Reality had to brake the fantasy of the moment—and she did it with regret. "Thank you, Garrick. For everything you have done for me. I feel much better and will leave later today after I play a game with the girls."

He frowned at her, a look that told her to never displease him. "You can't."

She cocked a brow. "Can't play?"

"Can't go."

"I certainly mustn't stay here." She yanked the covers higher to her chin. The way he appraised her, as if he drank her inside him, warmed her insides with all those eggs and sausage bits. But the outrageous allure must end. "First of all, isn't it against all propriety for you to be in my bedroom alone—and with the door closed, too?"

He smacked his lips together, marched over to the door connecting her bedroom to her sitting room, and pulled it open. "There. Proper. Now."

"Mr. Ruxton, I have no idea what you are about to order me to do, but I will tell you that I have no intentions of prevailing upon your hospitality any longer than I must. I will hire a hack—"

"No."

"To take me to the nearest postal stop to Lyme—"

"You can't."

She fumed—and continued. "—Regis. And go home."

"I forbid it."

Angry to the roots of her hair, she frowned at him. *"Pardon, je n'ai pas compris?"*

"You must understand. You cannot go. It is too dangerous."

"Explain that to me."

"You perhaps do not remember all that happened to you yesterday. Nor do you know all that happened. I daresay even I do not."

She folded her arms. "Now you speak in riddles."

He watched her covers fall.

She hastened to retrieve them.

He blinked, dragging his gaze upward to fasten it on her lips and, finally, her eyes. "Daisy. You cannot go home. Or go anywhere. The carriage you were in yesterday was attacked by four thugs. I do not know who they are or why they attacked you. But I will learn. It will take me time. I have to investigate. Until we know who it was who drove the carriage to the side of the bridge, it is unsafe for you to go anywhere."

She stared at him. His audacity astonished her. "I am your prisoner?"

"Not that. Not that at all."

"What, then?"

He strode forward, angry, hovering over her like a guardian.

And not an angel, either. "Our guest."

She sputtered in frustration. "I was to be your uncle's wife. Then your castoff. Now I'm your guest? Indefinitely. This is absurd. I will not do it."

She threw back the covers and got to her feet.

And promptly fell into his arms.

SUCH A LUSCIOUS armful of woman he'd not had in many months. And never one as warm and soft, without a corset and yards and yards of fabrics. She thrilled him. "You're hurt. And you're weak. Still."

"Only my knee." She pushed at his chest. "Do put me down, sir."

He fixed her with a dour look.

"Garrick! Garrick, put me down. How's that?"

"Better." He marched with her to the settee opposite her bed and plunked her on it.

"My robe, please," she said, and pointed to the rose-colored cotton draped at the foot of her bed.

He retrieved it and returned, holding it out to her as she shrugged into it and tied the bows at her neckline and her breasts. Her large, lovely…

How could he be thinking of her this way when he had so much more to consider? Her safety. Her health.

Although, to be sure, she looked very healthy, save for the big purple lump on her forehead and whatever was wrong with her knee. She could not stand, but fell into his arms.

He smiled. He shouldn't. But he brightened. "I should be impressing you with the need to stay here, be our guest until I can learn how much at risk you might be."

"Why would I be at risk?" She glared up at him, her arms crossed and her eyes fierce with affront.

He sighed then took the chair near her—and trained his gaze on her large brown eyes. "Very well. Hear me. Yesterday you left in our town coach. It is new, dark green lacquer, and recognizable. To too many. Far too many. The attack of the two cab drivers on the coach was coordinated and deliberate. The cabs carried inside them two more scoundrels, who attacked all of you. One tried to take you from the coach. You could have died."

"But I walloped him with that little boy's very sturdy broom."

"You did. And we are all grateful you did."

"So then?" She raised both her hands in exclamation.

He caught them and said, "Daisy! I will not allow you to make light of this. I do not want anything else to happen to you. Therefore, I deem it vital that you remain as our guest."

"And have you any clues as to the identity of these men?"

They were ruffians, not the men of status and wealth whom Daniel had so quickly listed for him last night as possible perpetrators. "Some."

"Any idea why they would plan such a thing?"

"A few."

She sat back. "Well, then I think you must share them with me."

"That would not be wise."

"Why?" She tipped up her chin, and he noted that even in defiance, she was breathtaking—her brown eyes bright, her platinum hair falling about her shoulders, the well-washed rose muslin robe draped about her curves and showing her pristine complexion to an ivory and pink perfection.

"I don't wish you to be alarmed."

She lifted her brows in a manner that he could only call regal. And it stunned him, humbled him, for he knew now the rightness of that assessment.

"Please listen to me, Daisy. Someone attacked our carriage last night. They must have assumed someone of significance to the family was riding in it. Why else would we bring out the town coach? Cab drivers don't make mistakes like those made last night. Drivers in this town read insignia on the doors. They know the width of streets. They don't crowd vehicles ahead of them or push others to the side."

"That's what happened?"

He'd told her as much yesterday, but she was not in any condition then to make sense of any of it. "Yes. Now I have hired a Bow Street Runner to track down the two hackney drivers."

"He can look for vehicles that have been damaged in just the right ways."

"Exactly," he said. Daisy Molyneaux could think through a problem. He valued that. "I expect results from him today or tomorrow."

"Then afterward I can leave."

"Not then, no."

"Oh, now, why not? You can prosecute them on grounds of assault."

He liked a woman who challenged him. A woman with spirit. And brains. He'd met so few over the years. Even when he returned from his post in Calais, weeks ago, his Uncle Daniel had insisted he meet all the latest beauties of the *ton*. They'd thrilled him as much as dried toast. "I believe that whoever hired the two hacks will strike again until and unless we find him."

She settled into the cushions of the settee. "And why would anyone wish to hire two hacks to attack your new carriage with a family member inside?"

A few possible reasons existed. "The only thing I can think is that someone wishes to hurt my uncle in any way possible. Perhaps that same man or woman has a resentment against him and will use any means to get an ounce of satisfaction."

"Resentments can be large or small. Murderous or petty. I know this firsthand."

He nodded, understanding that one who had lived as an *émigré*, running from French mobs, would know this intimately.

"I fear," he told her with distaste, "someone is big enough for them to try to bankrupt my uncle's shipping company."

She took in his explanation with a calmness that spoke of her own calculation of the complexity of that effort. "This person has been at it for a while, then."

"I must search for the answer to that. It takes me too much time. I must stop this drain of shipments from my warehouses. Here and in France. I must return to Calais, maybe Paris, too. I must match what I learn here with what I can glean there."

"Do you go, then, soon to France?"

"I will. Yes."

Her expression turned ethereal. She was captured by the names of cities. "Oh, you have lived in France. You were there. Did you like it?"

"Very much."

"Have you been to Rouen?"

"We have a small office there, yes."

"Is the town clock still in the old arch above the market-place?"

"It is. Huge and keeps good time."

She seemed to float, filled with pride. "No one tore it down. Good. Very good. The clock has always kept accurate time. The best watchmakers in Paris always take a boat to Rouen with their new timepieces and set them by the *Gros-Horloge*. It has stood there since my great…" She paused and considered her hands in her lap. "My many, many times great-grandfather."

"And what did he do?" he asked to draw her out, encourage her to remember the good things about her family and the past. Something everyone needed to do now and again.

"Ah." She smiled sadly. "He was a Dane, son of a Viking king. In Normandy, we were made dukes by William. Counts by King Phillip."

And princes and princesses? They must have married into the royal houses of the Valois or the Bourbons. She was from a handsome family. He could see it in her. Her bones. Her porcelain skin. Her hair, the stuff of fantasies. Her integrity.

"And where is your home?" he asked.

"South of Rouen and the Seine. The green hills and valleys of Normandy, washed by the rains from the Channel, drenched in the sun of the seaside, where the land is fit for cows and chickens, mushrooms from the loam of the forests, and parsley and basil." She paused, her lips parting as she sank down into her all-too-vivid past. "All the aromas of life wafting to your nostrils on the breezes…"

He could swear he smelled the heady blend of fragrances. "When were you there last?"

"In the autumn, when the leaves turn a rich auburn and the sky is the blue of sapphires."

It made sense if she had returned recently, as many *émigrés* had now that Napoleon was exiled to Elba and a new Bourbon king was on the throne. Had she gone to Paris to reclaim her home? "Have you gone recently? Home? Is it yours?"

The question shook her from her reverie. "Mine?"

"Yes. Have you gained it back?" The new French king, next youngest brother of the murdered Louis XVI, had been welcomed to the throne by the Allies, who had conquered French armies last April and forced Napoleon to abdicate. The new Louis had invited many of his nobles who had fled the country during the Terror and Napoleon's rule to return.

"From Louis? The Eighteenth? Ha." She scoffed. "No."

"I am sorry." Louis had not invited those who had in some way displeased his older brother or himself to return. During the period of the Empire, the heir had lived in little towns in Germany and, at the end, in England. He'd even received a monthly stipend from the prince regent.

"Louis and particularly his younger brother, Charles, did not care for my father." She lifted her face to him, defiance in her eyes and the tilt of her jaw. "My papa fought with the Americans, and when all assembled on the Tennis Court, he wanted a constitution for France. He was in the first assembly and the next. When he was on a mission to Baden for them, the minister of police ordered my mother and my two older brothers put in La Force."

The worst of Parisian prisons. Sentenced there by Police Minister Joseph Fouché, a devious man loyal to no one but himself.

"My uncle, his wife, and my cousin tried to free them, but Fouché would not let them go. We went to the Place de la Bastille the day they took them to the guillotine." She gazed beyond him. "They were brave. So brave. Tall and proud as they were led to the machine."

She had been a child, innocent of the world and naïve of the horrors man imposed on man. He took her hands in his. She was cold, stiff. She had been hurt by so many. He would not have her hurt by his family's anonymous nemesis. To allow her to leave and be caught in a misdirected assault on her person would be as criminal as those who sought to destroy his uncle. "Listen to me, Daisy. I will not have you suffer any more because you know us. I beg you to reconsider and allow me to shelter you here."

"You do not understand me at all, sir."

"I will not let you die."

"I came here to marry. That is true. But I was to marry your uncle for my own purposes."

"As he had his own reasons." *One was that you were French. And I don't understand why that meant anything to him.* "Daniel valued the fact that you were French. Why?"

She rolled a shoulder. "I assumed he valued me, my family, my past."

"You told him all of that?"

"I did. I told him who I was. The only survivor of my family. One steeped in knowledge of that family. Trained to be a lady of the court, even though there was no court. An expert pianist. A lover of books. A…a writer, when I have time and inspiration. But above all, I wished to marry to gain a strong husband who would help me present my case to win back my lands and the chateau. I care naught for the title. Let Louis and his brother keep it. I have the name. It is enough. But the land and my home, they should come to me."

His heart went out to her, and he drew her close to him. She came easily, and he sought to comfort her with more than the shelter of his arm. "It is my understanding that if your peasants agree, the land can return to your family."

She breathed in slowly, despair edging her eyes. "The new king's justices have been very particular with those like my family who were, shall we say, quick to work for a constitutional monarchy. But I must have the deeds in my possession. My father was sure to hide them. I knew where. And old as they are, they are the original grants."

"Without doubt, you should claim them and use them to regain your lands."

"But now, if Sir Daniel is not well..." Her words turned watery.

He would save her. Save himself. Do the noble and just thing. "I can offer you support to help you gain back your land and your home."

"That is kind of you, but you do not understand the fullness of what I require. To fight the French in their courts, I need a man. Because the French have the Salic Law, the Bourbons see a lady as less than she is. I need a man. Specifically, a husband."

He grasped her hands. The French had no respect for women inheriting. But he did. "Then marry me."

In her eyes stood so many emotions that he sat fascinated. Shock, humor, disbelief lit her expression in a kaleidoscope of acceptance and rejection. The flash of lingering delight, however, told him she welcomed the proposal. And him. He was not wrong about her appreciation of him. He was not wrong that she could feel...more for him. As he did for her. Amazing as that was.

She forced herself to sit taller, proud but a little shy with the compliment of his offer. "I must ask why you do this."

"Because it is a very fine idea." He dare not say *because I desire you*. That would shock her. "Because we get on well. We like each other."

"More than most who marry," she affirmed.

He smiled at her. "Yes."

"Does Sir Daniel know you ask me this?"

"He does."

"Why? Because he is so ill? Has his health failed during the night?" She clutched his hands, agitated by the possibility.

"Not because of his health. Because I am the best man to help you." *Better than Daniel. Daniel may want you for a mother to his daughters, perhaps to gain a son, but at his core, I know him. He wants you for a decoration, a social pawn, a piece to sparkle in his parlor. Like a doll. I want you for yourself.* "I know French law. I have dealt with it in many ways the past three years. Not so much about inheritances. But much else."

And besides, I want you. I want you safe and untouched. I want you…touched only by me. I want you whole and healthy, happy. Not by a thug from the streets or by my uncle. I want you with me where I can keep you safe.

"Daisy, will you marry me?"

She sat for a long minute as her eyes filled with tears and her lovely mouth quivered.

His heart dropped to his feet. She would reject him.

"Yes." She gripped his hands in hers and nodded eagerly. "When?"

He picked up her hand and kissed the back. But he wanted more than this. Much more. He needed her to want him completely as her husband and her lover.

He tipped up her chin and quickly took her lips. It was nothing more than a peck, but she came to him, open and willing. As he drifted away, her dark eyes went limpid with want.

She put her long, warm fingers to his nape and drew his lips down to hers once more.

Her kiss was a declaration, a statement of her claim on him, fierce and possessive. When she pulled away, her smile promised more than simple affection. "We should wed soon."

He curled her near, and their bodies melded together like two pieces of a puzzle. "Shall we say day after tomorrow?"

⇥⇥⇥⇤⇤⇤

WITH THAT AGREEMENT, he rose and excused himself to work.

She watched him leave her, and for the first time in her life, she felt honored. An equal, a man she desired, a man of purpose and kindness, wanted her. His words coursed through her veins and gave her courage and hope.

Could she for once in her life have all she desired?

She had only ever yearned for a good man as a husband.

But honor required that she revoke the first man's proposal before acting on the second.

Chapter Seven

A FTER TYING THE ribbons of her robe securely at her neck and waist, she stood and took steps with special care toward the hall. Standing there, hands supporting her on the hall étagère, she tried the stability of her injured knee. She inched along to the door closest to the top of the staircase.

Quietly opening the outer door, she slipped inside. The darkened sitting room and subdued lighting in the bedroom told her this might be Sir Daniel's bedroom. If he were asleep, she would not disturb him.

She paused to gather her wits. Sick rooms, people *in extremis*, hurt, dying, in agony, were not new to her. It seemed as if she had marked each year of her life watching those in her family in the throes of death.

"Tell him you love him, Marguerite."

"Pray for her, Marguerite."

"Come now, to the chapel…"

"Kiss him on the cheek, and say goodbye…"

That last made her tremble the most. For years, after kissing dead siblings and cousins, uncles and aunts in their coffins, she had slept with blankets over her head, her eyes and ears on guard…listening…watching for their ghosts to return and berate her for not wanting to kiss their cold, hard cheeks. She caught a breath, bit her lip, and put a hand to the door.

"*Courage, mon petite.* This one is not dead. No need to kiss him."

She clamped a hand over her mouth and swallowed her repulsion of her past.

They are gone. This man lives.

She stepped to the threshold of the bedroom.

The footman who sat at the head of the bed roused at her appearance. He tipped his head in question.

She raised her brows and glanced toward the bed. He caught her intention to approach.

She was surprised by the figure of the man lying so still. Like his nephew, Sir Daniel was an inordinately big fellow. On his back, head on the pillows, he seemed to sleep. His breathing was slow and deep as she inched forward. He was pale, his skin showing his recent agonies as it stretched over his sharp bones like wet parchment over rocks.

In the flickering light of a dozen or more tapers, she sat. This gave her an opportunity to examine the man she would have married. He, like his nephew, was a very handsome man. The very finely wrought bones of his cheeks and nose and jaw told of him as a Ruxton. A man of strength. Perhaps once he had been a man of ambition and accomplishment.

She had it in his own words that he had built his business of exporting goods to the Continent for the British Army's use. *One day,* he had written to her, *I will be as powerful as the king here and as important as the French king in your country.*

The words signaled a menace to his goals that she'd not perceived before this. Why that should be, she could only attribute to the fact that he lay here hurt. Disabled. And that the cause of that might well be someone's intention to do more than maim him. Furthermore, the attack on her might well be that same person's desire to hurt others in Daniel's family.

"*Mon Dieu,*" she whispered to herself. "*Qu'est-ce qui se passe?*"

Sir Daniel's cool green eyes, so like Garrick's, flicked wide open and locked on hers.

"Daisy. Come," he breathed, and cleared his throat, then coughed as he gazed at the footman. "You…go. Miss Molyneaux will be good company."

"I stand outside, ma'am." The servant dismissed himself with a bow and made a quick exit.

"Sit." Daniel indicated the footman's chair.

As she took it, he looked her over as if he were appraising a piece of jewelry.

She licked her lips and shifted. Such inspection reminded her of her Uncle Lamballe, her mother's cousin, who had run with them to England twenty years ago. He'd lived with them in the tiny cottage they first occupied in Kent, and he tried to seduce every poor girl in the village. By two of them, he sired two children. Neither of them had he ever supported. For years, he'd played the wily libertine, Daisy's aunt—his wife—ridiculing him in her loudest, crudest French. She threw him out after he'd tried to rape Daisy when she was sixteen. A more salacious rooster Daisy had never met.

Daniel reached out his hand and, in a surprise attack, grabbed hers. His hold was too strong, too demanding, like that of a snake. She wiggled far back into the chair, where he could not reach more of her.

"I am so glad you came."

I regret it. I should have waited for Garrick.

"You are lovelier than the poetry of your letters." His cracked lips parted to reveal a lecher's grin. "A lady to impress all."

He spoke with the syrupy charm of a seducer—and she could not run now. Where was her training? Her royal façade? She sat ever more erect and gave him all her reserve. "You are kind. I was eager to see for myself your health. Your accident is a terrible shock to you. I am so pleased you do recover."

"I wish I could marry you myself." He moved his hand, and it fell over her sore knee.

Swallowing her revulsion, she slid beyond his reach. "*Pardon.* That hurts."

"Je suis désolé," he murmured, but his eyes flared with carnal ambitions.

She swallowed her disgust. Was he ever sorry for doing whatever he wished? She doubted it.

"You and I," he crooned, "would have done well together."

She thanked her stars that could not happen. She would show him it could not be. "I met your daughters, sir. They are charming."

"They are. Like their mother, in that, they are." His pale eyes fell to her breasts. In the thin robe and night rail, she had thought she was well covered. But such a man saw through anything to his own desires.

She did not move a hair.

His gaze rose to her hair and lips. "You would have been a treasure to me."

Her stomach turned. She was here to do more than sympathize over his injuries, or worse, subject herself to his flattery. "I hope you approve of this marriage between your nephew and me."

"I do. I suggested it."

"How kind of you." She concealed the shock out of old habit to allow few to see her true feelings. *Marrying me was not Garrick's idea?*

"Prudent of me," he said in a prideful tone. "Yet I am sad not to have you for my own. I know you wish to go to Paris and argue your case for regaining your lands. Garrick can argue. Knows how to attack. He can travel, and I...I will not. Not for a long time, I fear."

Her gaze drifted to the space on the bed where his leg should have made an impression in the coverlet. For that lack, she had compassion for him. No one should suffer so. "I am so sorry this has happened to you."

"I deeply regret I cannot marry you."

But I do not. I prefer Garrick in so many ways. Even if...it was your idea.

She rose to leave, her heart heavier than when she arrived. "I will leave you to rest."

"Wait." He extended his arm.

She did not take his hand.

He noted her rejection, his gaze bright with the threat of reprisal. "We will see more of each other. Much more. Often."

She would make certain that was never so. He was exactly like Uncle Lamballe.

⇛⇚

THAT NIGHT, SHE dressed for dinner. Her knee still gave her a hitch in her gait, but she managed to walk downstairs holding on to the banisters and her newly assigned maid, Cora. Nuttley came to her at the foot of the staircase, smiled with benevolence, and offered his arm to help her navigate to the dining room.

She was happy she had a gown presentable enough to wear. It was not new. But it was of Lyon silk, which her mother had purchased from merchants in that French town and laid into her trunks decades before. The peach silk and white organza gown had been Daisy's finest creation, fitted to her two years ago by an *émigré* French seamstress in Lyme Regis. She'd had reason to wear it once. This afternoon, Cora had pressed the gown as well as petticoats. For the first time in years, Daisy looked like a lady in her own mind as she floated along, knowing that she would be a married woman soon. And one whom she had initially thought was wanted.

And now, with Daniel's statement, she questioned Garrick's motive to marry her. Initially, she found none. But then she pondered the possibility that Garrick may have asked her to thwart Daniel. Though on that, she knew not why. Family relationships left much open to all the raw emotions. She had entered this house and come in the midst of the two men's relationship only days before. She could question anything like this and not learn an answer in years.

Yet as she gained the dining room and saw Garrick standing there, his handsome face lighting up at the sight of her, she could believe he wanted her. And she could test that, if she wished, or simply ignore the question, and become the endearing wife she meant to be when she'd accepted his proposal.

Garrick strode toward her, his gaze that of a man captured by the woman he beheld. She had seen that in a few men's eyes, and she could not mistake fervid desire. Attired in black dinner clothes, her intended was even more appetizing than the aromas floating up from the covered silver salvers. Candelabra stood upon the sideboards, and the flames threw shimmers of gold upon his sun-kissed complexion and the dark waves of his hair. In the subtle shades of evening, he beheld her with a twinkle in his eyes.

He took her arm and lifted her hand as he had that morning, after he proposed. "I hope you do not mind that I have started us here and not in the salon."

She caught sight of the wine bottle in a silver bowl on the sideboard. "You are perceptive, and I believe we have dithered enough over details. I'm hungry too, unfashionable as that is to admit. Speed is a good thing."

"Be quick about anything you wish," he told her. His face wreathed in mirth was a sight she wished to see often in the coming decades. She was so delighted that Garrick's approval of her attire and her person filled her with a sense of pride—as well as a girlish enchantment with her new bridegroom-to-be. So unlike her reaction to the older man who lay upstairs and whose untoward advances had left her sickened that she might once have married him. "Whatever you want, I will support you in it."

Really? She let her heart dance upon the flickering rays of candlelight. His words opened up intriguing possibilities for their future.

She could not hide her approval of that, and so, with arched brows, she grinned at him and took her chair—thankfully, at his right hand. They were to be intimate at dinner. How welcome.

"Shall we have our champagne now?" he asked.

"Let's."

He glanced at a footman, who brought forth the opened bottle and poured for them both.

"You may leave it here, Collins. Miss Molyneaux and I will dine alone."

In England, it was not done to be alone with a man before marriage. But she was not English and not interested in keeping rules that deterred her from the intimacy she now required to learn everything she could about her fiancé.

"Oh, and Collins, do close the doors as you leave."

Privacy, too. Superb. She grinned.

"To you," he said with his crystal held high toward her. "You have braved much to be here."

"To us," she said, and pressed her own glass to his. "You have braved much to persist for your uncle, his children, his business, and even for me. Not many would have done that."

"I will take the compliment, though I must add I have not accomplished much yet." He took a drink.

"For me, you have." She sipped the bubbling wine. "Oh, that's very good. And I must tell you I am very happy."

"I'm glad to hear it." His good humor dwindled. "I want you to know that I will endeavor to be a good husband."

"A promise I match. I would not marry if I did not feel that could be so."

"Many marry with less understanding of each other," he said.

"For money or land. Titles, power. Not for love. Or affection. I hope we can find and keep that. As well as loyalty."

"I can promise you that, Daisy. Fidelity, too. I know the costs of breaking one's wedding vows." He glanced down into his champagne. "My parents were never faithful to each other. Nor were my older brother and his wife. Only Daniel and his wife stand as the shining example of a marriage well made and well kept."

Why or when Daniel became more of a libertine was an issue Daisy pondered then dismissed with rapidity. "I'm glad you have that example. In our family, my parents' marriage was a love match that brought all the benefits of wealth and money and prestige. No one else in their generation can claim such."

"And your generation? Your brothers and sisters?"

She was bereft. "My two brothers died on the guillotine with Mama. My two sisters died here in England of consumption. None of them was old enough to marry. I am the only offspring of my parents still alive."

He reached out to cover her hand with his. "I am so sorry to hear this. You have no family?"

"None." She stared into his sorrowful eyes. "Perhaps a few cousins still alive, but I know not their whereabouts. You will be my family."

He took her fingertips to his lips and blessed them with his kiss. "And you mine."

His promise gave her wings to fly. "We will make a new family," she told him.

"A strong one, and happy," he pledged.

Her next words were ones she would not suppress. "With children, I do hope?"

"With children. As many as we are able."

That affirmed for her his resolve to make theirs a strong union of affection.

If she could have that, she would count it as her success.

And yet…as they sat and conversed and the evening drifted toward its close, she vowed to make a marriage built on more than simple fondness. This man was worthy of love.

She could give it to him.

The only question remained was if she might summon the same from him.

Chapter Eight

February 25, 1815

S HE FLOATED DOWN the staircase to the salon three days later in a gown especially designed for her and made so rapidly she could not believe the skill of the London modiste that Garrick had hastily hired. In a confection of fine ivory tulle over an azure satin slip, Daisy imagined herself a true bride.

She would escape her lonely past, and help her husband do the same. She was determined that the problems they faced now could be addressed with time and attention. Daniel showed no signs of worsening health, and they would continue to give him excellent care. Garrick had promised her privacy, with a home of her own a few streets away in the house he had inherited from his maiden aunt. They'd open and staff it when they returned from France. By then, he promised her that he would have located the missing military supplies. Though the Bow Street Runner he had hired had not located all the ruffians who attacked them on the Westminster Bridge, the man had reported yesterday that he had tracked two of them to the East India docks. He hoped to arrest them soon.

The bigger challenges of her claim to her chateau and lands, and his to find missing items from his shipments, would come aright. Last night he had appeared quite late in her bedroom and promised both.

"Do you always take to walking about after midnight?" She had awakened, somehow perceiving his presence in her room, and wanted to raise his spirits.

He stood at the foot of her bed, his hands to the wooden frame, his manner brooding. "I do lately. Pardon me, I did not mean to wake you."

She patted the bed as invitation for him to sit. "No need for apologies. Will you stay and tell me what bothers you?"

"I will not worry you." He made to go.

"If you share your worries, I will take a portion and your burden will be lighter."

Halting, he cast about her shadowy room for his answer to that. "I want you to know that if you wish to refuse my hand, I will understand."

"I don't want to reject your offer. Truly. I think you and I are best suited. I want to make you happy."

"As I do you."

"We are agreed, then." She threw back the covers. "Will you stay and find some peace?"

He threw her a wry look.

"What matters one night together when I offer you comfort and you can sleep?"

He chuckled. "Other things can happen!"

"*Certainment!*" she shot back, but sobered. "But that's not what you require tonight."

"No! It isn't. You come to know me well!"

"I hope so."

He had waved *adieu* and left her alone.

She stood taller now as she rounded the threshold of the salon, her heart in her throat.

Garrick had clearly been watching for her because, at once, his eyes met hers and he came forward and took her hand. "You are quite lovely. We'll make of this a joyful day."

"And memorable."

"Without any doubt."

For his charm alone, she could love him forever.

THE WEDDING IN the salon went quietly according to plan. A small group gathered—Daniel's daughters, their ever-proper governess, a tall, dark gentleman and a lady who held his arm, the vicar, and a few of the downstairs servants. Throughout the short ceremony, Garrick gazed at her as though she were most precious to him. He held both her hands throughout the recitation of their vows. She lost all thought of what the vicar uttered, alight with her joy that this was her reward for placing a newspaper advertisement for a husband.

"You pronounced your vows like a woman who knows what she's doing," Garrick said to her afterward with a grin.

"Wed to a man I am so pleased to call my own." *As opposed to the one I might have married.*

"I am proud to claim you as my wife, Mrs. Ruxton."

"I do like the sound of my new name."

He wound her arm through his and patted her hand. "One you shall wear for decades to come. Allow me to introduce you to my oldest friend and his wife."

The couple stood talking with the vicar who had performed their wedding. He was a short, chubby fellow who had stopped twitching only during their wedding service. Uncomfortable with polite talk, he made his escape as quickly as he could to go upstairs to call upon Daniel.

The tall, imposing gentleman and his lady were the friends Garrick had drawn her toward. Both of them offered their congratulations in turn. From their ease with Garrick, it was clear that they had known him many years. The man was her husband's best friend Reginald, Lord Courtenay, and his wife, Dorothea. After a few minutes, Lord Courtenay asked if Daisy would excuse him so he might drag her husband away for a few minutes.

"Please do, sir," she told him. "You leave me with the good

company of your wife."

"Forgive them." Dorothea, Lady Courtenay, grimaced as her husband took Daisy's new one aside. "They have not seen each other in a few days."

Garrick had also told her last night that Lord Courtenay was the one who had alerted him weeks ago to Ruxton & Company's missing shipments. Yet she had no idea how much detail the man's wife knew of that matter. Nor had she any idea if the lady knew of Garrick's fears that Daniel's "accident" was no such thing. Discretion was called for here.

Daisy regarded the two men. "Friends need time together often."

"These two have known each other since they were eight." The lady's endearing regard of the men told of her fondness for both. "I'm delighted that now I can invite both of you to dinner. We just might get them to discuss something other than politics and supplying the army on the Continent."

Daisy grinned. "Crop production numbers can have their limits. Gossip too, I imagine."

"How long have you and Garrick known each other that you understand that so well?"

The lady's statement was meant to be jovial, but there was a quest in there for information. Daisy could give her only a tiny bit. "Not very long at all."

"So then." Dorothea arched a finely plucked brown brow. "Love at first sight?"

"You might say." Daisy nodded and glanced at him, dashing in his formal morning attire for their wedding. She had promised herself no such manly attributes in the man she applied to the *Chronicle* to marry, but accepted whoever the newspaper advertisement might bring her. Now, to her utter amazement, she was blessed with a husband who made her mouth water.

"He deserves a woman who adores him." Dorothea met Daisy's gaze frankly. "Since his return from France, others had begun to set their hearts on him. They will be disappointed they had no chance."

Garrick had told Daisy he intended to be faithful to her. She valued that and believed him. She did not want a husband whose mind wandered to another woman. That way lay disaster. "I believe we will be compatible."

"Garrick is an honorable man. He has worked diligently for his uncle and has re-established an excellent reputation."

Whatever Lady Courtenay hinted at, Daisy would wait to learn. She would not ask such explanations of this woman—nor would she use another's intimations to probe Garrick. He would tell her anything—she would encourage it. Furthermore, he would do it all in his own time.

"I see my husband's good character in his treatment of others." *Me, whom he hardly knows. The staff, whom he treats with respect. His best friend, whom he honors with laughter.*

Lady Courtenay's face fell to stark lines. "Forgive me. I did not mean to imply I do not approve of Garrick. On the contrary, I love him dearly. He has twice saved my husband's life and for that, I owe your husband my deep gratitude. Reg wishes to see Garrick successful. For his own sake as well as Sir Daniel's."

Daisy appreciated the lady's sentiments. "Everyone needs a friend in times of trouble."

"How is Sir Daniel?" Dorothea's gaze drifted toward the hall.

"Resting quietly. Improving daily, I am happy to report."

"But he cannot work, can he?"

"No. He is in much pain."

"And there is no fear of..." She bit her lip.

Gangrene. "The physician tells us he sees no signs that would indicate we should be concerned, no." Garrick had also had the local apothecary up to examine his uncle's stump, and he had declared the wound healthy.

"Thank heavens. May it remain so."

The two vibrant reasons for that sentiment approached Daisy and Lady Courtenay.

Little Susana sidled close to Daisy. The girl and her sister had played cards with Daisy these past two days, and Susana had, surprisingly, played without cheating. "Papa says we are to say to you to be happy."

"Best wishes," her older sister told Daisy in a tone that corrected her sibling. "We hope you are very happy."

Daisy thanked them.

"Are you?" Susana asked.

"I am. Very." *More than I ever expected to be.*

"You were to be our mama," Susana said mournfully. "But Papa said that you were better to marry Uncle Garrick. How is that if you wrote to Papa and he liked you first?"

Daisy wondered if Lady Courtenay understood that statement, but addressed the little girl. "Susana, your father and I did correspond. But your Uncle Garrick and I have struck up a friendship which we think will be very enjoyable."

"Papa says he'll find another lady to marry him," Elizabeth told her. "Do you think that's true?"

"I'm sure it is. Your father is an agreeable fellow."

"And he has money," Susana told her. "I heard the footman say Papa has more money than Uncle Garrick."

"Susana!" Elizabeth elbowed her sister.

"Do you like that wine?" Susana waggled her brows at Daisy and pointed at the glass in her hand.

"I do."

"Mama never did. But Papa likes wine. When is a lady old enough to drink it, do you think?"

"When you come out," Daisy announced. "You'll be eighteen."

Lady Courtenay swallowed her laughter.

Susana pouted. "That's a long time."

"True." Daisy nodded. "But you won't like it until then."

"How do you know? If I have a taste, I might like it now."

Susana's sister groaned. "Don't be a pest, Suz. Mrs. Ruxton does not need your silly ideas."

"Not silly." Susana made a face at Elizabeth. "If I could taste it now—"

"Well, you can't."

"Girls!" Their governess, Miss Pearson, rushed to Daisy's side. "I think it is time we leave the party."

Her charges argued.

"Please, please may we stay?" Susana batted her long lashes in determined appeal.

"Come away now. I see Nuttley calls us in for luncheon." Miss Pearson squired the girls toward the dining room and rolled her eyes in apology at Daisy and Lady Courtenay. "We can dine!"

Off the girls trotted, grumbling at each other as they followed the governess.

"They are quite a pair!" Lady Courtenay chuckled.

"A duet of conflicting melodies."

"Soon they will harmonize. Sisters are comforting. Have you any siblings?"

"None." Daisy silently acknowledged that her two sisters would be so happy for her today. They would not want her grief for them to creep into her wedding day. "And you?"

"None. Perhaps you and I might try to become good friends?"

"I would like that."

"As would I. Daisy, is it?"

"And you are Dorothea?"

"Thea," she said, and raised her glass in a toast to their future.

⟫⟫⟫✕⟪⟪⟪

"CONGRATULATIONS, MY FRIEND." Reginald lifted his glass in honor of the nuptials. "She is lovely. With all that blonde hair, I would say she must be Danish. Not French."

"My wife, Reg, is now officially English." It had taken Garrick two days to get the French ambassador's approval for their marriage. The old Comte de Nançay, said Daisy, disliked her father for his support of a constitution and made excuses to withhold his signature on the form. Frustrated by the man's delays, she'd insisted yesterday she go with Garrick to persuade the man. At her stubborn insistence, the king's man had thrown up his hands and immediately performed the French ceremony.

This morning's Anglican ceremony at home was easier and happier for them both. They said their vows in the main salon, not in front of Daniel in his bedroom. Daniel, in one of his rare strokes of humility, had refused to mar the event by people looking at him instead of the bride.

Indeed, as Daisy stood talking with Daniel's daughters and Reg's wife, she laughed more easily than ever. The past few days had lifted her spirits.

As they have mine. Despite no progress from Bow Street in finding more of the ruffians who had attacked her, Garrick and she had enjoyed each other's company dining together and discussing those little intimacies that made up a person's character. Garrick discovered in each new moment with her that Daisy was a woman of simple pleasures who had too long been without loving company. She liked to play the pianoforte. She wrote children's stories. She longed to have a joyous family filled with kindness and serenity.

He would give it to her. To see her laugh gaily, to watch her plush lips spread in joy, was a new torture for him. He ran his gaze down her body and, outrageously randy bridegroom that he was, undressed his new wife to her skin. He had married in haste. He prayed he would not rush her to her marriage bed in any time but a decent interval. *But what is that? Not today. Too rash. Not tonight. Not in a coach. Tomorrow? Next week? Hell.*

He took a long pull of his drink.

"Hello? Are you listening to me at all?"

"Definitely!" Garrick knitted his brows.

Reg snorted. "You are a fortunate fellow. Thea tells me that Daniel's daughters' governess told her this morning that your wife was to have married their father."

"That is true. I don't want to explain it now. Perhaps when

we return from our honeymoon trip." Garrick had not yet told anyone where he and Daisy were going. But he trusted Reg. Implicitly. Despite Daniel's recent hint that he suspected an illegal collusion between Reg and his cousin, Jacques Durand. Subsequently, Garrick had asked Daniel for proof, of which he had none. Rumor, Daniel had offered, was that Reg was miscalculating goods going to British troops protecting the embassy in Paris. But who would have given Daniel such gossip? He saw no one but those serving him in the house. And newspapers had not printed any such scurrilous stories.

Reg had consulted with Whitehall on the Army Commissariat for more than six years. Though Reg and he had gone to school together and been fast friends since age eight, they had also worked together since Garrick had first gone to Portugal after the accusation of his assault on Adam Foley. Never had Reg believed Garrick killed the man. Never had Reg given Garrick any indication that Reg himself had been dishonest in his work with army supply. As for the assertion by Daniel that Jacques Durand was corrupt, Garrick was inclined not to believe it. For many reasons. But as with much else in this mystery he must solve, he would test such an accusation.

Reg eyed him. "Is it a secret where you are going for your honeymoon?"

"You never told anyone where you and Thea went." Garrick made his point with humor.

His friend shook his head. "Useful for a honeymoon trip. But I am shocked that you leave the house. After what happened to your wife days ago?"

"We do." Garrick had gone to see Reg the day after the attack and told him all. "I added numbers to our footmen, you might recall, after Daniel's accident. They are rough-and-tumble men, and now on alert to every tiny thing. Daisy has recovered from that ordeal. So has our coachman."

Reg took a swallow of his whisky. "I've had time to think over your issues. Have you considered that the attack on Daniel and on your coach with Daisy inside might be related?"

"Indeed I have. I have Bow Street on the matter. So far, nothing."

"The mysteries pile up. I'm worried about you and your wife. Might these two accidents in any way be connected to that *particular* deed that exiled you to Portugal?"

"It has occurred to me."

Reg referred to the accusation that Garrick had killed the clerk Adam Foley, one of Ruxton & Company's employees, after which he'd been forced by the analysis of Bow Street to go abroad to avoid a trial. When Garrick had gone to Porto, Portugal to run his uncle's office there, he thought he'd lost everything worthwhile. His future as his uncle's manager and heir was the most significant. Close in importance was the loss of the woman who at the time Garrick considered the love of his life. But Maribelle Swanson had quickly taken the proposal of another man.

Viscount Gordonston's deathbed confession two weeks ago was a surprise to Garrick, Daniel, and Reg. The man had blubbered that he had conspired with another man and given false witness that he saw Garrick push Foley to his death. The viscount had not, sadly, revealed who that other man was before he passed away. All they had was Gordonston's breathless description of "an evil man of genius."

"But at the moment, Reg, I see no direct relationships. I ask about for Gordonston's closet friends, but he seems to have cut himself off from everyone in the past few years."

"That fellow did become a recluse."

"That's what I hear. So I continue to hunt and look at everything."

Reg downed his whisky in disgust and nodded at Garrick. "We all know you were innocent."

"Not all, Reg." Garrick pushed away his anger at the accusation his uncle had made days ago. Venomous as Daniel's words had been, Garrick had put them down to a sick man's drugged babbling. If indeed they were more than that, he would not forget them and would deal with them in time. At the moment, he was only thinking of the lady who had captured his interest from the first moment he looked upon her. "Trust me. I look into every matter you've brought to my attention."

Reg turned his back on others in the salon and locked his dark gaze on Garrick's. "Meanwhile… Discovered anything more about those missing items?"

Garrick waited to reply while two ladies passed them, headed for the dining room. "Nothing on the French shipments yet. That's why I go there to examine things with my own eyes. For all the shipments here, I've confirmed the number of saddles arriving from the Yorkshire workhouses here. I checked with the factor who receives them. I trust him. A good man. He did a thorough review of numbers and of the honesty of our men. We did receive the right numbers in our warehouse near St. Katherine's dock, and they have not drifted away to thieves unknown!"

That dock east of the Tower of London was one of the oldest in the city, and smuggling was nigh impossible there because it was so exposed on all sides to the greater public.

"That is good news." Reg took another swallow of his whisky. "Don't you think many of the details about the missing items are odd?"

"I do." *Just bits and pieces, like ones that used to go missing from our Porto shipments before I took over six years ago. The last year from Calais before Bony abdicated and I got to Calais to stop the flood.* "Blankets. Tents. Shirts. Items that anyone can use and sell."

"Similar thefts to items stolen from shipments to Porto before you went there."

"Yes. The numbers are puzzling as well. I will find them. I promise you, Reg." The alternative was to be prosecuted for failure to deliver goods to the military during an army occupation of conquered territory. "I plan to visit with Jacques Durand and ask for his insights."

"Going to Calais, then?"

Garrick needed Reg's current thoughts about Durand. "Your

cousin continues to prosper now that the little corporal has gone to Elba."

"Durand knows how to turn a good coin within and without the law. He makes no secret of the fact that he hated Napoleon. His family was destroyed by the Republicans and by the Bonapartes. Jacques prefers to stay out of politics and focus on his ships and his nice profits."

Garrick cocked a brow. "He made good money during the wars shipping contraband French goods into Brighton and Portsmouth."

"That was yesterday's secret. Now he is legitimate. And rich. He's good at this, and he's proud of it all. After all, his father was one of the late king's courtiers, and a sycophant of whom all made jest. Jacques wants respect. And he earns it."

Every word Reg spoke was from his heart. More, Garrick felt them to be indicative of Reg's cousin, the Frenchman, whose integrity Garrick thought to be impeccable. He also knew that if anyone understood the interior of France these past months since the abdication, it was Jacques Durand. Garrick needed his insight for his missing items and for Daisy's chances to regain her family chateau.

"Give him my regards," Reg said with a nod.

"I will. Tell me about two men, will you?" Garrick spoke low and turned toward the wall. "Kirby and Richardson."

"The first used to be a friend of your uncle. The second never was."

"Why is Kirby no longer a friend of Daniel's? Any ideas?"

"They fell out about politics. Argued at a house party one night while in their cups. Never spoke again. All over their view of Napoleon."

Garrick recalled his uncle's vain desire to become prime minister. "But both are supporters of the government and the war against France."

"Shades of difference. Shades, my friend."

And shades of ambition? "Does Kirby seek a position in the government?"

"Not that I have ever heard. He is rather…hmmm…a bit of a fool. Who would want him in Downing Street, eh?"

Were Kirby and Garrick's uncle rivals for the same post? "Anything else of note? About Kirby or Richardson?"

"Both are hotheads."

"Would they try to hurt Daniel?"

"Together? I doubt it. Neither has more than two friends, one of whom they see in the mirror."

Just like Gordonston. "Find out, will you, while I'm gone?"

"Certainly. Meanwhile…" Reg smiled, examining him with a glint in his eye. "You just got married. Not the best time to be investigating mysteries."

"Don't worry." Garrick turned his attentions once more to his new wife, who laughed with Daniel's girls and Reg's wife. The hour drew nigh when he could take Daisy away and explore the dynamics of his new life as a husband. A devoted one, at that. One who helped her gain her heart's desire to get her home returned to her. "We'll do only what's necessary."

Reg sidled nearer to lower his voice. "You should be doing other, more enjoyable *things.*"

Never doubt me on that score. "It's a new beginning for us, Reg." *For me. I have a new way to look at life, and I wish to keep it.*

"Sir, sir!" Nuttley scuttled to Garrick's side. Agitated, the elderly man who was so afflicted with his palsy was even more agitated and moved his head in repeated little jerks. "You…you have a caller."

The scowl on his butler's wrinkled face told Garrick the visitor was not one who came to join the wedding festivities. In fact, he was one of whom Nuttley disapproved—and Garrick knew at once the person's identity. "Where is he?"

"In the small parlor, sir."

"Excuse me, Reg. More business."

THE WIRY FELLOW who stood awaiting him in the back parlor was the Bow Street Runner whom Garrick had hired to investigate those who had attacked Daisy and his men the other day. The fellow was amiable and thorough, considering he had not ever found who really murdered Adam Foley.

Standing in profile when Garrick entered, the Runner appeared as tall as the door lintel, and so slight, one might shake him and find nothing inhabited his dark blue suit but air.

"Afternoon, sir." The fellow removed his hat and ran a hand through his unruly hair. His blue eyes riveted on Garrick, assessing, appraising. Always working, this man missed little.

"Good to see you, Thynne." A more properly named fellow there never was. They shook hands. Garrick wanted to get right to the matter at hand. "Do sit down."

Thynne complied, his skinny legs out before him, twirling his hat in his hands.

He was a creature of constant activity. Garrick remembered that of him from six years ago, when Thynne had been the one assigned to investigate Foley's death. He did not take easily to the violent creatures he pursued. Though he often seemed in haste, the Runner was very methodical and careful. That was why Garrick had asked for Thynne to investigate these attacks for him. "You have news?"

"I do, sir. The easiest information to get was that you requested about Viscount Gordonston."

Garrick had requested Thynne learn who the man's closest associates were. "Go on."

"He was often seen in the company of Peter Hamden, Viscount Willoughby, and William Kemp, Baron Ward. Both are men of title, wealth, and reputation as well as ne'er-do-wells in their politics. They are Whigs, sir, and did not support the wars against Napoleon. Do you know them?"

Garrick recognized the names. "Not me, personally, no. But many years ago before my uncle, Sir Daniel, married, he kept company with the three men. After my uncle eloped, he no longer consorted with the three." But had the four remained friends? Garrick had not heard Daniel speak of them, but he needed to learn.

"A good thing they parted. From what I see—and I will be frank, Mr. Ruxton—Willoughby, Ward, and Gordonston were known about Town as the Three Awfuls, Wily, Wicked, and Wurst."

"And now that Gordonston is dead?"

"Willoughby and Ward remain a lively pair about town, sir."

"Is either one man known as a 'genius'?"

Thynne looked like he was ready to scoff at that, but worked at his lips to hold his emotions in check. "No, sir. That I've not heard about either of them. But you say someone reported to you about Gordonston's so-called confession just before he died."

"That is true, Thynne."

"So you have reason to believe the person who reported that to you, do you?"

Nuttley's best friend had an only daughter in service to the Gordonston household, and she had been in the room when he faced his last few hours.

"I do, Thynne."

"Not the words of a man out of his head, are they?" Thynne was bold.

Garrick would draw him out, wishing to be clear about his own knowledge. "They did not seem so. Gordonston appeared to be looking for absolution. Please to tell me what you mean by saying they're 'ne'er-do-wells in politics'?"

"He didn't want to spend money to give to Allies to fight Bony."

Garrick got a bitter taste in his mouth. He remembered the debates in Parliament. "Thought it a waste of money, did they?"

The Runner nodded.

"Pardon me." Daisy rushed into the room, smiling and apologetic to Garrick. Her cheeks were pink. Had been all morning. Excitement was good for her. Him too, as he had an equal portion of it since he'd proposed and she'd accepted. "I hope you don't mind I've come?"

He was happy to see her interested and involved. No delicate flower, his Daisy. "Not at all. Come in, my dear. Meet Mr. Frederick Thynne."

"Oh, good." She smiled so eagerly at Thynne that the poor fellow nearly swallowed his tongue. Brushing aside the silken skirts of her new gown, she sat beside Garrick. Her hip warmed his own, her nearness to him new and evidently so acceptable to her that he hoped the rest of this interview would be short. He preferred to get on with securing the affections of his bride if he could end this sordid interview.

"I wished to hear what progress you've made," she told Thynne with anticipation. She had been in such poor condition the night of her accident that she had gone to her rooms and not met the man when Garrick hired him. But the next day, she had expressed her wish to do so in future. Garrick was proud she did not flinch from the opportunity to talk with the man who'd find those who had hurt her.

"I do have word for you about that accident." Thynne latched his gaze on Garrick's and laid his hat to the table. "I've been to Seven Dials and Houndsditch, a few times. We got word one of the four's an upright man who's in a mob."

"Rivers' or O'Neill's?" Garrick named the two most powerful gang leaders.

"Rivers, but not for certain. We think this Jack McDoughal's one of the four that attacked you. Got a few with my word out for them. Not much coming to me yet. But there will be. Rum coves like that, they don't get far when they fail. Get laughed at. Thrown to the dogs. For failing. It isn't good to do that."

Daisy reached for Garrick's hand. "You think others will tell on those who did this?"

"Not so, miss."

"The lady," Garrick told him with a grin, and squeezed her hand, "is now my wife."

"Begging your pardon, ma'am."

She cast Thynne a forgiving look. "You could not have known, sir."

Garrick was most concerned that the man who'd attempted to hurt or abduct Daisy would be caught and punished. "No news of who might have had the skills to jump the family carriage?"

"On him, I do know a few things, sir." Thynne sat straight as a poker. "The one who tried to take you, Mrs. Ruxton, I found this morning. He was flat on his face, in a ditch. Dead. Stabbed."

Daisy clutched Garrick's hand.

"Any idea who may have killed him?" Garrick asked.

"Not yet, sir. I'm asking."

"And this Jack McDoughal?" Daisy ventured. "Can you find him?"

"I've got a trail and I think so. If he's still alive, ma'am, I'll get him."

⫸✳⫷

Nuttley showed the Runner from the room.

Daisy stared after him. "What do you think?" she asked in a voice so soft that Garrick barely heard her.

"Look at me." He smiled when she finally did. "We let him do his work. And we get on with enjoying our wedding day. We'll dine, then tonight we will leave for Dover as we planned."

She frowned at their entwined hands. "You are not concerned about leaving Daniel and the girls?"

"They are well protected. We will be, too. We travel as Mr. and Mrs. Charles Evans. I carry only French silver and copper coins. Miller goes with us as far as Dover and returns to join the other footmen to secure those in the house. All the men are very skilled. And as for the other work here, Lord Courtenay has it well in hand, as does my chief clerk in the office on the docks. You and I go on our honeymoon trip to work, but also to become accustomed to being husband and wife."

"I wish we might do only that."

"We will." He put his hand to her soft cheek. She deserved a honeymoon trip devoted only to her and their union. He would spend the next few days attempting to tame his urge to have her, all of her, as soon as gentlemanly behavior allowed. "After all this is done, we'll take another trip. The two of us. Devoted to each other."

"Without worries."

"Full of hope and the promise of the future." He lifted her hand and kissed the back. Time would provide them the element they needed to become friends. And soon, lovers. "For now, we have a few guests to see to. Shall we?"

Chapter Nine

DAISY PUT THE last of her new muslin night rails into her valise and told herself to focus on her new husband. She'd concentrated too much on Jack McDoughal and the other fellow who'd died in the worst way.

No. She was going away from all this. Escaping the disagreeable demands of Daniel. His odd requests to visit him each day. To feed him his meals. To read poetry to him. Love poems written by cavaliers, no less.

She set her teeth and took another glance around her rooms.

"I've closed your trunk, ma'am." Her new maid Cora was her lively self. "There is no more, I do believe."

"You are right." Daisy glanced at the pink and white ribboned garters on her nightstand. To take them would mean she promised herself to follow through on her desire to make more of this marriage than the friendly agreement that cemented it. "Thank you for your help today."

The girl curtsied, ever eager to please her. Too much so, it often seemed. "My duty, ma'am. I hope you'll choose me when you return."

"I see no reason why not, Cora." Daisy really had little for which to criticize the girl. Though she was congenial and efficient, Cora missed nothing. Sharp-eyed and meticulous, she had qualities that recommended any maid. Yet Daisy had this eerie feeling around her that she could not shake.

Yet whether to keep her was not a decision she needed to confront now. Her bridegroom waited for her downstairs. The man whom she'd wed with an eager heart and without doubts. She rushed to pick up her traveling pelisse and new kid gloves, ready to meet her husband.

On the landing, she stared down at the man who had surprised and honored her with his proposal. His generous mouth spread in a grin as he beheld her, and she was once more absorbed by his suave demeanor. An impulse sang through her, and she raised her hand to him. "Something I forgot."

A minute later, she sailed down the staircase, where her husband awaited her with a teasing glint in his pale green eyes.

"What did you remember?" he asked, and took her arm to loop through his.

"I had set out my mother's last set of silk garters and put them on my dressing table." She handed over her valise to him, then followed his lead toward the back of the house and descended the kitchen steps into the small garden. He had told her they would take hired carriages to Dover to avoid detection by those who might do them harm.

"You forgot to pack them?"

She'd be honest with him. What else was marriage built on but truth? "I kept looking at them. Mama left them to my older sister, and I inherited them. They are, according to family legend, passed down through my mother's line as good luck to wear for brides. I've kept them, hoping I might have occasion to use them on my wedding trip. And so..." She gave a lift to her shoulders, a careful and impish gesture.

"Ah, well. I look forward to seeing them." He looked away, his lips pressed tightly together, and handed her up into the hired hackney coach. Was he trying not to appear too interested?

"You are a diplomat." Laughter danced inside her as she watched him settle in across from her.

"I am certainly trying my best." He feigned a frown.

"I appreciate your efforts." She folded her gloved hands and fought her chuckle. "But we mustn't avoid this discussion."

"We won't." He met her honesty with his own measure. "I thought we would use this journey to walk into a closer friendship."

No wedding night for us to force an intimacy we've not yet cultivated.

She was content with it. "Why don't you start by telling me how we will travel?"

The jarvey gave his whip to the horses, and off they went.

"This carriage, then we change in Southwark." When she shook her head, Garrick added, "Across the Thames in South London. We travel onward, south to stop at a carriage inn in Rochester to change coaches. Then go on through the night to Dover. We travel in anonymity without our Ruxton-marked carriages. I thought it best to change carriages and drivers and not to stop, and I hope you agree."

"I do. You've traveled this route, I assume, often, and you know it better than I ever will."

"Thank you." He did look immensely happy over that, and handed her one of the two carriage blankets folded beside him on the seat. "I know a comfortable small hotel in Dover which caters to travelers. I've never stayed there before. I like it for this trip because it offers a fine view of the Channel. We can see across, and the skyline gives a good perspective of the weather. There, we will wait until the Channel is clear."

"But is there a chance of that? It's the end of February, and the start of spring is never kind, no matter the terrain."

"We won't wait forever. But it can clear. Trust me."

She regarded him with newfound delight. How wonderful that that feeling never seemed to stop? "I do," she said. "I'm grateful that we wait to sail in good weather. I don't remember much about our crossing when I was six, but I do recall how very ill I was."

"Storms in the Channel can be disastrous."

"Yes," she said, and nodded, gazing out into the dark night. "I'm not certain now that there was a storm when we sailed, or if the terror of the trip was all in my head."

"Who in your family fled with you?"

"My father. My mother's sister, her husband, and their two daughters. Another uncle and aunt. My two sisters, one older and another younger. My father's steward and valet. Two maids." She saw them as she often did in her reverie, parading before her as last she saw them, gray and gnarled with anger. "We came with what we remembered to pack. The rush…"

She winced at the shroud over her poor recollection. "The rush to escape the Paris mob was…like a lightning storm that never ceased. My aunt and sisters crying, shrieking. Running around me in circles. Crazed. Hurried. Each of us had a trunk from the cellars. Ours to fill. Most of our servants had run away, and Papa ordered us to haul up what luggage we could to the grand salon. He yelled that we were to wear our heavy coats. But it was June…and hot. We obeyed, but I remember, all the time we were crying. Papa filled two trunks. The only one who had two. But one was for his court attire and his badge of *Saint Louis*. He vowed he'd go nowhere without them. Poor man. So lost."

She pressed a hand to her throat, the memories like stones she could not swallow. "When he died, we buried him in his frills. His badge upon his chest."

Garrick rose and sat beside her, his arm around her shoulders, curling her close. "You need not tell me more."

"I will. I can. Honestly, once I start…" Always when she walked into that last day in Paris, she sank into it as if she were cast to the water, swimming, frantically pulling herself to shore. Only by rushing through the flood of yesterday could she gain land and breathe.

"Papa hired four carriages. Our *majordome*, Monsieur LeClerk, found them. Papa said *the monsieur* was loyal. We got away, no farther than to the Invalides when the mob recognized us and ran after us. *Majordome*'s little curricle was the last of our line of carriages, and they got him. Tore him from the carriage. We stopped, circled, but the masses were intent on us, and Papa yelled to our drivers to run, run. We never saw Monsieur LeClerk again." She closed her eyes. Behind her lids, the ravenous crowds clawed at the paint on the carriages and stabbed at their horses, screaming at those inside the coach to come out, come out. She pressed her cheek to her husband's chest.

He curled her closer. "Darling, you need not tell me more."

She shot backward in his embrace—and saw her father's drawn face. "They wanted Papa. 'Bring him out,' they yelled, and he banged on the roof of the cab to harry the driver to go faster. He did, but he ran over someone. I heard them cry out. We felt the bump and heard the crunch of his body. But we did not stop. Could not. 'Them or us,' Papa shouted. 'Them or us.' Our horses were strong, fast. *Mon Dieu,* so fast."

Her husband stroked her hair, the old comfort one her mother would do. And she sank into his arms more deeply, sighing, sheltered from the horrors of the past by his firm body.

"What we took with us was laughable," she went on. "Later, years later, in our rented house in Lyme Regis, my aunt and my sisters, on the anniversary of the day we ran, we would recite the day's events and list the items they had found in their trunks."

Garrick removed her little hat and kissed her forehead. His arms wrapped around her as she poured out the rest.

"You would not believe what anyone afraid for their life will choose to save. My aunt took her Haviland china and six rouge pots. My sister Chantelle took her porcelain doll, but only two of her own dresses. And her winter coat, of course. We all had our winter coats. My aunt burned hers one year on the anniversary. Uncle d'Harcourt took three of his watches and two engagement books." She scoffed. "As if he'd receive his minions in a new domain called England.

"Some of those goods, we used. We sold them to pay our rent and our greengrocer. Sold them all very carefully. Uncle d'Harcourt would go to London to dealers who bought French goods. Each year, whatever he sold—even if a duplicate of what he'd sold the year before—brought less. Papa's complete silver dinner service for thirty-six. Given to him by his grandfather, Louis Quatorze. He would sell one complete setting per year. We ate with utensils *mon père* purchased from a smithy, and on the day he'd sell them, we ate beef and drank good wine.

"But the money would always run out. Always. So then we had to learn how to support ourselves. In a country where we had to learn to speak more like our neighbors, we had to apply to work. Some in the family could never accept the need. But as the dealers in Clerkenwell paid Uncle and Papa less to pawn our goods, many of us resigned ourselves to the necessity of labor."

Garrick pushed back curls around her ears. "What did you do, my darling?"

"I tutored many young girls to speak French. I was hired by families and by a local school. A fine one for young ladies who were to go into Society. None of that paid much, but it was money we needed.

"My father took a position as a tutor of French to young boys. My Aunt d'Harcourt was very skilled in making bobbin lace, and sold it in yards to local seamstresses. My sister, Liliane, who was ten years older than me, suffered the most for our exile. She was in love with the vicomte who held a domain south of ours, and she was affianced to marry him, but he, too, was carried off to the guillotine. After his death, the life went out of her. She wrote of it all in a diary she had started on the day she met him, when she was twelve. She entered her thoughts each day until she died three years ago. Her words are eloquent and heartbreaking."

Garrick hugged her near. "You've kept it?"

"I have." *I reread it to see my loved ones when they were safe from harm, confident and carefree. Before the deluge and the living death.* "I keep it with me. In my trunk. It's with me. I brought it. And so it is in the boot."

He cupped her cheek. "Then you must seek to have it published."

"Who would want to know her trials and tribulations?"

"Many would. What has happened in France these past decades needs to be understood by all. Mistakes have been made. Hearts broken. Much of it unnecessarily and without any compassion."

She wrapped her arms around her husband's chest. The humiliation and desperation her family had endured weighed like stones in her heart. "Even now, many suffer. To try to correct the past is such difficult work for anyone who emigrated. Even now that the Bourbons are back, I've written and appealed to so many to right the wrongs. But it's difficult. Even to gain help from an old friend can be a nightmare. So many have changed sides that one does not know who is a friend and who will turn you in for no reason at all. One of those is the military governor of Rouen who administers Normandy. He is an old friend of my father's. I have written to him twice. He does me no service, but puts me off."

"Jean-Pierre Jourdan." Garrick practically spat the man's name.

She pulled back in surprise. "You know him?"

"I know of him. He has turned his coat so many times from Republic to Napoleon to Bourbon last year, we know not whom he truly supports."

"One cannot trust him. He moves with the wind. At first, he wrote last June that he would help me. In December, he refused my request to review my claim to our domain. He says he knows not if our peasants have bought any parcels of our land. I think that is a lie. He knows. How can he not?"

"Exactly." Garrick scowled. "If Marshall Jourdan is to collect the taxes, he knows precisely who owns what lands. Do you know if any of your peasants bought it up over the years?"

"No. Many domains had been parceled and sold to their tenants since the Revolution. Papa wrote often to our steward LeClerk and asked, but we never received a response. Perhaps Papa's letters were confiscated. Or LeClerk died that day we all ran. Or he may have died later, or simply was unwilling to tell Papa. When I wrote and told Jourdan this, he told me I must present the property deeds."

"And do you have them?"

"The royal grants?" She hated to answer. "No. They are in our family chateau near Rouen. In Papa's safest place. Or so he said."

"Which is where?"

"In the library overlooking the Seine. In the wall near the former castle wall's solar."

"Hidden in the wall?" He was aghast.

"So my father always claimed." She shook her head. "I know which panel. We will have to pull them out. If the documents are still there. If the parchment is intact and the old French is still legible. If, if, if. So tenuous, eh? If they exist, then we can wrap them up and take them to Jourdan and hope they don't disintegrate in our hands."

"You and I will pay a surprising visit to the old marshal of France."

"Do you think he will receive us?"

"I supply the British Army on his northern border. I may not know him personally, but I am certain when you appear with me, he will receive us and be inclined to aid you."

"I doubt he'll be too happy to be cornered. Oh, Garrick," she breathed in awe of the news, "thank you for this."

In the shadows of the darkened cab, he beamed triumphantly. "It will be my pleasure to call upon the less-than-honorable fellow."

The driver slowed their carriage.

In the still of the night, people scurried about to get out of the chill.

"The coach stops."

"Don't be afraid."

She clutched his hands. Her gratitude to this man, her husband, overflowed. How was it possible she had found a man so charming and yet one so daring as to help her? Would that she would never disappoint him. And that he might find in her characteristics to admire…and cherish. "I'm not concerned about the sea."

"No? What, then? Tell me and I'll—"

She wrapped her fingers around his nape and kissed him madly. His mouth was all that she remembered. Firm and fierce. Warm and hers. Now hers by all rights to enjoy. Hating to end it, she mewled and broke away to consider the shock she'd given him.

First he stared. Then he grinned. One side of his mouth cocked up. Then he reached for her and, with his arms around her back, sank her to the squabs with measured ease. His lips, when they took hers, were all a husband's should be. Reverent and hot. Questing and demanding. Domineering. And when he drew away, his gaze was searching, molten, alight with desires she knew matched her own. "My darling wife, would that we might go on."

The coachman rapped upon their door and called to them to leave.

"But I fear our driver is a stubborn fellow, and this is the most uncomfortable position for us to continue."

She smoothed the arch of his cheek with her thumb. "But we will…won't we?"

"I promise you, we will." He sat back and pulled her to a sitting position, then helped her replace her lopsided little hat. "We change here and go on to Rochester and Dover," he told her as he lifted her coat collar about her throat "Come. Stay warm. We have a long night ahead of us."

⟫⟪

GARRICK, ROUSED BY her advance, told himself to relax into the squabs, and drew her back against his torso. He'd be a cad to take her in a carriage. One that had stopped, no less. The driver was anxious to get rid of them in the middle of the night. Garrick put himself to the goal of abstinence.

But his body did not want to obey. He had wanted her from first sight of her. Her body, her elegance and kindness—even her vulnerability drew him to her. For he could stand strong for her as, he somehow understood, she stood valiant for those she loved.

"Sleep," he urged her, and wished he could instead encourage her to kiss him again. Capture his lips as she had his mind. But no. Tonight was not the right hour or place. And he'd have her in all the correct ways in the fullness of time.

He ran his hand over her shoulder to curl her nearer. "We've far to go tonight. Tomorrow will be bright."

She kissed his ear, his charming wife, then snuggled close and rejoiced that she could grant him such trust. Small it might be that a bride might give to her new husband such faith. But Garrick could wait to consummate their union. With her kisses, he knew she wished it as much as he.

Certainly, he was feeling more like a bridegroom than he had during the ceremony. To comfort and to cherish was part of a husband's vows. He'd had no one since his mother's death who had shown either of those qualities to him, but he had longed for them. As a child. As a young man. As an older one. Now.

Though others might deny they wished comfort and care from others, he could admit it and not think it detracted from his masculinity. He knew who he was. Whom he valued and why.

He valued Daniel, less so these past few days, but still had to give the man his due. He trusted his uncle more than he ever had relied on his father or brother. Daniel, alone among the less-than-stellar members of his family, had been admirable. He had shown he valued Garrick and saved him from trial and prison by sending his nephew abroad to work on the peninsula for the company. Garrick, when a child, had always enjoyed Daniel's strength of purpose and ambition. If his uncle was rather too driven in his desire for politics, Garrick had forgiven him his obsession.

Until now, when he questioned what Daniel truly wanted and what he had done to achieve it. In the past few days since Daisy arrived, Daniel had presented an extraordinarily different man. A man whom Garrick thought he'd known. And known well.

Daniel now was irritable, constantly complaining. The physician repeatedly gave good reports of Daniel's recuperation from amputation, and for that, he should be grateful. But the man acted like a petulant child. He ordered hot chocolate with every meal. New nightshirts washed to a thin gauze before he'd don them. He even requested one specific housemaid to wait on him. An upstairs girl, no less, the one Garrick had assigned to Daisy. The girl did not complain and performed both sets of duties in quick order. About the servant, Daniel had no complaints.

But he'd focused his ire on Daisy. His attentions were certainly misplaced, especially after Garrick told him he had proposed marriage and Daisy accepted. Daniel became picky and insisted she visit. She had done so. Daniel had reported to Garrick that she appeared two or three times each day in his rooms. But she did not give him all he craved. He grumbled that she was too polite. She needed to sit with him. Read to him. Feed him his porridge or soup. But she had cut her visits short and spent only two or three minutes in his company. Then she would hurry away, pardoning herself to tend to some matter to do with the wedding.

Her seeming uninterest fueled Daniel's foul disposition. If he was not complaining about her lack of interest, he was needling Garrick about his progress finding the discrepancies in the warehouse records. The physician had warned Garrick not to disturb Daniel with business matters. But his uncle was persistent, and Garrick gave him short bits of news. But Daniel grew only more frustrated. Garrick would sort this out in Calais. The problem that had existed before he'd taken over in Porto was the same type that had existed in Calais before he hired Monsieur Henri. None of the people who had worked in Porto had ever worked in Calais. Who stole these goods, and why and how, eluded him.

But he would learn. His future—a very bright one with his new wife—depended on it.

Daisy sighed in his arms, and he shifted to find a more comfortable position for them in the far-too-small coach. A bride and groom needed better accommodations than these to start their marriage.

He'd see to it. In Dover in the morning, he would take a room for them in an inn different from one he usually took when he embarked to Calais. The one he had in mind was used by aristocrats when they traveled. It was a grand establishment, with bigger rooms, better fireplaces, and finer food. For their sail across the Channel, he would be careful to hire one of the newer, sturdier packets. That would offer less chance of seasickness for Daisy. The newer boats were costlier, but he would not pinch pennies to make her comfortable. The newer ones also carried fewer passengers. She and he traveled under assumed names, but the less they conversed with others, the greater their secrecy to land and do their work successfully.

Intimate and binding, the vows they exchanged meant much to him. Alone as he'd considered himself to be for all his life, to marry this woman, this seeming stranger, thrilled him more than he had expected. Now to be able to hold her and comfort her as if they were more than strangers gratified him immensely.

Not only was he pleased because he and Daisy were to be alone to begin their journey to deeper friendship, but also because he was happy to be far from Daniel.

He had decided long before Daniel suggested the marriage that he would wed Daisy and seal the agreement that she had made originally with his uncle. She appealed to him. He wanted her.

She had few artifices. He had once thought he loved a woman who employed them fully, and learned all too painfully what mattered in a person's character was the kind respect for others.

He had discovered that bright young things who sailed through the *ton* with visions of wealth, a title, and servants to order were not for him. He had always desired someone to marry with whom he might find common cause. Upon meeting Daisy, he had been imbued with an intuition that they had longings and attitudes in common.

Her recollections of her family's tribulations had given him proof his instinct was correct. Hers had been a family in life-threatening crisis, and they had reacted as anyone would. Fleeing bloodthirsty crowds would never inspire logic or caution. They'd done what they must and fled with their possessions, hastily chosen and, in the moment, dearly prized. But as they achieved safety, they had as individuals lost much of their reason. A new way to live, hand to mouth. A new place to live, in diminished circumstances with less money, fewer friends and chances to prosper. To each other, they seemed incapable of giving much emotional support. Yet they had done as well as they could.

Daisy, like the others, survived but did not flourish. Their abilities to do so were limited. By time, money, location, and politics, they were closed to the social order they lived among. And in the limited means they had, they each pondered means to adjust. Many had failed.

Yet Daisy had saved herself. Through it all she had found ways to live in such a manner that she *could* flourish. Even to the point where she decided she could and should marry someone with whom she might be friends.

He shared that belief and hope for himself. Now came the opportunity to do that. The conditions for their union were not perfect. They had left for France with two goals in mind. Hers to regain her family's chateau and domains. His to solve his mystery.

Neither had anything to do with establishing any kind of rapport between them. But they could use the time and the shared goals to forge a firmer bond.

That was a real possibility, and Garrick would provide the

means. Their mutual fondness for each other could provide the foundation of the passion that he sought.

On a small laugh to himself, he prayed he might overcome his bride's lack of patience to make their first time together one on which to build a lifetime of happiness.

THE NEXT MORNING, the two of them bade farewell to Miller in the public room of the inn Garrick had chosen. Exhausted from their poor night's rest from the bumpy ride in the sparely upholstered carriage, he led Daisy up the stairs to the largest room in the old inn.

The porters carried up their trunks and valises while the innkeeper stoked the fire higher. Within minutes, the newlyweds were alone.

No sooner had he helped her off with her pelisse, she spun to face him, her gaze full of a lazy speculation that endeared her to him more than seemed usual for a new bride on her first morning—at the ungodly hour of eight.

She pressed her hands to his chest, her fingers upon the buttons of his waistcoat. "How adept are you, sir, at being a ladies' maid?"

He understood the many questions she sought to have him answer. He cocked a brow at her, and covered her hands resting upon his beating heart. "I have had a little experience. But I will seek to perfect my skill with only you."

She lifted her chin, bravery the first look on her lovely face, coquettishness the next. "I have no experience as a valet. But I want to become accomplished. With only you."

"How good to know." He grinned and cupped her cheeks. "Might I kiss my valet?"

She chuckled softly and tipped her head to and fro. "Well… If I can kiss my maid."

He traced his thumb along the edge of her lower lip. "Please do."

She rose on her toes.

He brought her against him, sliding his arms around her slim waist, her lips a breath away from his.

At the first touch of her mouth to his, his mind went blank. Her skin was silk. A smooth brush of her flesh on his, and his hope soared high. Her kiss was fresh, naïve, and hot. His response was careful, tender. She leaned against him, her search for something more apparent in her haste. And he gave it to her.

Crushing her close, he braced himself to hold her tightly to him. This time, he bent and captured those lips that had tormented him since she had kissed him nights ago. This time, he showed her how a groom kissed his bride. He could not bury his need, and he took her with a desire that shocked him.

And to his surprise, she did not pull away but met him, kiss for kiss, until, breathless, she pulled away.

She tipped back her head to examine him, her brown eyes dancing in the dim firelight. "If I'd known maids kissed like this, I would have tried it sooner."

He threw back his head to laugh. He should let her go. He was a cad to possess her so, but he wanted her ever nearer, around him, inside him. "The valets I've known never offered much appeal."

She touched a fingertip to his mouth. "I'm pleased."

"We have years to learn the art."

Her long, dark lashes fluttered, and he saw in her eyes how relief warred with want and won. "I am tired."

"Turn around."

She presented her back. He undid her garments, even the hated half-corset with all the mistakes of his fumbling fingers. When she clutched her undone garments to her shoulders, he drew her back against him and blessed the long, graceful arc of her throat with his lips. "Climb into bed, valet. It's cold and we are both tired."

She whirled to face him. "And you will come to sleep beside me, won't you?"

There was only one bed and only one place he wished to be.

"I will." He touched the tip of her perfect nose. "Go."

When, minutes later, he climbed under the heavy quilts to lie down beside her and curl her against him with an arm across her waist, she snuggled backward. "We'll stay warmer if we share our heat."

He wanted to groan, but from somewhere he found forbearance and repositioned his hips to be less suggestive. "A challenge for me, Mrs. Ruxton."

"I know," she said, sending a little giggle to the night air. "Thank you for everything."

"There is no need for that."

"Oh, but there is, Garrick. I must tell you…I must. I did not want to marry Daniel."

In her stilted words Garrick found confirmation of what he'd suspected with her avoidance of his uncle the past few days. Some humor would do in lieu of a discussion of her meaning. "He would have been a terrible maid."

She flinched at his words. "I could never be his valet."

"No, my darling." Garrick kissed her shapely, bare shoulder. "You are mine."

Chapter Ten

SHE AWAKENED THE next morning to the flash of lightning and the rattle of the rafters in a horrific rain storm. Drowsy with sleep, she had her hand to her new husband's chest and her legs aligned to his under the covers. She'd slept with her two sisters when she'd been younger, before all in the family had learned to pawn their goods and work to afford them a bigger house and individual accommodations.

But this arrangement, she could live with for decades...she hoped. Niggling at her was Daniel's declaration that he had encouraged Garrick to marry her. She pushed it away. What she saw in her new husband was a man who had eyes only for her. Courage was a useful trait, and she squeezed shut her eyes looking for it. In their relationship, there was so much to value...and discover.

"What do you think?" His bass voice reverberated inside her like a seductive melody.

She opened her eyes to see him peering down at her with devilish intent. "I'd say you're warm and just what I need to chase this storm away."

"Maids do that well," he affirmed with the assurance of a stuffy old servant.

"Let me see..." she murmured, and draped her arm around his waist so that she could meld against his firm, hot body and reach up to peck his lips. "You're right."

He splayed his fingers into her hair and held her for a long minute before he took her mouth in a deep and daring claim. "Valets have all sorts of talents."

"They wait upon their employers with speed and efficiency. And they don't wait forever." She caught him close and brushed her lips on his.

He rolled her to the mattress, and as her legs twined in his, he pressed his open mouth to her chin, then descended. Her gown was a thin and useless barrier. She'd known it from the start.

Her breasts grew hard and needy. Her hands sought knowledge of the man who wended his way down to her cleavage and sighed as he put a searing kiss between her breasts.

"Might we dispense with this muslin?" he asked against her skin.

She'd love nothing better. "If you will remove yours as well."

"Why not?" He cupped her cheek and laughed into her eyes. "I want you as God gave you to me. Without frills. Just you."

They rustled about, throwing their garments to the floor and collapsing back into each other's arms with chuckles.

Their laughter suited her. Nerves were a terrible thing to have at such a glorious moment.

He bound her to him, and at his strength, her insides melted. "You feel wonderful."

"As do you."

He stroked her spine. "I wish to make you feel wonderful inside."

"I wish you'd tell me how to make you feel the same," she told him, wide-eyed.

"No one has ever taught you any of this?" His question sounded as much a need for knowledge as assurance he might be her only amour.

"Ah, well." She had to admit her experiments. "The baker's son had aspirations."

"Did he succeed?" He nuzzled between her breasts and blew

hot kisses on her shivering skin.

"His kisses were…tepid."

"Hmmm." Garrick caught her gaze as his hand weighed one breast and rubbed her tingling nipple with his thumb.

She arched up to beg for more. "I told him."

"Bet he didn't care for that," he said as he rolled her nipple to a little point, and she clamped muscles inside her loins she never knew she had.

"He worked in the heat of ovens all day long, so he said he never liked to get too hot elsewhere."

Garrick broke into gales of laughter. "Poor bugger. A likely excuse. Did you correct him?"

"I only knew whatever he did wasn't…"

"Enough." He swooped down to take her breast into his mouth and lick her to a high point. He broke away with a sharp sucking sound. "It wasn't enough, was it?"

"Nooo," she whispered, and bowed higher into his palm.

"Any more?" His hand covered the full mound of her very happy breast.

"More of that," she shot back in mindless petition. "Please."

"I meant, my darling, were there more than just the baker's son?" He sent one hand down her ribs to her hip and stroked the skin above the hairline of her mons.

"Mmm," she crooned at the sensation of his fingertips, back and forth, back and forth. Her eyes stung. Her heart raced. The spot between her legs grew slippery and oddly…hungry. "There was a viscount."

"Ah." Garrick slid between her thighs and supported himself on his elbows. As he nuzzled her belly and the skin he'd stroked so well, he said, "Did the viscount gain any ground?"

"No. He had enough land."

"Darling?" In frustration at his delay, she opened her eyes. He peered down into hers. "I don't care about his estates. I care to learn what he had of you."

"Oh."

"Did he?"

She bit her lip and nodded. "Kisses."

Garrick paused above her belly button. "Where?" he asked, and dipped his tongue into the recess.

She squirmed. "My back."

"I'll do that next," Garrick said, and threaded his fingers into her nether hair.

"Oh, superb." She sighed in relief as he slid one thick finger inside her. His possession was at once enough…and yet not. Her eyes fell closed. She felt fulfilled yet needed more.

"Look at me."

He was her angel come to make wicked love to her. A vision in taut skin over bulging muscles, his sparkling eyes on her, he sat on his haunches. Later, in more light, she'd see him. But now, his midnight hair mussed upon his brow, his chest heaving, his cock oh so long and erect and soon to be hers, he was her dream, her husband, come true. And with her smile, he sent her a lopsided grin—and her reward was a finger to join the other.

"Oh…that's…" She ran her tongue over her lips.

"I can tell," he murmured. "Look at me."

"My, what the baker's son was missing."

He hooted. "You're telling me."

"And the viscount."

"What a rogue."

Whooping, she scooted nearer to him. "It's you I cannot get enough of."

"My darling," he said, his brows high, his eyes wide, as he parted her legs and settled down to view her very intimate flesh, "I am determined to prove you wrong."

She dug her fists into the bed. Embarrassed, wanton, she was a mess of emotions. "Do it!"

"What?" he said with a smirk in his voice. Then he blew his hot breath on her cold, wet lips.

"That! That! Anything! More!"

He caught her wrists. "Stop. I'm going to give you everything."

"Oh, you'd better."

"And you are going to be quiet."

"I am?"

"And lie back and let me have you."

"I will?"

"Ever so sweetly."

"Will I enjoy you?"

"I aspire to it."

She liked his narrowed gaze upon her, his focus sweetly savage. "You're rather mad, you know."

His face lit up with the devil's own sin. "I am. For you. From first sight."

"Really?"

"Truly."

Her nipples ached. Her insides swelled. "Do hurry."

He sank to her body and, with careful fingers, parted her folds. "No need to. You're ready."

"I am."

He gave a laugh. Three fingers gave her a long, smooth massage. "You're very wet."

"You're very chatty."

"I want you to be done with talk, because when I come inside you, there'll be no need to utter a word."

"Prove it."

"Oh, Mrs. Ruxton, you will have all of me." He disappeared from her view, and she heard him part her drenched lips and breathe so hotly upon them. He found some spot that shot her to the stars.

She grabbed his hair. "That."

He caught her gaze, one brow high. "What?"

"That…that place you…um…licked?"

"This?" His pale green eyes wild with laughter and desire, he reached out and, sight unseen, found the bit and pinched her.

She gulped down her delight. "Yes, yes. That! How did you… What is that, and where has it been hiding all my life?"

"Ah, well. A treasure hidden away just for me." He put his

lips to it to suck her hard into his mouth.

She keened. The *hotelier* would throw them out. She slapped a hand to her husband's shoulder. "Garrick!"

For answer, he opened her wider and sent his fingers inside while he flicked that tender spot to an urgent point of madness. He was thorough. He was kind.

His tongue was long. And very skillful.

Her mind was gone. And very craven.

He gave her all she cried out for, and left her climbing high to a pulsing satisfaction that left her panting and wrapped in his embrace.

When she thought there could not be more, she realized he must have his own satisfaction.

"What?" she asked him, unsure how to make him happy.

That was when he laid her back, spread her out, and crawled between her thighs to slowly, slowly fill her with his cock and make her want and whine and purr once again. She was spent and done, and breathless when he kissed her on her cheek.

Then he rose to leave her boneless on the bed. She watched him walk away, watched the muscles of his ass and thighs working in a symmetry she could appreciate now that they had worked for her pleasure as well as his.

He came back, then lay down beside her with a cloth to clean her thighs and kiss her lips in sweet benediction. When he left and returned, he curled her against him. "Rest. Breakfast won't be served for another hour or more."

She wiggled herself backward into his full embrace. "I cannot move."

He nuzzled the hollow behind her ear. "You'll revive."

"And do this again?"

He kissed the curve of her shoulder. "In all the ways that make us happy."

"In all the ways we are perfect together."

"Forevermore," he confirmed, and hugged her tightly, skin to skin, the warmth of their union filling her heart to the brim.

Chapter Eleven

THAT MORNING, A terrible storm blowing a very hard gale rained down with thunder and lightning that shook the rafters of their inn. But they were oblivious to the tempest outside.

In their cozy room, Daisy viewed their lovemaking as prelude to hours of magic in her new husband's embrace. As they dressed to go down to the public room for breakfast, she needed to do nothing more than glance at him to know she was eager to taste again the thrill of his tenderness. He read her overture as invitation to return to their bed, and they tarried in their adventures for so long that they nearly missed the breakfast service.

Upstairs later, Garrick settled at one of the two tables, took out his spectacles, and began to doodle on paper he had purchased from the innkeeper. When she asked what he did, he told her that he often thought best with quill in hand, drawing nothing but circles and triangles, boxes and lines. "I discover new ideas. Things I'd never thought of before. I've not had a chance to do it these past few weeks. One thing and another has happened so quickly. I need to let my mind wander to figure out the problems I face."

"I understand that. I began a project when I encountered difficulties teaching my students. It's taken the form of a children's book. Perhaps one day I might sell it, if a publisher thinks it might have merit."

"Did you bring it with you?"

"I did."

"May I see it?"

"Of course. It's rough. But it represents my attempt to think of a project in a new way." No one else had ever asked about it, and she doubted she would have readily handed it to just anyone. But she had no compunctions about showing Garrick.

Daisy removed a sheaf of papers from a portfolio in her valise and set them out upon the other table in their room. "Like you with your random drawing, I haven't done any work on this in a while. Since I left for London, in fact. It's an instruction book I wrote for children to learn French."

He leaned over her at the table and skimmed her words. "Remarkable. Have you been at this long?"

She leaned back against his chest, his tender assurance all she'd never had. "I began two years ago, but changed last summer the direction of what I'm doing. At first, it was to be more of a lexicon. Now it is a story in English and French. A new way, I hope, for children to be entertained while they learn a new language."

He read a few more lines. "A story about a fox and a rabbit?"

"*Oui, monsieur! Renard et Lapine* live together on the edge of a forest bordering two estates."

"But they are antagonists, aren't they? One the hunter of the other?"

"In real life, it would be so. But Monsieur Renard and Mademoiselle Lapine have a challenge to overcome. You see, the people who live on the two estates are always fighting each other. They keep destroying the forest, and the two animals realize one day they must settle their own differences and learn how to work together to save their homes and find some peace."

"Like humans, eh?" He lifted her chin and planted a kiss on her lips. "Perhaps this tale is as much for children as adults."

She pointed a finger at him. "When they succeed in becoming friends themselves, they plan to teach the people how to cooperate."

"And how is that?"

She shrugged. "All ideas are welcome, sir. I've started down this road and, at the moment, have no idea where I'm going. I think some days to give up."

"I venture many an author has come to an impasse and thought to stop. Don't." He grinned. "You could have a fine idea there and sell many copies to aspiring French students."

"I have enjoyed the writing. But some days my mind is not on my characters."

A glint of interest flashed in his eyes as he offered his hand. "Such as today?"

"Such as now." She rose to follow him to their bed and sit in his lap.

He ran his palm up her leg and toyed with the garter he had so recently tied on her thigh. "New ideas come in extraordinary ways."

"We need to try that premise," she whispered as she splayed her fingers into his thick satin curls.

The story that needed to be written at the moment was the beginning of her romance with her husband. The characters were new to each other but eager to learn where to kiss. Behind an ear. Beneath a breast. Inside a thigh. Along a long, hard, silken member. Between wet, willing folds that parted and were filled.

With sighing satisfaction, afternoon came. Daisy returned to her writing, and Garrick asked if he might read her sister's diary. She dug it from her trunk, and he sat in the old, overstuffed chair by the one window and read until daylight disappeared and it was time to emerge from their room for dinner.

Afterward, forged together in the cocoon of their room, they gave a nod to the storms outside that grew more wild, and they were naked once more, marveling with compliments and kisses at their complete surrender to passion.

WHEN THE INNKEEPER offered up his chess set the next afternoon, the two of them played each other with a growing fury. Each took from the other victories in equal number. They celebrated with lazy hours entangled in each other and rose to dine, only to return and pleasure each other once more.

At last, on the third morning, they heard no thunder and saw no lightning flash. After tea and toast and eggs, they stepped outside just as the clouds parted.

"How many crossings are there each day?" she asked Garrick.

"A few. We'll go for a stroll, take a look at the currents, and decide if we want to chance sailing today."

"Shall we go to your docks?"

"No. Remember, no one knows us. We book passage on a post packet as Mr. and Mrs. Evans from Canterbury."

Within minutes, they were warmed by the sun and encouraged to cross by the sight of calm Channel waters. They decided they would indeed buy tickets to travel that noon. Inside the packet office, other customers gathered. One gossiped to his friend of a merchant ship that had come back from Calais because of the storms the previous days.

"Pardon me," Garrick interrupted the two. "Do you know the name of that ship?"

"The *Old George*, was it, Carmichael?" the man asked his friend.

"Aye. Tha's the name."

"Is that one of yours?" Daisy asked Garrick as they hurried back to their inn to pack.

"It is."

"Is its delay a problem?"

"Not really. We have to account for storms. Our schedules keep us efficient, but God knows the weather he sends us is His purview, never ours."

"It seems so odd that to cross here is so treacherous when one can see Calais before us."

"It's only twenty-six miles, but dangerous." He squeezed her hand. "Not today, though. We sail in calm waters."

"And in excellent company," she said to him with a serenity that surprised her. "I'm ready to go."

Hours later, as the golden rays of the day cast shimmering shades upon the waters ahead of them, they boarded the public packet. The crossing was smooth, and the packet moved along at even keel. They stood on the deck apart from two other passengers who braved the air, Garrick's arm around her.

"The other night," she said, "when I told you I was happy to be your valet and I thanked you, I did not mean to offend you when I said I had learned I did not wish to marry Daniel."

He reached over and caressed her cheek. His lips were close, and his breath was soft and sweet. "You didn't." And then, as was his wont these past few glorious days, he hovered over her and kissed her. His possession bold, he took her mouth in one strong claim, then another.

Her eyes closed, she drifted in the euphoria his kisses bestowed upon her. "You could kiss me a thousand times and I'd never have enough."

"I shall test that." Upon his breathless words, he took her mouth in a searing kiss.

"Please do," she told him when at last he tore away. "But I…I must tell you why I could not marry Daniel. Talking with him those past few days, I learned I could not want him. He was not the man I perceived in our letters. Not kind or respectful. No. He…he leered at me. Spoke to me as if I were…his to rule. My skin prickled, and I became frightened of him, even though I knew he could not rise from the bed. I knew, and yet…"

She bound Garrick tightly.

He buried his lips in her hair and clutched her close. "I understand, my darling. I know him not since you came to us. He became demanding, critical. Particular. Calling on the maid,

Cora, to wait upon him to feed him and fetch for him."

She caught Garrick's gaze. "Cora? He had her to wait on him?"

"Yes. I know not why. I never noticed anything particular between them previously."

"Not even now," she said, recalling that Cora had been in Daniel's bedroom a few times when she herself had called upon him. "They maintained a proper decorum between them when I was in his rooms. Yet…yet Cora did bring me messages from him that he wished to see me. I thought they were requests he had sent through Nuttley. But I might be wrong."

She grew silent. Speculating on the maid and Daniel's relationship brought her no clarity. "What could be the reason for that? Other than the fact that she is agreeable. And she is. Most agreeable."

"Perhaps too much so."

"Perhaps."

"She asked me to remember her and request her services permanently when we return."

"Did she?" He gazed off into the gathering night. "Odd."

Daisy pressed herself against her husband.

"You needn't have her, Daisy. When we return and move into our own home, Cora will stay in Chesterfield Street. But when we return, you need not have her then either. We shall see if Daniel is insistent she stays there under his employ. Of that, I don't care. He can do as he wants. It is his house, and he can have those whom he wishes to wait upon him. But you and I do not need to subject ourselves to his whims. Certainly not now, or even when we return and move out." Garrick regarded her with an endearing light in his pale green eyes. "You are my wife, and you may have anyone you wish."

She rose on her toes and placed her lips on his in a kiss that told of many delights for which she yearned. "I wish only for you."

"I KNOW YOU will like our chief clerk," Garrick told her the next morning as he helped her into their *hôtelier's* borrowed *cabriolet*. They had arrived in Calais late the evening before and gone straight to the hotel, where Garrick had never stayed. As soon as the concierge showed them to their room and their possessions were brought up, Garrick and she refreshed themselves in the house restaurant. They went straight to bed and arose early. Garrick wanted to set off immediately to take care of business. "Monsieur Henri has been with me since last August."

"A Frenchman! I should have known." She was so pleased that Garrick invited her to come along to his offices. Promising not to interfere in his discussions, she was happy to do something other than swaying to the incessant waves of the Channel. She'd not become ill on the journey. She'd feared it more than was warranted. Now she was proud she had held her own. But today she needed to walk on solid ground. Take the air. Hear the birds chirp. "I'll be happy to meet him."

Only a few streets away from the quay, the building was an old stone edifice that had once been the French Empire's customs office. Since the peace, Garrick told her, they needed larger quarters. The building was now rented to various merchants. They climbed the marble stairs to the second floor.

Monsieur Henri must have spied them arriving from his window—he came to the top of the massive staircase, arms out to greet them. A man of forty or so, with a hearty smile, he wore his coal-black hair pomaded straight back from his face, with thick glasses perched upon his long Gallic nose. He received Garrick in unrestrained and booming English that echoed in the cavernous hallway.

After Garrick introduced Daisy, Henri greeted her in English with the *savoir faire* of a Frenchman taught well by his mama to honor all ladies he met with grace. "Madam Ruxton, I welcome you to France."

"*Merci beaucoup, monsieur. Je suis Normande.*"

The big man was impressed. "You are French, *madame?*"

"*Oui.* I am delighted now to be Monsieur Ruxton's bride and can claim to be English, as well."

Henri lost himself in profuse exclamations of joy at her presence and clasped his hands together in apology. "*Excusez-moi,* Monsieur Ruxton. I get carried away. You are newly wed?"

Garrick chuckled. "Only four days ago."

"Oh, well! You are a bride, *madame!* My felicitations to you both! We should have a champagne, *oui?*"

Garrick refrained. "*Monsieur,* we have no need."

Daisy suppressed her delight. Henri seemed much too eager to impress her and make this meeting into a celebration instead of a necessary meeting about missing stock. She would not see Garrick disappointed in his quest for information.

"But we should! The new bubbly white is the best way to celebrate. Napoleon said it so, and our new Louis likes it, too! I will send out one of the men from the *entrepôt.*"

"Why not join my wife and me for a drink later after we finish our discussion?"

Pushing his disappointment aside with a reluctant shake of his head, Henri agreed. "As you wish, Monsieur Ruxton. Do come in."

His desk, a huge, old thing of nicked and scuffed varnished oak, commanded the expansive room. At all four walls stood oaken cabinets composed of shelves and a few tall drawers.

"Please to sit here, *madame.*" Henri swept up a pile of documents from one large wooden chair. As he nodded toward a matching chair for Garrick, Daisy wondered if Henri's messy desk signaled that he was not very organized.

The two men spoke of minor matters, who among their men was ill or had recently married or welcomed babies.

"You know why I have come, *monsieur.*" Garrick sat back, the lines along his mouth severe. "I wish the news on efficiency. Tell me about the numbers of our stock reaching their destinations."

Henri checked Garrick's expression and Daisy's.

"Do proceed, *monsieur*. My wife may hear it all."

The clerk's *bonhomie* vanished. "I wish I could share good tidings, sir."

Garrick frowned. He had hired Henri last August soon after he took over. Before that time, items shipped through Ostend and Calais went missing in odd lots. Diverse items of odd numbers, all of which were unnoticed until the quantities totaled huge amounts. The reason why Garrick hired Henri and replaced the former clerk was to stop the leaks. "You have found no new evidence of how these goods are disappearing?"

"Some. Some." The man shook his dark head and pushed his spectacles up his big, hooked nose. "I have not solved the problem. Not found who does this. Or how. But I have located a hole. A…a place where they disappear."

"A leak." Garrick sat forward, hoping it was not through Calais again. "Describe it for me."

Henri's long, square jaw dropped lower. "Our goods for those along the northern lines?"

"Yes. The Lille fortifications and east?"

"*Oui*. They have been delivered. All are accounted for. Each crate. Each number inside them is correct. Shirts. Boots. Tins of grease for the cannon."

"And those going to Paris?"

"The numbers of crates on our ships from Calais to Le Havre and into the Seine are also intact. When they reach the docks in Rouen, the right number is loaded off and put to the warehouse. But when they must be loaded on to the barges to Paris the next day or the next, the numbers are wrong. They are fewer."

Daisy watched, helpless, as Garrick worked the muscles in his jaw.

He sat forward. "Are our own dockworkers stealing the supplies? Our man there, Michaud, has a record of ethical business practices. I hired him last June after great examination of him and his work. Henri, I have never questioned his integrity."

Henri nodded. "Alphonse Michaud is a good man. I doubt he would suddenly change. And I have no idea why he would. I mean, what has changed since the spring? Nothing."

"And," Garrick said, "he assured me he hires honest workers."

"Just so, Monsieur Ruxton. But I have had letters from him, and he has not been able to learn when or how the crates disappear."

"What are the numbers? What exactly is missing as of today?"

"Still random. Five crates of this and three of that. Or six the next time. Four of that."

Daisy fell back, befuddled. "They care not how much they take? Such thieves never know their profits if they have no constant chain of supply."

Garrick stared at her, but spun to ask Henri about it. "For them, is it always a matter of opportunity?"

Henri sagged. "I do not know, *monsieur*. It baffles me."

WHEN GARRICK AND Daisy settled into their borrowed *cabriolet* once more, she regarded her husband with sympathy for his plight. "We go now to Rouen for another reason besides my own, don't we?"

He ran a hand over his eyes and sighed. "We do."

"Do we hire a *diligence*?" She'd heard of the traveling coaches one could hire in the port cities to make quick work of trips to the interior of France.

"No. We see a friend of mine who will give us passage on one of his ships."

As night enveloped the city, she suggested to Garrick that they go for a walk along the boulevard. "A change of scenery will do us some good. We can change our thinking, and inspiration may strike."

With a smile that he clearly did not feel, Garrick had agreed.

She welcomed the time to reflect. Her recollections of Calais amounted to shadowed impressions, so like the rest of her flight with her family. She had long since resigned herself to faded memories full only of sounds or smells and flashes of light. For the first time in her life, she was content with that. She absorbed what she saw here now of the city whence she had fled a terrified French child and where she now arrived a very happy married woman of French descent and English ties.

Since they had left the meeting with Monsieur Henri, Garrick had turned quiet. When they left his man, Garrick had taken a few of the lading documents with him to study. But she had persuaded him to put them aside and leave them until the morning to examine.

"We'll share a bottle of that champagne Monsieur Henri was so eager to offer us," Garrick told her as they strolled toward the city's Notre Dame. Henri and Garrick had been in no mood to celebrate anything after they spoke of the missing items. Henri had returned home, but not before offering them the use of his carriage. To that, Garrick politely refused and told his man he would hire a small fiacre. Daisy and he were here in strictest secrecy. Henri was to tell no one of their presence in the city. Nor was he to write to Alphonse Michaud in Rouen to tell him of their discussion, of Garrick's presence in France, nor his intention to confront Michaud.

"We'll rejoice that we have a few answers," she said, and hugged his arm. "And we will soon have a few ideas as to the nature of our theft."

"Will we?"

She traced her fingers over his brow to banish his skepticism. "Dinner first, then those ideas on the theft." She gave him a consoling smile, and he agreed to push his concerns aside during their walk and dinner. She had kept her thoughts to herself, not wishing to intrude on his efforts to untangle his mystery.

After a fine dinner of roast beef, creamed, sautéed potatoes, and turnips in a delicate white wine sauce, he banned any talk of his problems.

She did as he asked, not wishing to deny his wishes.

They went back to their rooms, and she sought to improve his mood.

As he did her the service of undoing all her clothes down to her skin, she turned in his arms and traced the outline of his lips. "Might I entice you to kiss me, sir, and put aside your troubles for a few minutes?"

He rubbed his nose against hers and chuckled. "Might I entice you to spend more than a few minutes teasing my worries from me?"

She grabbed handfuls of his shirt and drew it over his head. With kisses to his marvelously broad chest, she brushed her breasts against his molten skin. "Tell me all your cares, sir. I have no need to sleep when your heart is so heavy."

"Be careful, wife." He lifted her up in his arms and strode with her to their bed. There, he devoted himself to rousing her to new planes of desire. "I may keep you awake all night."

"I will never object," she told him.

When the two of them found a breathless satisfaction, he took her lips and smiled into her eyes. "My heart, my darling, is lighter now that you are mine."

For such loving care, she knew now she would always be his. Always.

But she lay awake long after he fell to a deep sleep. His refusal to discuss the new information gained from Henri caused her to pick through random thoughts that had occurred to her during dinner. They were odd ideas.

Old stories, tales of daring, in cellars and caves. Her brothers laughing at the table about a day gone exploring.

Why she should think of that when she had not in decades was curious. She perceived they certainly would sound so to Garrick.

So she smiled at the scintillating echoes of a family laughing together, and faced her husband, content that the past came to her in happiness and that her future promised a lifetime of more.

Chapter Twelve

T HEY ROSE EARLY the next morning and took their breakfast quickly.

"I apologize for rushing you," Garrick told her as they emerged from the hotel to the street. He took her arm, then led her away toward Notre Dame. They were going to see Lord Courtenay's and his friend, Jacques Durand.

"Don't you want to use the hotel's *cabriolet?*"

"I want to hire a different hack."

Alarm had her clutching his arm. "Do you think we're being followed?"

"I've not seen such, no. Have you felt someone staring at you?"

"No, no." She had always had a keen sense if someone were observing her overlong. She hadn't felt that here.

"Good. I simply wish to be careful here in all things. I am wary now that Monsieur Henri tells me items are missing and my man in Rouen may be to blame. Forgive me. I do not want to frighten you."

"You don't." They climbed into a shoddy old cab he hailed, and Garrick sat beside her. She took his hand. "And you need never apologize to me. I know you are worried."

He scowled. "I am frustrated. I thought I could trust Michaud. I don't think of myself as naïve. But I have spent my life relying on my own instincts. A few times, I have been wrong. On this matter, I cannot afford to be."

"I understand. I do." She did not want to counter Garrick's conclusions. Nor did she wish to upset him any more than he was. But something about Monsieur Henri was too…perfect. Too accommodating. She found him agreeable. But trust him? She conceded that she needed more than twenty minutes in his company to decide. Garrick knew his man better than she, and she would abide by her husband's judgment. "You will meet Michaud again in Rouen and investigate these charges. You will rely on your instinct if he tells the truth. Then time will tell if you can find evidence that implicates him."

"You are right." He inhaled and picked up her hand to give her a kiss. "And with you by my side, I'll welcome your impressions."

"I'd be honored." She wanted to help him, but she was not going to add more possible questions to his mysteries. Not unless she had further indications after meeting Michaud in Rouen that she could not trust him. And she would certainly not entertain that her odd little thoughts might mean more without evidence.

THE CAB RETURNED to the port along the lower banks and stopped in front of a large ship, anchored at the quay. During Napoleon's reign, Garrick had told her, Durand had been a smuggler. Now he worked legitimately with his ships registered in London. Durand knew so many along the French ports that some had assumed he'd worked as a British spy. No official, French or British, questioned him.

"Your friend works here?" She was surprised at the size of the ship. Guns lined the deck, the muzzles staring down at them.

"He's been so long at his trade that he spends his days now on the water but sailing as little as possible."

"Unusual man."

"He is. This is his home most of the year. It is a French frigate which he captured in 1810 in Brest."

"He went into the port to take it?"

"He did. Intrepid man."

One look at the fellow and Daisy knew the description well applied. She thought she was looking at a man who had plied the rough and ready seas of a century ago. Jacques Durand was an arrogantly handsome man. With inky-black hair long to his shoulders, one eye beneath a dark leather patch, and one blue eye staring at her, he was dressed as if he were a British gentleman ready for tea. In a bottle-green frock coat and gold satin waistcoat, sparkling white shirt, and fawn breeches that fit him like a skin, he bowed over Daisy's hand and, with a flourish, offered her a seat on his damask-covered settee.

"Where did you acquire such a lovely bride?" he said, his eerie blue gaze riveted to Daisy's.

"She advertised and was to marry Daniel," Garrick told him without one second of hesitation.

Durand snorted in surprise. "Is that so?" He directed the question to Daisy.

"Every word." She liked this man. His subtle mix of English and mellifluous French. His gruff manner.

"Intriguing." His eyes narrowed in assessment of her. Yet he was respectful, sizing her up for his friend. "I must hear that tale."

"Would you like to enlighten this man, Daisy?" Garrick asked.

"I will give you the brief version," she replied.

"By all means." Durand swept out a hand and sat, one long leg crossed upon the other, to hear her story. At the end, he shook his head and laughed. "I think, Garrick, you have the better of that advertisement. Daniel must be furious."

"He may be, but Daisy and I are meant to be."

The words told Daisy nothing about Daniel's claim to have suggested the marriage to Garrick. She would let her concern about it recede once more. They had many issues to resolve that were of the moment. She would raise this one later, if ever she had to.

"But to business," said Durand with a slap of his hand to his thigh. "I understand there are problems in Rouen."

"You know this." Garrick appeared unsurprised. "How?"

"Rumor. My own network still works, even if we are no longer at war, my friend."

"Your rumor. Is it a whisper or a roar?"

Durand inhaled and rolled his eyes. "Better. A combination."

"Tell me."

"You experience problems in your business. No different than many, living and working in this sad and desperate country. Since Napoleon went south to Elba, much is in disarray. The peasants reel and rebel under new royalist taxes. They hate that our new king invites the courtiers to return to grab their land and possessions. The old till barren fields. Their sons lie dead in foreign fields cultivated by Napoleon's cannon. No one has any money. The new copper and silver *Louis* are worth half their value."

"So I have seen," Garrick said. "We are paying here only in coin."

"You are wise. Who are you, by the way? Certainly not Garrick Ruxton."

Garrick told him their assumed names. "Because we have not yet learned who attacks us in London, I thought it best to come abroad secretly."

"Go to Rouen the same way. Tell no one you go or that you will see Michaud at your depots."

"There are no rules any longer."

Durand curled up his lips in distaste. "Every vagabond and thief who could not operate under the little corporal now tries his hand at thieving. There is no honor among them."

"Was there ever?" Garrick asked. "Aside from you."

Durand flicked something from his kneecap. "And that is why

I am still here. The new French royalists like me. What can I say? I was once their friend. Then the Bonapartes' worst nightmare. Now? Ah. *Quels sont les dommage?*"

Garrick sighed. "Tell me. Do you know my man in Rouen?"

"Alphonse Michaud. I do. A very good businessman. His sympathies have always been to the best of his abilities regardless of who sat on the throne in Tuileries."

"Would he create a small business for himself with Ruxton goods?"

Durand scoffed. "He'd be a fool. Your shipments are meant for your army."

"And the items missing are of little value per piece. A small number here, a different number there. Even in bulk, they cannot be sold. Who would want them?"

"So they have stolen nothing that's worth their effort. Odd. Odd."

Garrick shook his head. "They've taken dribs and drabs of this and that. Nothing that makes any sense. If I ship in a cargo of diamonds, will they bite?"

Durand shrugged. "You are right. And what does Daniel say of all this?"

"He does not say much. Pain rules him. He grumbles and gives orders."

"And you have not found the culprit for his accident or the attack on your wife?"

Daisy was taken aback. They had not spoken of that here today.

Garrick pursed his lips. "Your rumors travel quickly."

"It's what I pay well to learn." Durand regarded Daisy with kindness. "I am quite thrilled you were not hurt, *madame*. But Garrick, an attack on those in your house is ugly. So I ask why that is." Durand folded his long fingers together.

"If I can answer that, I will know much about this problem," Garrick said.

Durand got up to pour them all glasses of *vin rouge*.

"We go to Rouen tomorrow," Garrick told Durand as they finished their wine. "I will ask you the favor of sailing there on one of your ships."

"Of course. A carriage ride would be tedious. You will have my schooner. It is faster."

"Thank you. I knew you would have men you can trust."

"I will give my captain papers for you to clear customs in Le Havre. That means you do not have to pay the immigration tax or declare your nationality."

As THEY RODE back to their hotel, Garrick sank to the seat with his problems weighing down on him. The discovery of his identity and Daisy's was a tiny fraction of Garrick's concerns. He negotiated in London to ship a very valuable cargo to Paris. Not diamonds. Infinitely more useful and appealing to everyone— thief, priest, commoner, or king. But if he could not guarantee the safety of shirts and cannon grease, he could not win the contract for this precious item.

Daisy had just settled when she curled her arm around his and asked him about Durand. "He knows so much. Is he that widely received?"

"He has many friends. Some are not on the right side of the law or the right side of the blanket. He makes it his business to listen to all of them. It's how he has survived."

"Might he know the military governor of Rouen?"

"Jourdan? I am certain he does." Garrick drew her against him in the carriage. Her nearness was becoming for him a talisman against all ills. "His mother's family is the same as Jourdan's wife's."

"From the house of Vendôme?"

He should not have been surprised at Daisy's question. "You know the family?"

"Not I. But my Aunt d'Harcourt claimed that the old Marquise de Vendôme knew everyone in Paris, where they slept with whom, and why."

Garrick snorted. "Durand has inherited the trait. What he said, you can record in stone."

What worried him more was what Durand had not said. Durand had not given any indication that he could transport anything into France safely. And if Garrick could not find the source of these piddly thefts, he could not in good conscience take on the job of transporting Rothschild gold to Britain's allies.

THAT NIGHT, GARRICK insisted they take their meal in their rooms. He disliked brooding, but he could see nothing but an abyss ahead of him. Today, neither Henri nor Durand had been of any help.

He paced the floor.

His wife had declared she understood his reasons to think over this situation, and allowed him his brown study. But as they undressed for bed, she came and wrapped her arms around his back and sighed. "I think Monsieur Durand had a few good points today."

"He did." Garrick covered her hands with his own, grateful for her comfort. He truly hated to be such poor company.

She turned in his embrace. "Have you considered that the attacks on Daniel and me are meant to ruin your reputation?"

"Oh, yes." *They will whether I solve these problems or not.*

"And have you any idea why someone would do that?"

"To prove me incompetent to run the business." *Or to bankrupt it.*

She brushed her hands over his cheeks, her soft brown eyes so honest and forgiving. He recalled no one who'd ever been so sweet to him since his mother when he was very young. "So that you would step down?"

"Or be forced down."

"And who would benefit from that?"

"Daniel is the sole owner. He would be in charge again."

"If he is capable."

"If. Yes."

"Would he sell the company?"

He frowned. *I doubt that. He is too proud.* "I've never had that conversation with him."

"Perhaps it's time you see if he has that on his mind."

He spread his fingers into her hair. "It is. When we return."

"And what if—forgive me for this—we return home and his health has worsened? Who inherits the company?"

"He told me I do."

"Have you seen his will? Do you know that for a fact?"

"No. I have only his word."

"I see." She nodded, grim. "Do you trust him?"

The very question he had not answered for himself in so very long.

"I—I cannot decide. He is so closed. Now, since his accident, he is even more so. Certainly, your insights to his character disturb me. His attitude toward you. And the business with the maid."

She stared at him, worry lining her features. "What else? There is more. What is it?"

If he did not share the answer with her, would she be able to entrust him with her own fears and problems?

"I am not a man who shares my troubles."

"Is it time you did?" She tipped her head to one side.

"It is. I allow them to haunt me. That's why I walk the floors in the middle of the night."

"Why you came to me in my bedroom in London?"

"Oh, yes." He sank his fingers into the wealth of her long, pale hair. "Aside from the fact that I could not bear the fact that you would belong to Daniel when I wanted you for myself? Oh, yes, my darling. I walked the floors in agony over how I wanted you. And I would not take you from Daniel…"

"Because you thought it was not ethical."

"Yes. That and because I was not worthy of you."

She reached up and took his mouth in an earnest kiss. "Never say that again. You are more than worthy. Look at what you have done. Worked at your uncle's behest for years. In Portugal and here in France. Sought to aid him in his dire hour of need after someone attacked him and tried to kill him. Oh, my darling husband, how can you say you are not worthy of him when you have been his savior?"

He set his jaw and walked away to the other side of the room. Raking his hair, he spun to face her. Ready to tell her all.

"There is one person who has just reason to see me disgraced. It's possible, though she has not the connections or the means to pay ne'er-do-wells to push Daniel to the street or to stage a carriage accident."

Daisy stilled. "A woman can do so as well as a man."

"I agree. But these acts are not like her."

Daisy walked over to the chair, sat, and waited. "What would be her motive?"

He inhaled. "Six years ago I worked as chief clerk in Ruxton & Company's warehouse on the London docks. I had worked for Daniel since I graduated from Cambridge, and I was responsible for keeping the London import-export ledgers. I found a discrepancy in the numbers. Crates of candles from our suppliers in Abbey Street and Pill Lane were missing. I brought up the matter with the young man who was responsible for counting all the goods. He became angry, defensive. We argued. Loudly. I told him he had to find the items. He told me I had miscounted. We parted, each furious with the other. Minutes later, I heard an argument. Then…a cry. I hurried to find him. He had fallen two stories down to the hard earthen floor. He was dead. Four men in the factory had heard our argument, and minutes later, another. Then the cry and the thud of his body. I was the natural suspect. I was the *only* suspect."

"No. Then what happened?"

"Bow Street was called in. They took stock of the body and the scene. My four men told them they heard us arguing, and that was enough. I was accused of murder."

"But that's ridiculous! You argued, and it does not mean that you—"

"It does. No one else had cause."

"Did you ever find the missing items?"

"No."

"Odd. Don't you think? That sounds like the same thing that's happening in Rouen."

"It does." He strode to the table where the concierge had left a bottle of brandy. "Exactly like it. I think whoever did it is up to it again."

"And who could that be? Do you have any of those men working for you still in London or here in Rouen?"

"No."

"Friends of theirs?"

He shook his head. God, she was fierce in his defense. He could almost summon a smile. "No."

"And this woman. Who is she?"

"The wife of the man who died. Mrs. Adam Foley." *Belinda.*

"And she has a grudge against you because you did not go to the gallows?"

"Because my uncle made an agreement with the magistrate that I was to go abroad and work in Portugal in his warehouse. The Peninsular Wars had begun, and Ruxton & Company was the major supplier into the ports. I was needed. I was essential. To have me hang, Daniel told the authorities, would have been a waste of good talent at a time when Britain needed every man to its cause."

"And you went abroad. And no one was sent to gaol for the death of this man."

Silence fell over them.

Daisy stirred. "Who took over for you at the London warehouse?"

"One of the four men who had sworn I was the one who argued with Foley. And before you ask, know that he was no longer working there when I returned to London to resume my previous role."

"When did you return?"

"June."

"After Napoleon was gone to Elba, Paris was occupied and the northern lines were to be supplied."

"Yes," he said, and sank to the chair opposite her. "When the fighting had stopped and supplying the army was less critical. When no one would die from the shortages."

"But someone would know. Someone would learn."

"And they have. My friend Courtenay works in the commissariat. He knows very well."

She narrowed her eyes upon the far wall. "He does not appear to criticize you for the losses."

"Not me personally. But he knows the tendency may be there. My sin—shall we call it?—is well known. This current matter may become a larger issue to the government if the goods are not found or the bleeding is not stopped."

"And your uncle knows this."

"Quite well. He is a member of Parliament. And…"

She blinked. "And what?"

Garrick paused. Daniel's old ambition rose to hover over this discussion. "He had ambitions to become prime minister one day. That is done now."

"My darling man," she said, and raised high her elegant brows, "a prime minister does not need two legs to govern."

"But he needs to have a family without murderers among the lot."

"Right you are, my dear husband. Good that he does not."

His heart leaping in his chest, he watched her rise and settle into his lap. Her belief in him humbled him. Few had ever bestowed on him such an honor.

# Chapter Thirteen

THEY BOARDED JACQUES Durand's schooner the next morning for the sail along the coast. The weather once more bowed to Daisy's wish for calm seas, and she and Garrick strolled the deck as the boat sailed south.

Daisy grew tense. He saw it in the way she knitted her brows. The way her hands would clench and she would stop and shake her head or sigh.

He opened his greatcoat, wrapped it around her, and brought her close, his lips next to her ear as he cradled her near him. "Do you think you will remember much of Rouen?"

"I hope it is the same. My childhood was filled with trips to the city from our chateau. Mama would lead us down the old market streets like a mother duck leading her ducklings. All in a row. The clock above the main street is what I recall most. Large and lovely, it tells much, but I cannot recall it all. What I do remember is that it is just up the lane from our townhouse, and I wonder if it still stands."

So much of her return to her homeland was difficult for her emotionally. He was careful of bringing it up. "Shall we go see?"

She made a face at that. "I am not certain I want to. It was a few houses away from an abbey, and you know what the French did to those of the cloth during the Revolution."

Ran out all in robes, killed many, then burned to the ground many of the churches, abbeys, and monasteries. "Did you ask Jourdan about that house?"

She shook her head. "No. It's the chateau in the country that I want, the one I remember most, and I fear if I expect too much to have survived, I may cast a spell on the rest."

"You do know that there is no such thing as a spell."

"I do." She smiled at him. "And I don't. I am so new at hoping that anything might be returned to me. I've waited so long for the chance, not even knowing I might have it."

"Think on it. We do not have to go see it if you decide against it."

THAT NIGHT, LATE, they walked up from the schooner tied at the quay and sought accommodations on a side street. A gray and white half-timbered structure, the hotel appeared to have been built centuries ago.

"These accommodations are rumored to be excellent," Garrick told her. "They do not know me here either. But the chef is supposed to be excellent. Our warehouse is that one." He pointed to a brick building facing the Seine.

Inside, they were shown to their rooms, but the kitchen had closed hours before.

"We can go to a bistro which I know will be open," he told her. "They serve good calvados apple wine and excellent cheese pies. Shall we go?"

They stuffed themselves so much they fell into bed, arms around each other, and slept without moving until late the next morning.

"I WANTED THIS to be a surprise visit to Monsieur Michaud,"

Garrick said as they gazed up at the red brick warehouse. Two men bustled about the far doors, loading crates at the quay. He recognized one of his own small Ruxton ships, its name emblazoned on the side in bold black letters. "You need not come inside with me. You can sit on that bench over there and watch the ships go by."

"I'd like to come. If you want me."

Her willingness to sort this through with him filled him with gratitude. "Do come, then. I want you always with me."

He led her up the steps, feigning a nonchalance for the coming confrontation. Inside, men hurried to and fro, sorting crates and opening them to sort items into piles.

He sought the office to the left. He knocked on the closed door, expecting to see his man Michaud. But the place was empty.

He emerged and hailed one of the passing laborers. In his best French, he asked where Michaud was.

"He is not here," the man told him with a decided once-over to him and to Daisy. The fellow was one Garrick did not know. New and surly, too. "At home. Ill, says his wife."

"*Merci*," Garrick told the man, and decided he'd call upon Michaud's house. Sick or not, Michaud needed to provide answers.

Outside, Garrick nodded toward a row of old stucco townhouses in the next street. "Michaud lives there."

One sharp set of knocks upon the red lacquered door and a white-haired, portly lady opened it wide.

"Madame Michaud," Garrick greeted his man's wife. He'd met her last spring. "I hope you remember me."

In French, she welcomed him with hearty words and a handshake, then stepped aside to have him and Daisy enter. To his wife, the lady was most pleasant, and to them both, she offered cake and coffee.

"*Merci beaucoup, madame*," said Garrick, "but I am in town and have heard at the warehouse that your husband is ill."

"*Ah. Oui. Non,*" she said with sadness in her tone and a drooping face. "He is not ill, Monsieur Ruxton. But gone."

"Gone?"

"Please to come inside, *monsieur*. I will tell you."

"I am in a hurry, *madame*. Please tell me now."

But she shook her head at his less-than-perfect French and rattled off more words he could not decipher.

Daisy stepped into the breach.

"Madame Michaud says," she told him with a consoling smile at the lady, "that her husband left home day before yesterday. He told his men that he was ill and would not return until he was recovered. He left on business."

"Where has he gone?" Garrick checked the woman's expression for signs of her veracity.

Another barrage of French had him gazing at Daisy for help.

Daisy listened to the lady with growing concern lining her face. Then she turned to Garrick. "He knows he is missing items for the Paris shipments, and he has become distraught. Unable to learn who was stealing from him, he went to search himself. He told his wife he would not return until he knew who did this to him and where his goods had gone."

Garrick thrilled to the proof of his man's innocence—and the confirmation that Michaud was concerned about the thefts. "Where has he gone?"

Madame Michaud shook her head and replied in her rapid and sorrowful French.

"He would not tell her," Daisy translated. "To the south, is all she knows."

"South where? To Paris?"

The woman looked bewildered. She had understood his question. "*Non, monsieur.* Across the Seine." They expressed their thanks to her and made to leave when she shook her head and said, "He went in a rush. But he was sure to pack his riding boots and many candles."

There was little more to say. He and Daisy emerged onto the street.

"LET'S WALK," DAISY said to him, and curled her arm through his. Why would a man be certain to take on a journey his boots and a good supply of candles?

It niggled at her.

The sun was bright today, the wind off the river brisk. In minutes, they stood upon the quay and watched once more two men unload crates from the Ruxton ship to the dock.

"I've known the terrain of this town as a child," she told him. Some of it had returned to her like a map she'd hidden from herself and found once more in the precise place she remembered.

With it came a replay of Madame Michaud's words. And the family dinner scene with her two brothers joking danced back into her reverie. Their escapade was a family story retold many times over the decades, a way to remember those who had been lost to them so cruelly.

The two had gone exploring one morning and taken two of their father's best hunting horses. When they returned, her father had delivered a tirade, unusual for him. The boys had planned their expedition well and asked their chef to prepare for them a picnic luncheon, complete with sandwiches of chicken and a bottle of good applejack cider. They had planned to escape the chateau and their father's chores for the day with the herd of dairy cows. So what they found on their excursion had delighted the entire family, including sisters and Mama, and finally even Papa.

Her nails digging into Garrick's arm, she considered the opposite shore as she recalled the story. There the quay was not as wide or deep, and fewer people walked along the river. The town of Rouen had always spread to the north more than the south. And that was because the south was filled with chateaux like her family's, rolling hills, many rivers and streams, and crevasses in the stone. And of them all, the Normans told tales. Lots of them.

Like this one of the family Molyneaux.

She would not blurt out all she recalled. She would not raise Garrick's hopes beyond reason. But her heart filled with the possibility that she might have a notion as to how items might be hidden.

And, of course, she knew not who had taken Ruxton's missing items. Nor did she know why or how the goods might have gone astray. But where they were, she might know. Might help with.

Might.

All her knowledge came from her family's fables spun like gold at other dinners, or as children's fairytales full of warnings and morality lessons. Even in her story about *Renard et Lapine*, a few of the old legends abounded, about those descended from renegade Vikings who lived on the outskirts of Rouen and the law—and who stole for the fun of it.

Then took the stolen goods and hid them. Very well.

"Shall we walk toward the clock and see if my family's townhouse still stands?"

"If you're sure," Garrick said with a frown.

She patted his arm and nodded. "I am. I want to tell you a story. A long one. Are you ready?"

As the great clock beneath the old Renaissance arch moved its hands toward eleven, the two of them rounded the cobbled street.

Daisy had begun with the old tales of Viking conquests and the French Capetian kings' hopes to suppress the growing influence of the men in the northwestern provinces. But the invaders from the colder lands had proven inventive and surprising. They'd turned from warriors to farmers and craftsmen. What they hadn't had time to create, they often stole from their French neighbors. And what did they do with that booty? They hid it.

"So you are telling me that stealing goods is an old Norman practice?"

"Not alone are the Normans for taking things that are not theirs."

"That's for certain." He scoffed and shook his head, then strolled along the market street with a sad smile.

She licked her lips. "What I want to tell you is that stealing is one thing. Hiding is another."

Garrick paused. "Meaning?"

"French land is rich in stone."

"Yes. And…?"

"The Palace of Versailles and the great *hôtel particulier* of Paris, even our family house in the Rue Croix, are built of the same stone from a quarry north of Paris. My Uncle d'Harcourt spoke of Creil limestone used to restore his family's chateau just before the Bastille was raided. It was very expensive, and he often wailed that he'd never see it again."

"I don't understand."

"I know. Let me tell you more. You see, in Normandy, our chateaux and churches are built not of Parisian stone, but of stone cut from deposits nearer. We have quarries all over Normandy. Many of them are so old that no more stone is cut from them. Thus, we have caves. Old, empty caves. Where some stolen goods have occasionally been found."

Garrick's eyes lit with interest. "Did you go there? How do you know this?"

"My two brothers went on an escapade one day to a cave near our chateau. The tale became a family story we all loved, because we could laugh at them and their adventurous nature. And this was long after they had sneaked out with Papa's best hunters with a picnic full of treats from our chef. When they entered the caves, they found boxes of different things. Old, rotting. Newer. A mix. I don't remember what they were precisely, but the items had been stolen and hidden there."

Joy dawned on Garrick's face. "Are you telling me that Monsieur Michaud may be onto an old Viking tale?"

"Just as my two brothers were. Yes. I am."

Right there in the street, he gave a great whoop, picked her up, hugged her, and whirled her around.

Though she laughed with him, she sobered, put a hand to his chest, and urged caution. "I could be wrong."

"You could be."

"It is a possibility."

"Indeed." He inhaled as if to clear his head. "A good one. And so now that I am fully prepared to be overjoyed or suitably disenchanted at that outcome, shall we go to your family's townhouse?"

The delight she'd given to Garrick drifted from her like the wash of a wave receding from the shore. Her feet rooted to the ground, she stared at him. "No. Oh, what am I saying? Yes. Yes, we will."

She grabbed for his hand.

In this town filled with strangers, what did it matter if the two of them were behaving like two lovers who could not keep their affections to themselves? They were that. She would not change it.

"Stop. Please. Just for a moment." She squeezed shut her eyes. "It's so unnerving to be here. For this to be possible. I have a time responding to it. Thank you for humoring me."

He lifted her chin and rubbed his thumb along her cheek. "We are here. It is prudent for us to seek it out. The same way we might look for a teashop whose fare we enjoyed the last time we were there. What say you?"

She agreed.

With slow and careful steps, they took the street away from *Gros Horloge*. It was a narrow lane, lined on both sides with half-timbered houses, many four and five stories tall. With tradesmen shops on the street level, the buildings housed merchant companies of every type above.

She looked from side to side, recalling nothing specific except the warm and cheery charm of the architecture.

But at the wide corner, she halted. It stood here. Once. It had stood here next to the tall abbey where the nuns sang at odd times of the day. Here, where that tall steeple still rose and marked the shoemaker's shop where her father had taken her to have her feet measured.

And so with her husband's hand on hers and hope in her heart, she winced and looked up at her family's four-story-tall home.

Her husband let out a sound of shock.

Her heart pounded and fell to her feet.

The skeleton with four holes for iron-cased windows gazed down upon her. The glass was gone. The iron rims rusted. The shutters banged against the pocked red brick like the cymbals of a dirge. The door, a lacquered royal blue, loomed like a gigantic sentry upon the broken pieces of the front step. From each of the orifices spreading upward to the caverns of the roofless edifice were long black smears of the fires that had raged inside and destroyed all but the façade of a once grand and happy abode.

Speechless, she stood like a child who knew not the language spoken here. What had happened here. Who had done this. Why. All were empty words, unable to be questions posed, for there would be no answers. Ever.

She could not imagine the savagery of those who had burned her house to its shell. How did one do that to another? Another question. Another without answer.

Her cheeks were wet. Tears spilled from her eyes, and she could not push them away fast enough.

From her chest, great, heaving gasps of sorrow seized her breath, and she was shrieking.

Sobbing.

Sobbing.

➤➤➤❮❮❮

"ASHES," SHE CRIED. "All ashes. I hoped... Oh, Garrick, I hoped something would stand."

He crushed her against him, and his heart broke for her. She had hoped to change her life, to marry a man who could give her companionship and happiness. She had hope that defied the destruction of her past and those who, in their own desperation, had given her little of themselves. She had endured because of her hope, and now, to stand here, she thought it gone.

"Something does stand, Daisy. It does."

He lifted her chin. Her eyes swam with tears, and he wanted to kiss them all away. He would tonight. But at this moment, his mind took flight with the gift she had given him. And he would share it with her because she needed it and she needed him.

"What stands, my darling, is your enduring hope that your past might be assuaged. That your family's life here might stand in the stones and the wood and the glass. That you might see yourself here as a child and rejoice in the remembrance of what your family were as individuals and as a whole. They are gone, but you have marched on valiantly to save yourself and share what you know is true. You write *Renard et Lapine*. You've saved your sister's memoirs. You will give the world the lessons you have learned from these years and man's inhumanity to man.

"This house is gone, my darling, but the ground it lies upon is yours. The heritage of it is yours to claim and restore. You can fill it with the essence of what the Molyneaux family were at their finest. Before they were besieged and destroyed by others who, in truth, knew them not."

She regarded him with pain. Her pink lips trembled and her brown eyes glistened with tears. "I do not see how you can see this."

He filled to the brim with the answer. One that had eluded him. One that rushed toward him like a flood that refreshed and renewed. "That's such an easy answer, sweetheart. You have shown me so much of your own hope that I have new hope for myself."

She tipped her head into his palm and smiled.

Now his own eyes watered.

"Ashes they may be, darling. But they are ashes of yesterday. And you and I are alive and well. And today, we can build for all our tomorrows."

She reached out her arms and clasped him to her.

There in the street, dozens of people passed by. They murmured as they went. Some laughed. Others shook their heads. All hurried on. They all disappeared from his view. He hugged his wife, who trembled with the trails of her tears. She kissed his cheek and his lips, and thanked him once again for his words.

And he led her back to their little hotel, and with nary a word, they each undressed the other with only sighs to mark delight and kisses for the proclamation of desire.

They missed the supper service, hungry for each other more than the allure of any other corporeal need.

Chapter Fourteen

"N OT FAR NOW," Daisy told him as their hired coach rounded the bend in the road and the two horses clomped more slowly along a pebbled drive. Snow had piled high in a storm days before, and drops of ice encased each little leaf in blinding beauty across the landscape. Today the sun beat down from a cloudless sky and all would soon be water and mud. "Those are our stone boundaries around our chateau. Oh, I can't look." Turning away, she squeezed Garrick's hand and held her breath.

Garrick gasped, clutched her fingers, and said, "My darling, I think you must look."

"Tell me what you see."

"I know not words."

She seized her old fantasies about her home and focused as the blurry oblong structure came into view as they approached. "Oh my. It is not burned. The windows shine in the sun and…and…the steps are swept clean of snow and leaves and grass."

She sat back and forward again. She blinked. She was not wrong. The house of five broad bays with wide white blocks of stone and sharply slanted slate roof stood like the *seigneur* of all it surveyed, untouched, unharmed, unbowed.

"Stop. Stop the coach," she begged of Garrick.

And he called to their driver, who did as he asked.

"I...I want to walk. To feel the earth. To know it again."

"Look at me, Daisy."

She could not ignore the demand in his bass voice.

"It is not wise you get out, my darling. You said you have had no word of who is here. Who has mended the drive or washed the windows."

"Oh, but I—"

"*Princesse Molyneaux.*"

His use of her title made her start.

"You must take care." He swept his hands over her cheeks and nodded toward the long building with wooden doors flung open. "Look there. The stables are inhabited. I can see the horses. And the smoke from the smithy."

"I do." Instinct had her looking the other way toward the gardeners' block. Those doors were also open. "You're right."

She sat quiet, but alive with fraught nerves, as their carriage made is way down the drive. With reverent pace, their cab passed the old Rococo parterres, now barren in the late winter and dotted with snow here and there. A circular drive near the entrance steps allowed for carriages to make a majestic sweep before one side of the chateau. Their driver came to a slow and graceful stop before the grand staircase up to the grand double doors of filigree and glass.

She nibbled at her lip as she examined the chateau, now so near, so dear. Memories swamped her and tears clouded her view.

A tall, dark male figure emerged from the main doors. Two more figures scurried out of the similar single doors to either side, one male and one female. All three dressed in drab crossed the portico and stood together, hands clasped, to await the visitors.

Garrick narrowed his eyes on them. "They appear to be curious more than—"

Daisy was bedazzled as if she'd been struck by lightning and seen all of them in dreams. Younger and laughing, kind and...

"Oh! I know them. I do! That's *majordome*! And Madame Boucher, our chatelaine! Garrick! They are still here." She had her hands on the handle of the carriage door.

Garrick stayed her hand. "And the third? Do you know him?"

"No. No. But he looks familiar." She worked the handle.

"Wait, Daisy! Let me get out first."

She searched his worried eyes. "Yes, yes. Do it."

The driver came to the door, positioned the step, and opened it for Garrick.

He stepped out to the pebbles and spoke in French. "Good afternoon, *madame et monsieur*. I am Mr. Garrick Ruxton of London England, and I have with me my wife."

Though their attention was drawn to Garrick by his introduction, the three kept returning to peer into the window of the carriage.

The older man paused upon the wide portico and, looking down at Garrick, responded in French. "Welcome, Monsieur Ruxton. I am the man in charge of Molyneaux Chateau, and this is my housekeeper, our chatelaine, Madame Boucher. Our younger fellow here is Monsieur Corbin, my assistant. We see not many strangers to our home. Why are you here, sir?"

"I travel in France on business, *monsieur*, and I have brought with me my wife, whom you may know."

"How would we know her, sir?" The older man was as cautious as Garrick. "I see her in the window, sir, but I must see her in the full. Will she step out?"

Garrick paused and took a breath. "My wife comes today seeking knowledge of her past. I do earnestly hope she might be received in the manner in which she arrives. Humble and in search of fond memories."

The older man took a step down and halted. The woman gasped, tears in her eyes, and said to him, "Charles, she may be one of ours."

"I am. I am," Daisy said in French, and pushed through the carriage door down to the pebbles crunching beneath her feet.

She brushed at her skirts, shy and ebullient, clearly full of the urge to run to them and hug them—and cry. "I am Marguerite, *majordome. Et Madame Boucher.* I know you not," she told the younger man, "but you do appear familiar to me. I've come home, and you...you needn't think I've come to hurt you or...or..."

But the older two were suddenly down the steps. The man worked at suppressing his tears, arms out in greeting to lead Daisy up the steps. The woman gave no attempt to hide her emotions, but flung her arms wide and sobbed a garbled, happy welcome as the two embraced.

"Come in, do," the *majordome* encouraged Daisy.

She turned to her husband and held out her hand to him. The two climbed the steps and crossed the wide portico to enter the semicircular foyer of marble and glass and gold filigree.

She was home, and the majesty of her family's abode was nothing compared to the joy that she had come here with her husband's encouragement and that she could share it with him.

GARRICK HAD SEEN her in so many situations. Arguing her case to meet with Daniel, reeling from the carriage accident, rebelling at marrying his uncle, thrilling to his proposal, but never had he viewed her as she was now. Reacquainting herself with the magnificence of her family home, she blossomed.

In truth, the chateau was more than a house or a home. It was a palace. It took his breath away. The black and white and rose marble in the foyer. The gilded sculptures of Apollo and Diana above the arches. The huge rooms. The main salon, with faded pink satin on the walls. The dining room, a vibrant grass green. The royal bedroom, never used, but ready for a French king. Most of the woodwork and furniture was carefully dusted and washed, though the walls needed new coats of paint.

The breakfast room was smaller, more intimate, with a lively yellow and pale orange upon the walls, the furniture serviceable, a farmer's white. The family sitting room furniture, like the others on the first floor, was draped in old cloths. But the outlines gave evidence that the appointments were numerous and lavish. Even the rugs, rolled up and positioned to one side of each room, looked of thick, lustrous quality.

In a mix of English and French, mostly to be polite to him, the servants and Daisy began a conversation to enlighten all to the facts of the past. They adjourned to the breakfast room. Madame Boucher rang a little bell, and a young girl appeared, to whom the lady gave orders for tea and *déjeuner*.

"No one has used the family's rooms, princess," Madame Boucher told Daisy. "We gather in our sitting room off the kitchen and take our meals in the servants' dining room down-stairs."

"How many care for the house and the estate? Is it only you three of you?" Daisy asked.

"Oh, no," the lady said. "We are eight in all. We have lost so many men to the army and the battlefields. Our women could not bear the work in the fields, and most have gone to the city to find employment. We have not seen or heard from them again. Only LeClerk, Corbin here, and I care for the house and the vegetable garden. We sell the vegetables to villagers, and that is how we have earned coin. We take that money to buy seed to plant grain in the southern fields. We have four more, all older, who work the fields—two men and two women. One of our women is the widow of the blacksmith, and she has taken up his trade. We care for our cows and sell our milk and cheese."

"And with all that to do," Daisy said, marveling at their indus-try, "you have kept the house in such a good state."

"It was our responsibility, was it not?" Monsieur LeClerk said. "It was our pride to keep it up."

"Our house in Rouen," Daisy told them with difficulty, "was burned."

"I know," LeClerk told her. "Madame and I went to Rouen—I would say it was in 1801—and we saw then it was gone. Who knows when it had been set aflame? The servants fled. None came here, although we never knew why not. If they wished to stay, they could have lived here with us. But," he said, and cast his arms wide, "they chose to do other. May God help them."

"Have you heard about our house in Paris?" Daisy looked fearful to ask.

"In the Rue de La Vrillière. *Oui.* A tragedy. The Tribunal made it *bien national*, national property, and that scoundrel Napoleon took it a few years ago to make it the seat of the Banque de France."

"Gone, then." Daisy sighed, then her sorrows cleared at once. "But you here have managed to keep yourselves alive and well. That is a feat. I am awed at your resourcefulness."

Madame Boucher reached for a handkerchief from her pocket and wiped her eyes. "We are awed by yours."

"You must tell us, princess," LeClerk said, "what happened to all of you."

"After you were taken from us in Paris?" she asked him.

"You remember that?"

"I do. The memories are more impressions than facts."

"You were a small child. So sweet, and to suffer that? Horrible."

"But, sir, it is a miracle you are alive. I remember the crowd seized you."

"They let me go when Madame Boucher came to *La Force* and testified I was but a servant."

Garrick winced at the name of the fortress used as a gaol by the revolutionaries. Most died there or were hauled off to the guillotine.

"But you must tell us, princess, of all your family," LeClerk said. "We heard nothing."

"We sent you letters, sir. I know Papa sent many. But we never heard from you, and so we thought we had lost you to the mobs or the army."

"*Non.*" LeClerk rolled a shoulder. "I received no letters. Ever. I worried over all of you. But Madame Boucher and I kept the house and the land ordered. We thought it the best we could do for you and for us." He sighed and rubbed his fleshy jaw. "We have been at war for so long, and frankly, I could never trust the mail when we were at peace."

"Only a year, it was," Garrick said of the period of peace between the two countries more than thirteen years ago. "Now with Napoleon gone to Elba, we have it again."

"Long may he remain there, too." Young Corbin roused to the name of the former emperor. "We have not prospered. We are lucky we have any of our cows. And our prize horses? The army would come each spring and conscript them."

"Papa was very proud of his herd. How many do you have?" Daisy asked.

"Six. Only six. Two old. Two but colts. But they are of the best stock, princess," he told her with pride. "We breed again since the peace. Good Percherons, we will have."

"To fetch a comely price," she said, and grinned at the young man.

"Your family," LeClerk said once more. "Tell us what happened to them. Where are they? How?"

Daisy lifted her chin.

Garrick saw her rally her courage. She swallowed, refusing to shed tears that would mar the stories. Her family, each one, deserved a proper tale.

"It will take me some time to recount all that occurred to them. But I may need days," she said with a smile and a flourish.

Madame Boucher squeezed her hand. "Take weeks! Years! Take your time. We are here and go nowhere."

Garrick frowned at that. Daisy and he could not stay days. He had to find his missing goods or who had ordered them. And he had to return home to see to Daniel. *Does Daisy want to stay? Without me?*

"Ah. Well." Daisy drew back. "Time. That is a problem."

"Why?" asked LeClerk.

"I must prove I own this land and the house."

"But...but..." LeClerk blustered, "of course you do!"

"I have not the deeds. And the military governor will not grant me the right unless I have the deeds."

LeClerk's eyes went to beady little slits. "Jourdan? That bastard. Turning from one victor to the next, like a hungry dog."

Madame Boucher shushed him. "When you arrived here from Paris, did not your father take the deeds with him to England?"

"No. I come here in the hope that they are here—" Daisy began.

"They must be!" said LeClerk.

"Why?" she asked.

"Well, no one has been in the house except us," he assured her, then got to his feet.

"Well then," Daisy said, rising and rubbing her hands together as she beamed at Garrick.

"Let's go!" he said, and stood aside for LeClerk to lead the way.

Chapter Fifteen

T HE CHATEAU, GARRICK soon saw, was a structure of newer and older portions. As the five of them hurried to the library, they passed room after room done in a similar grand style. But at the far end, the house extended through a hall to a circular turret reminiscent of a medieval tower. They climbed a circular staircase and emerged into a large room, the walls of which were lined in old oaken bookshelves. These, holding hundreds of books, were a more modern addition to the room, which appeared to have once been a ladies' solar. On one side, three arrow slit windows stood side by side. Glass had been added to cover the stones, and the view was out to a panorama of the Seine flowing past.

"Papa often spoke of how his own father had this room made into a library," Daisy told him.

"It's lovely! And the books," Garrick said as he fingered a few large, leather-bound folios, "are centuries old."

But the papers are dry, flaking. Falling apart. After years exposed in the turret to cold and damp after the family had gone abroad, the old manuscripts were fragile.

What if Daisy's deeds were in this condition? Even if they retrieved them in some viable form, they might disintegrate in their hands.

He feared all her hopes would be dashed. After they'd come

so far, she would be crushed. And he would be as heartbroken as she.

He strode near her, his arm around her shoulder as LeClerk and Boucher stood admiring their delight in the room. "And you know what you seek here. Do you see it?"

"I do," she said, her lips pressed together in expectation. To the others, she turned and said, "I have nothing but praise for how well you have preserved this room and the whole of the chateau."

LeClerk gave her a little bow. "Shall we leave you to your exploration?"

But the man did not wait for an answer. He gave a nod to the chatelaine, and off they trotted, young Corbin in their wake.

Garrick, casting his fears to the wind, grew excited for Daisy. "How do you remember where this is? How to access the papers?"

"Papa spoke of it all the time. I think he knew that if any of us lived to see the day when we might reclaim our land, we should know where the deeds are."

"Wise man."

She clasped her hands together. "I will do this," she said like a prayer.

Then she whirled toward the inner wall of the turret that still connected to the more modern chateau. She stood before the shelves closest to the hall and counted silently upward from the floor. "Five. This one! Now...if we can find the *Roman des rois*...out of order. Out of place. *Roman des rois. Roman...* Here! The little Benedictine monk would be so happy to know that we kept his copy of the history of France with our history of our..."

She halted.

Scowled.

"What's the matter?"

"I thought the next book was to be *Cinderella*, the fairytale by Perrault. But it is *Puss in Boots. Le Maître chat,*" she rambled on, then paused, her fingers on a long illustrated folio. "Here."

She removed folios carefully, handing them to Garrick until they had a pile on the carpet. Behind the folios appeared a little wooden door of polished oak.

"That," she said with reverence, her hands on her hips, "is the safe."

But she did not open it, instead whirling toward the room, and, with narrowed eyes, scanned the meagerly furnished turret. One large black lacquered *chiffonnière* stood on the far wall. She walked to one, licked her lips, and counted four drawers up from the floor.

After yanking it open, she fished around inside and came up with a long iron key.

"Discovered!" She brandished the thing as if it were made of gold, then strode to the little wooden door, sank the key in the lock, turned, and pulled it open. She faced him fully, her brown eyes twinkling like stars, reached inside, and came out holding a small leather pouch and a half-size leather portfolio.

Her hands shook. "If this is not…"

He went to her and wrapped his arms around her. "We will find it. Continue, darling. It is here. You know it."

"It is," she announced as if it were law. "It is." And she handed him the pouch and gingerly opened the leather leaves of the folio. Inside were parchments. Thick and old. Crinkling as she read one and the other. Then returned to read the first.

At last, she lifted her gaze to his. With a reverence one reserved for moments of one's life, she looked at Garrick. "These are them."

And then she was in his arms, clinging tightly to him, gasping, shuddering. "Oh, Garrick. I could never have done this without you."

He drew back and smiled down into her dark eyes brimming with tears of joy. "This is your victory, my darling. Yours. I am but a companion on the way to the celebration."

"You are my companion. Mine. The celebration would not have happened without you." And she kissed him. Kissed him with the exuberance of her discovery and a passion that he welcomed—and knew he could not live without.

"Come sit down." He led her to one of the two large medieval chairs that adorned the library turret. They sat side by side as she opened the documents again and shared them with him, translating the old French where she could.

At length, they sat back and sighed.

It occurred to him that he still held the little leather pouch. "Shall we open this and see what is so important that it ranks with the deeds?"

"Do," she said, and nodded.

He pulled open the old, withered leather strings, and he was able to open it with the use of two fingers to stretch it wide. He stuck a finger inside, and many small items, smooth and oddly shaped, slid around. He turned the sack on its side and emptied into his palm hundreds of tiny stones.

Daisy gasped.

He hooted.

"Did you know about these?" he asked her when he finally caught his breath.

She clamped a hand to her chest. Wide-eyed, she shook her head.

"Put your hand out, my love."

And she did.

He emptied the lot of them into her palm. "At least a hundred of them," he murmured.

"Diamonds," she said as carefully as if she spoke some unusual foreign language. "Diamonds.

THE DAY HAD been a blur for her. Daisy clutched her robe to her and sank to the bed in the master suite. The huge bed had been dressed by Madame Boucher with the fine linen sheets and silk coverlet that had adorned this bed for her mother and father. It gave with her weight. Now, this bed was hers and her husband's. She could not believe she'd achieved her dream, that she and Garrick had found the deeds…and more.

Tomorrow, God willing, they would go to the caves west of here and find in their craggy depths Ruxton & Company's missing goods. She prayed that would be so. Then they would go on to Paris to present her deeds and claim her house and lands.

She scanned the bedroom with its creamy walls, vaulted ceilings, and gold filigree. The house was her fairytale memory, preserved, come alive. To be here was more than a fantasy.

How Garrick and she had arrived, how the house looked, how her family's servants had stayed and maintained the home for themselves and for others, was little to the inordinate delight of possessing the deeds. The old, yellowed, weathered deeds, one signed by the Norman Duke Rollo, another by the French King Phillippe, and two others signed by those whose names she could not decipher. Many of the words were in obscure and unintelligible old versions of the language. But the rights to the lands, the diagram of one, the land size and description of the other, all were definitely the domain of the Molyneaux family.

She smiled to herself.

Her satisfaction to come here was complete. Her days of wishing, wanting, planning to regain them during the past months, hoping to have a husband help her, marrying a man she did not know—and yet desired—all of it was worth it.

And then there were the diamonds.

She gazed at the leather pouch upon the dressing table.

Garrick rounded the corner from the master's boudoir bathing room. He was nude, a towel around his waist, his feet bare, his hair wet and tousled upon his brow. He saw her, stopped, and grinned. "What goes through your mind, princess? You look like you have just won a fortune!"

"And I have, haven't I? Haven't *we*?" she corrected herself.

"No, no." He waggled his finger at her. "Not mine. Yours.

Your fortune."

She went to him, determined he'd see her point of view, and wound her arms around his waist. He was warm and supple and wet. "Enough for us to live on for centuries. To maintain this. To do the repairs to the roof and the stables. To help you in your business. To—"

"I will not take a penny from you. My business is my responsibility. I will not have you giving me the fruits of your family's labors."

"And our peasants, I would guess."

"Even so, if you sell even one of those diamonds, I would hope you'd use it here, for your people. Not me. I am not one to be saved."

"You have saved me."

"You would have found a way to come here, Daisy."

She peered into his tormented green eyes and pressed against him. Her robe parted, and she had the sighing satisfaction of feeling her skin on his. "But I chose this way. With you."

He splayed his fingers up into her hair at her nape and drew her close. His lips brushed hers. "God knows I'm honored, my darling. But you must give yourself credit."

"As must you." She nestled her nose under his chin. His body smelled of soap and musky man. She'd made love to him so many times since that night in Dover, and he'd created a hunger in her for his hands on her, his body inside her. Today, since the discovery of the deeds and diamonds, he'd become distant. Cool. She wanted him back. That man who kissed her freely and whose arms bound her to him in passion and fulfillment.

"Go. Take your bath. Your water will get cold." And then he set her away from him.

Disappointment flooded her. She wanted him. To celebrate with him. But he denied her because he did not feel the same euphoria. For her, yes, but not for himself. She wondered how she had failed to impress on him how she valued him.

She tipped her head in question. But without an answer, and

stung by his rejection, she could not find the right words to convince him of her quest. Lost, she shrugged and walked away.

He watched her. She felt his eyes on her.

And as she turned at the corner to her own boudoir to gaze back at him, to catch him looking, she let her robe slide from her shoulders, to catch on the tips of her nipples and then on over her belly and thighs to the floor.

His eyes went dark. His jaw dropped.

So. She could indeed affect him.

Fine.

We shall see, my husband, how well you keep away from me.

She strode into her bathing room and grumbled to herself. *He would be stubborn? He would be prideful?* She could let him be all that. But she would bathe. And pout. And wrinkle her nose. And win…

With a quick this and that of soap and towel, she washed then rose with a splash from her tub. Garrick had told Corbin and two footmen not to worry about retrieving the two tubs and water until the morning. She would have no one to interfere.

Good.

She dried off and left a few drops here and there in strategic points and curves. Then she strode into their bedroom, naked as she'd planned.

It took her husband, who sat up in their bed, two seconds to notice she wore not a stitch.

"You'll catch cold," he said after she waltzed around the room, feigning a search for clothes she did not need or want.

Then she whirled, stood at the foot of the massive bed, one hand on a hip, and said, "I expect there are ways to get warm."

He curled his fingers at her. "Come. I'll show you."

She tapped an impatient foot. "I never want you to address me as 'princess' again."

He closed his book. Rather, it was her sister's that he read now and then. The look on his face was new to her—bewilderment. "Why?"

"I am Mrs. Garrick Ruxton." She put her hands to the foot of the bed, and on her hands and knees crawled up the length to hover over him.

His seafoam eyes turned green with wickedness. "Indeed you are, madam."

Even with the coverlet between them, she could smell him. And yes, beneath the layers of linen and silk, she could feel the point of his cock, too. "I am your wife."

He put the book on the end table. His gaze traveled from her lips to the tips of her breasts and back up again. "I want no other."

"How do I know?" she countered.

He lifted his hips, and the point of his penis nudged her thigh. "Proof."

"Hardly. How many have you had?"

"None worth an ounce of you, my darling." He curled his long fingers around her nape and tried to bring her mouth to his.

He failed. She would not surrender. "How do I know?"

"I can spend my life proving it to you." His offer was the low growl that vibrated through her and turned her loins to gushing heat.

She caught a cry at the back of her throat. "Why not now?"

"Now," he crooned, and lifted one of her breasts to lick her nipple round and round. "What would you like this night?"

Possession. Declaration. Undying love!

That broke her. She leaned closer for more of his mad caress. She caught a sob, for if she wanted undying love from him, she realized she gave it of herself. She loved him. Loved him.

He played with her, pinching her nipple and sucking the whole of her other breast into the furnace of his silken mouth.

She was afire, wet and needy, and she groaned that she was failing to make him want her forever.

He whirled her down to the bed. "My turn, my cat." He grinned and ran a hand down her hips and along her thigh to lift her leg and play amid her wet folds. "What is your pleasure, wife?"

"Your tongue."

He arched a long brow. "Where?"

"There."

He parted her drenched lips with his fingers and found that special spot that made her keen like a witch. "Here?"

"Please."

"So polite," he said, and blessed her lips with a quick buss, then slid down her body. His skin rough and smooth, his breath hot and moist, his fingers artful and delicate, he had her open as he settled between her thighs and took his damned time getting to work.

She slapped a hand to his shoulder. "Do it."

"Wife"—he chuckled and pinched that nub she wished he'd suck—"you are demanding. But this is best done slowly."

"Who said?"

He choked on laughter and massaged her with talented fingers. "Oh, hell," he said.

And then he went down and did that marvelous service to her poor, neglected body that she'd pined for lo these past few nights.

With his tongue, he did more than his duty by her, fulfilled more than her simple request. He petted her, stroked her, tamed her, made her a flaming mass of need. At his lavish kisses, she surrendered and rose like fireworks at a feast. She yelped, she cried, she ground out her completion in a long, low groan.

And then her husband was inside her, his penis as long and thick and hot as she recalled. He rode her, hard and fierce, his own summit as noisy and raucous as hers.

They lay together, her lips on his hairy chest, his fingers on her hips, their legs twined about each other's. She toyed with his nipples.

He clamped one of her hands to his flesh. "Time, my wife, is needed to do this all again."

"I'm just using the minutes wisely." She waggled her brows. "Do you know, sir, that Perrault's fairytales each have a moral?"

"No," he said, his voice husky, as he sucked a spot beneath

her ear. His cock twitched in interest. "Will you tell me?"

"I will. You see the hero of *Puss in Boots*... Oh!"

He sent roving fingers inside her. "Using my time well, that's all." He gave her a lopsided grin. "Tell me about Puss."

"The important point to remember about Puss is that he was the hero of the story because he possessed the charm and dedication to win the heart of his princess."

"I see."

"That's you," she said with solemnity.

"I thought I was not to think of you in that way any longer?"

"You're not. But you perceive the moral of the story anyway."

"I do. And I thank you, my darling, for the compliment."

HOURS LATER, AFTER they had enjoyed each other twice more and he had called her *his* and *wife* and *mine*, he questioned if he possessed the charm and tenacity to keep his wife with him to the end of time.

For now, she had all and more than she had wanted. She had her home, her deeds, and the rights to her past. She even had a fortune to keep the house and the land in excellent condition. She did not need him.

But he loved her. God help him. Loved her as he had never loved anyone his entire life.

And he wondered if she could, beyond the bedroom, beyond this moment, beyond this house and land, want him.

Chapter Sixteen

"THESE CAVES STRETCH along the Seine for miles." Daisy stretched up from her saddle and pointed to one grim, looming entrance to the Caux caves. "Many of the entrances are all over this terrain. Stonemasons have been chipping away at these resources for centuries, so there is much to see."

Much to explore. Sad to say. Garrick nodded to his wife.

Early this morning, they'd left their bed to dress and dine and take two of the riding horses from the family stables to find the caves. Daisy did not recall going there herself, but LeClerk and Corbin gave directions.

"It's Sunday and many of the peasants will be in church," LeClerk had told them as they said their goodbyes in the kitchen. "That's good for you. You can pass through the villages without being noticed. Do not trust them. They could decide to attack you. The old fever never broke, you know. Though most of ours are kindly."

"Still," Madame Boucher added, "you cannot be too careful. Take these and hurry home." She gave them a flask of apple cider and a small sack of bread and cheese.

"Be quick," Corbin said.

"And home before dusk," LeClerk said.

"It looks like thick brush," Garrick told her now, returning from an exploration up the hill. "We should tie the horses here and walk."

No one was about. The sun provided warmth, and the wind refreshment. Conditions were as good as they could be. Garrick had his doubts as to the outcome. Something rankled him about the looks of the caves. Their position near the river. Close enough, but too far away to be a possible hiding place for anything but people on the run.

Daisy, who had insisted on wearing one of his own pairs of breeches instead of a gown to ride, hurried up the hill ahead of him. Watching her *derriere* sway as she took giant strides forward was certainly the most intriguing part of his day so far.

He loved her. He did.

The thought had him wincing before pushing it away, fixing his straw hat on his head, and marching on.

She was a princess. Of royal blood. They had just found proof of her rights. And why wouldn't she want to claim it all and live the glory of it, too?

It stabbed him and made him bleed. Bleed raw as he never had before.

Because he had loved. He had. And though he remembered how his mother had cared for him, he had often loved others. His father. His brother. His uncle.

His problem was that he had loved them all, and one by one—save for his mother—he'd learned they did not know how to love. Nor honor. Let alone cherish. They were scoundrels, liars, and cheats. Now, even his Uncle Daniel had marks against him. Uncouth and forward to Daisy. Creating some sort of pact with a housemaid to spy on her. And lately, as Garrick progressed in his pursuit of the unraveling of his missing goods, he heard disturbing bits that made him distrust Daniel.

"Look there!" Daisy caught her wide straw bonnet in the wind and pointed toward a nearby entrance. "We don't have to walk up there. Here is good to enter."

"Do you think it's safe?"

"I do. Children play in here. My brothers did. Maybe not this entrance, but still. Occasionally, some still carve out blocks for sculpting. LeClerk told me so this morning."

"Good. Take my hand. Let's go." Together they made their way gingerly down the slope and into the cool gray stones that slanted at all angles from the masons' tools.

"I feel...as though I shouldn't be here," she said to him, her voice echoing around the walls as she crossed her arms in the cooler air.

"We won't be long. I'll go look into the tunnel there. Stay here." And off he went, to return a few minutes later. "That leads nowhere, and there's nothing there."

"Let's go out to that other entrance we saw."

"It's higher, Daisy. The climb is steep."

"But it's a possibility."

"I doubt it. How would anyone transport crates up there?"

"Oh. You're right." She faced the entrance. "There are more. We should look."

"Only if they are closer to the river. Easier to access."

"All right. Let's do that."

By afternoon, they shared their bread and cheese and finished their cider. The horses needed a drink.

"One more," she said. "I see an old well down there." It stood outside what appeared to be an abandoned village with a wooden dock upon the riverbank.

He agreed to it, but his heart was not in it. Though for the sake of the health of the horses, he'd do it.

But when they arrived at the well, they needed a bucket. Daisy volunteered to search one of the huts. But when she didn't return to the center of the cottages and the well, Garrick went looking for her.

He found her when she called to him. "In here, Garrick!"

He stepped inside a ramshackle stone cottage and could not move. Piled high were crates. His crates. Ruxton & Company. Ten of them.

"We need to search the other cottages," she told him.

Off they went. He, his heart racing. She, grinning in anticipation.

Minutes later, they faced each other, shocked, laughing, dumb with delight.

Four other thatched roof huts contained boxes not only of Ruxton goods but of two other British shipping companies. A few of the crates were so old, they'd deteriorated. The Ruxton boxes were in fine fettle.

Stunned, Garrick stood hands on his hips and just smiled at Daisy.

"Didn't need to hide them in the caves, did they?" she laughed.

"Just offload them from the river into a few abandoned houses. Who was to guess?"

She broke into a grin and ran to throw her arms around him. "Only us!"

He whirled her around.

"How are we to get them back to Rouen?" she asked him. "Hire boats?"

"We'll return to Rouen tomorrow and notify Madame Michaud. We'll tell her to have her husband take a few barges down here and haul them back." *We still don't know who is responsible for this. I'll have to figure that out somehow.* "From Rouen, you and I go on to Paris."

She hugged him, happy as a two-year-old with a present. "A good day."

"A very good one."

She frowned. "We can't lock these up."

"We have to take that chance. At least now, Michaud can trace who has time and access to the stock that they can then hire boats or barges to bring the goods here."

WHEN GARRICK AND she arrived back at the chateau, they headed straight for the stables. But Corbin met them with a worried look and told them he would care for them. "Monsieur LeClerk wants to see you both urgently. He and *madame* are in the kitchen waiting for you."

Relief at the day's discoveries draining from her at the young man's dour words, Daisy met Garrick's gaze with trepidation. He took her hand, and the two of them ran to the chateau. They dashed down the winding stairs to the warm, cheerful kitchen where a fire blazed behind the grate. LeClerk stood to one side turning the ancient spit.

"Good evening!" she and Garrick bade the *majordome* and Madame Boucher.

But the servants were anything but delighted at the greeting.

Daisy put a hand to her throat, so dire did *madame* appear. And LeClerk was waving them to the old wooden dining chairs.

"Sit, please. Both of you," said LeClerk.

"What's wrong?" Garrick asked them as he took a chair beside Daisy.

"The worst news." LeClerk shook his head.

Madame looked strained, older than her years. "We are so glad you have returned, safe and healthy."

"Why wouldn't we be?" Daisy asked them.

"I went into the village earlier today," said LeClerk. "Everyone is alive with news from Rouen. A young man who had taken his pigs to the abattoir in Rouen yesterday returned this morning. He bought word from Paris."

Daisy could see the reluctance to pronounce whatever news they had on the face of both. "And? What is it?"

LeClerk flinched. "Napoleon has escaped from Elba."

"Nooo." She was appalled. "No, no. How could he? They have guards around him. Don't they?" She gaped at Garrick.

"How did he leave?" Garrick asked them. "Where is he?"

"They say he fooled the guards," LeClerk said. "Left in the middle of the night, sailed up to Cannes, and marches up the north road to Grenoble."

"How far away is that?" Daisy tried to envision where that town was. She'd frequently studied maps of France as a child. "Does someone stop him?"

LeClerk shook his head. "It is said all the army turns to him."

"What?" She clutched Garrick's arm. "That cannot be. He has taken everything from them. How can they want him back?"

Garrick took her against him. "He was once their savior."

"He killed thousands with his wars. Made poor the lot of them." She gazed at LeClerk with unbelieving eyes. "Surely someone will stop him."

"The news is no, they won't. He comes. And all bow before him. I hear that your duke, your Wellington, readies to ride from Vienna and the Congress. They do not want to fight again, but they will if Napoleon returns to Paris. Rumor says that the little corporal demands all bow to him. They must turn their colors. And his old generals who went over to Louis? Ha. All happily accept him."

Madame Boucher wrung her hands. "You both must leave. Return to London. *Madame et monsieur*, it is not safe for you here."

"You cannot go by Rouen," LeClerk warned. "Jourdan hints that he will turn back to Napoleon. He could close the port and all small ones up the river to Le Havre. People riot and demand Louis abdicate his throne."

Daisy shook her head. She could not believe all her hopes were dashed. "Garrick?"

"We go home to England, Daisy." Her husband rose from his chair.

"Not to Paris." Her hopes, so vivid after they'd obtained the deeds to the land and the house, went now to dust. *All of this will never be mine.*

"No, we cannot chance it, my darling."

"You are right, Garrick. Of course you are. So we will leave," she told the two servants. "No one can then accuse you of collaborating with a princess or an Englishman."

"Monsieur LeClerk," Garrick said to the man, "I must ask you to deliver letters to my man Michaud in Rouen. Only to him. No one else. On them hang the fate of my business and my life."

"*Oui, monsieur,* all that you ask, I will gladly do. Give them to me when you are ready."

As LeClerk left the room, Garrick said to her, "Daisy, look at me. We go tonight."

She was ready to ask him why they left so soon, but tears scalded her throat and her eyes. The part of her that remembered the sounds and smells and colors of flight knew the answer. Dread paralyzed her, cold as ice in her veins.

But her husband took her in his arms, kissed her hair, and imparted the only warmth in all the world. "Pack only what you need. Wear your trousers."

"Yes." An old memory weighed heavy in her mind. There was one essential piece they must take. "We'll wear our winter coats."

Chapter Seventeen

March 6, 1815
On the road to Honfleur

AN HOUR AFTER sunset, the two of them set off west along the village lane. They rode two of the older Molyneaux horses. LeClerk said they were hearty and were, by all rights, Daisy's. He would not hear of them walking. Not when they needed to travel as quickly as they could. Garrick promised to send them word about the animals' whereabouts—if not by post, then by messenger.

"We will try to sell them, *monsieur,*" Daisy had said to LeClerk as they stood outside the stables in the moonlight.

"We will not abandon them," Garrick promised Daisy more than LeClerk.

"They should take you at least to Le Bourge," Madame Boucher said. "Stick to the lower road."

"Don't go north near the Seine," LeClerk added. "By morning, you will be along the road near the remains of a Benedictine abbey. Rest inside. The monks built it like a labyrinth, and you will be safe to sleep there. If you find water for the horses and they can go on, try to make it to the village. I doubt if anyone will have the money to buy the animals there. But if you barter using them, the villagers will give you food and water. Thereafter, to reach the coast, you may have to walk."

"How far from there to Honfleur?" asked Garrick.

"With horses?" The old man ran a hand over his face. "Another full day. Without? Walking? Days. Two. Three!"

"So we will buy horses."

"But you have not that kind of means," Madame Boucher said.

"They will be costly," LeClerk warned.

"We'll find a way," Daisy had promised the two, then mounted and bade them *adieu*.

Without backward glances, they left. Their few possessions were in the saddle packs. Among Garrick's possessions were a change of clothes, a pistol belonging to Monsieur LeClerk, and the records that Madame Michaud had given him from her husband's latest papers. Among Daisy's were another gown and knit shawl, the Molyneaux family deeds, her sister's diary, her own folio of *Renard et Lapine*, and half the cache of diamonds. For safekeeping, she and Garrick had divided the number between them. Daisy had sewn all but two small stones of her half into the hem of her trousers. Into Garrick's shirt hem, she'd stitched the rest.

By dawn, they gained the medieval abbey that LeClerk had told them about. The ancient wooden doors were charred, but lay wide open. Inside, thankfully, was a well. The ropes were not frayed, and Garrick hauled up water for all of them. With fresh water for the horses and themselves, they washed their faces and hands and partook of the cheese and bread and ham Madame Boucher had wrapped up for them. Afterward, they lay down inside a monk's cell upon an ancient, creaky wooden bed.

Garrick found old rushes that he put to the rough slats. Then he pulled Daisy to him.

"We've done well," she told him, and kissed his lips. Proud of them, their endurance, and the horses, she was not afraid tonight. Not as she had been last night.

"We have the old monks' protection, too. I'll awaken you and we'll march on tonight."

WEARY FROM SLEEPING in an aged bed, they rose at dusk, ate, and washed, fed the horses bits and scraps they had from their own meal, and mounted up. The weather was fair for the first of March, their biggest deterrent a whipping wind from the west. Hours later, their route led them to a small village.

"Shall we chance a good meal at that inn?" she asked Garrick, and indicated the sign upon the post, slapping to and fro in the breeze.

"We can."

"It's best, don't you think, if only I talk?"

He grinned at her. "*Oui, madame. I* am at your service."

Inside, a few villagers took their ease. Eying the couple with a bold curiosity, the proprietor brought them their bowls of the night's meal, onion and potato soup with bread.

"*Vin rouge,*" she told Garrick when she set a mug of wine before him. "*Bon appetit, monsieur.*"

They ate in silence, paid in coin—and left.

Well out of town down the road, Garrick chanced a question. "Were they asking about us?"

"I told them we were from Rouen on our way to visit my former home. I am introducing you to my parents because we are just married. You are my mute husband."

"I bet that thrilled them."

She tipped her head. "They made me a few offers."

"Ha! I bet they did!"

"But I told them I prefer a silent husband." She winked at him. "Makes a happier wife. Not so many demands, eh?" Her good humor vanished. "They also said they have heard that mobs are attacking the old nobles who have returned to their domains. One family was burned out of their chateau in Aizier."

"It's a good thing we've left, Daisy."

She shivered with the old fright that she had to abandon her country once again.

He reached across to her and lifted her chin. "Listen to me, my darling. Home has many meanings. With you, I learn its dimensions anew each day. Never more so than now, when wherever you are is my most cherished abode."

She clamped a hand over her mouth, but her sobs broke out.

He danced his horse closer to hers and brought her against him, her head to his shoulder. "Don't cry, my darling. We rediscover old mansions only to find new ones for ourselves."

BY DAWN, THEY were exhausted and sought somewhere to stop. It was an hour later when they came upon an elaborate chateau.

"I've never seen so many turrets and gargoyles," she said.

"I hesitate to ask for asylum," he told her as they gazed at an old brick and stone manse upon a high escarpment. "Knowing what we do of the current mood, we should ride on to the next village and sell the horses."

"They have done well. I hate to leave them, but we must," she agreed.

"First, we will eat and sleep." He pointed to a two-story carriage house that appeared to be an inn. "There."

Once more only Daisy did the talking, negotiating breakfast of eggs and bread, a room for the day to sleep, and hip baths for them both.

When they were suitably refreshed, they retired for the day in their room, their horses cared for by the innkeeper.

"We may be able to make it to Honfleur by tomorrow morning," he told her as he pressed his lips to her forehead and settled them both into a comfy old feather bed.

"And not sell our horses until we get there."

As the sun set that night and they rode out of the town, they went heartened by rumors that a royalist army gathered south of Paris near the Loire River. Napoleon might not stand a chance.

Except as they left the little town, they heard groups singing raucous old revolutionary songs and shouting chants to bring back Napoleon and kill old, fat King Louis.

March 8
Northern Normandy

GARRICK WAS MORE than pleased with their progress. They'd managed to eat and rest while keeping their horses. But most unsettling were the rumors of Napoleon's continued acceptance by royalist forces and the civilian populace. Fearing for Daisy's safety at the hands of radical mobs, he'd been delighted to leave Molyneaux so quickly and to travel without any interference.

They seemed to have everything they needed to make their journey quick. He was eager, however, to get to Honfleur and hope to God he could book passage for them on a vessel leaving for an English port. He knew the shipping lanes on the French coast to Kent, north to Norfolk and Yarmouth, and beyond the Scottish ports. But what he feared now was that Frenchmen in the ports would turn their allegiances to Napoleon and cut off traffic between England and France, assuming the two countries were at war.

Today, they had stayed in an inn near the edge of the village. As they secured their packs to the saddles of their horses, he saw streaks of lightning cross the blue-black sky. They would travel into a thunderstorm. Even though they were attired for the cold, they were not prepared to journey in rain. He did not like riding horseback in it. He doubted their mounts would, either. But that was little compared to the other thing that disturbed him.

He heard a growing chorus of shouts and chants coming from

the center of the village near the smithy. In the gathering shadows of night, he could not see anything too far ahead on the road before them. Not wishing to alarm his wife, he went about his business to secure both their horses and concentrated on the sounds of the angry crowd growing louder…and coming nearer.

Daisy's fear of noisy crowds was one Garrick shared. In the London assault on her carriage, she'd instinctively jumped from the melee to grab the broom from the child in the cross street and hit her attacker. She'd done well, until it was over and she could collapse from the fright. Here he was her only defense—and by God, he would be. He reached inside his coat pocket to pet his pistol.

"You are quiet," she said to him.

He gave her a half-smile as he helped her mount her horse, then swung up into the saddle.

"I hear them too, Garrick."

He looked at her, fingering his weapon. "There is no place to hide. No forest. No cover of buildings. Nothing. Only to go back inside the inn, which is no choice at all."

"How well do you race?" she asked him with a flamboyant toss of her long braid hanging beneath the wide farmer's hat Corbin had given her as they departed the chateau.

He loved her stamina. "Let's," he said, ready to give spur.

But a flash broke over them, soundless and bright, and the rain poured down. In a sheet, it soaked them all at once. The horses did not care for it and whinnied. Daisy huddled into her coat and worked to control her prancing steed.

A man broke from behind a cottage and grabbed the reins of Daisy's horse.

"Let go!" Garrick yelled at him, pointing his pistol at the creature.

The fellow only laughed, held tight, and wrangled the horse around and around, away from Garrick's line of fire.

Another man sprang from the bushes and hid himself well behind Daisy's horse. She beat him about the head with her crop and sent him scurrying away, crying and holding his head.

"Here! Here!" The innkeeper, an older man, ran up and yelled in French at the two. "Stop this!"

A crowd of four advanced behind him.

Garrick slid from the saddle, his pistol pointed squarely at the first man who had held Daisy's mount. Up to then, he had not uttered a word, as per his and Daisy's agreement. "Let her go. I will shoot you."

"*Anglais! Anglais!*" the man shouted, and gestured at Garrick. "*C'est un Anglais!* He's not dumb! I told you! I told you! Get him!"

"*Non! Non!*" the older man shouted. "Leave them!"

But one man sneered at the older. "Take him away, Allard. The *gendarmes* will want this Englishman."

"No, they won't! Let him go now!" Daisy demanded in French as she led her horse backward and pointed her own gun at the crowd. "Monsieur Allard," she shouted to the innkeeper while her gaze was on the other men. "*Je vais tirer dans les dents.*"

When the first fellow who had attacked her was reluctant to back off, the innkeeper cursed at him. "What can you want from the English? To kill him? What good is that?"

The string of French that oozed from both of them was invective Garrick could not translate fully.

Two men pulled at his leg.

Daisy fired at the feet of both.

They yelped and did a little two-step backward, hands up.

"We are leaving," she told them in French, her lips pursed in a sardonic smile. "You will not follow."

With a kick of their heels to their horses, she and Garrick raced away.

THEY WERE WELL down the road a mile, far from sight of the village, when the rain moved to the valley beyond. Garrick motioned for her to go to a walk and stop. She expertly controlled her horse, but when she faced him, she appeared dazed, far away.

He took her chin in his hand. "Listen to me, my darling. We can go more slowly. Long gone from them, we are now."

"I am shaken. A little." She sniffed. "That is a lie. I am shaken a lot."

"No need to dismount?"

She arched both brows. "You mean, no inclination to faint?"

He blinked in answer.

"No. I can ride. The rain has stopped. The horse is good. Most of all, you are beside me."

He leaned over and kissed her luscious, rain-kissed lips. "You will tell me if you have the urge."

"I promise."

"Good. We'll walk a while." *As a precaution.*

A few minutes later, when the blood flowed back into his head in a steadier stream, and his breathing rate went to a more normal pace, he admired her profile, graceful and strong in the saddle. "You didn't tell me you had a pistol."

"Before we left home, I found it in my mother's dressing table. I wanted to bring it with me. Fitting, I thought, to remember her by." She gave him a beatific smile that in the fresh night air was a subtle inducement to laughter.

"I shall honor her always with fond memories myself," he said as they let their horses walk along the old road to Honfleur.

"A great lady," she said, holding up the small lady's pistol for him to admire.

"She had good taste," he offered with a grin. "Back there in the village, I did not get all that they said."

Daisy smirked. "A good thing. They were not very gentle-manly."

He snorted. "That I got. But…do tell me. Did you say at one point that if they didn't let me go, you would shoot them in the teeth?"

"I did."

"Could you?"

Her large eyes twinkled like stars in the sky. "I can. Papa insisted we each practice targets regularly."

"Good to know." They rode on in silence until he was driven to add, "I hope you never have to display your skills."

"So do I."

March 9
Honfleur, France

AS THE SUN rose over the waters of Honfleur, Garrick and Daisy rode their weary horses slowly down the road along the docks. The port was abustle with incoming schooners and barges, small frigates and packets from Havre, the larger port across the entrance to the Seine. The quays were abuzz with pedestrians and carriages, carts and horses of all shapes and sizes.

Garrick had been to Honfleur often last May and June, and he knew where Jacques Durand's offices were located. He led Daisy to the far end of a pier, tied the horses to a post outside, and escorted her up with him into the small brick building.

"Wait here," he told her, pointing to a bench inside the foyer. "I won't be long."

He took the stairs two at a time to the office where Jacques and his assistant worked.

When he reappeared before her minutes later, he was not happy. "Jacques went to Ostend yesterday. The English are fleeing Belgium in a panic. King Louis prepares, too, to leave Ghent. Jacques's assistant will take care of our horses and send them back to the Molyneaux chateau. But Daisy, you and I have to move quickly. He gave us passage to Brighton. But the ship leaves in twenty minutes. We have to hurry, and it sails from the north pier." He took her hand and pulled her to her feet. "It is the last ship out of Honfleur to the English coast."

Worry darkened her eyes. "The last? Until when?"

"We know not. Napoleon keeps coming north. The Allies have sealed off all communications between France and other countries. And Jourdan the military governor closes the northern ports by seven o'clock this morning."

"Surely we can go home."

"Only if we are on a cargo boat under the English flag sailing within the hour."

Chapter Eighteen

March 12, 1815
Brighton, England

THEIR SAIL ACROSS the Channel had been a nightmare for both. Chased by French privateers out of Honfleur, their aged boat evaded the two masted ships only by deft maneuvers in a coming storm. Battered by the rough seas, the Frenchmen gave up and put back. Soon after, the captain of Daisy and Garrick's ship, who was an English seaman of leathery skin and crusty demeanor, announced to them and the three other passengers that they would arrive home, but not necessarily quickly.

The crossing took a day longer than usual. The storms tossed and turned them with a vengeance. Throughout, Daisy stayed below, sick in their cabin. In the wee hours of the night, the ship drew into the small port serving the fashionable town of Brighton. Garrick and she, bedraggled and weary, sought shelter at the Old Ship Hotel on the coast.

Exhausted, Daisy could do little. In the dining room as they awaited their breakfast, she could only sip her tea. "Forgive me, Garrick. I must go to bed."

Garrick had told her he intended to go out to learn the latest news. "Sleep. You'll feel better."

She hurried to their room and fell upon the bed, fully dressed.

She hated to climb under the sheets until she had a bath, but she was incapable. The chase from Molyneaux to Honfleur had taken much out of her. She would never tell Garrick that, for she knew he'd take it as a failure on his part. But the fact she'd endured it as well as she had was all his success.

Truth was, it was she who suffered from her old insecurities. The dread had come upon her as it had after the London carriage attack. Not as severely as then. For that, she counted her blessings that she had made the ride out of that village away from that mob. She also gave herself credit for not fainting in panic afterward. Garrick had praised her countless times for that, as well as for having the presence of mind to bring her mother's pistol—and to use it. Of course, she could take credit for all of that. Though she had progressed, she still labeled herself as weak. She'd not tell Garrick, for he would never allow her to criticize herself that way. But in her solitude, she knew she was not healed. Perhaps she never would be.

She drove her fists into the mattress and stared at the ceiling of their bedchamber. When and how did one heal from childhood fears and traumas? Never? Little by little? In one swelling moment?

Tears burned her eyes. She knew one true thing: being wedded to a man who had as his goal her safety and protection had raised her spirits. Healed a part of her wounded soul. Being wedded to Garrick, who had aided her in regaining her lands, had lifted old sorrows from her heart. Gratitude was the primary emotion she bore for him, love the ultimate affection she would always give him.

With that, accepting she might one day recover completely with his help, she sighed and rolled over to fall into a deep and peaceful rest.

STROLLING ALONG THE main thoroughfare of the Steine, Garrick had bought two London news sheets. One had more news of Napoleon's progress. The other had gossip of King Louis's panic and his younger brother's flight from Lyon north to the safety of the Allied line. Neither paper knew more than Garrick himself.

Going into the Lanes where shops and public houses abounded, he searched for a modiste and a tailor. Daisy and he would need to burn the clothes they'd worn for days during their escape. She had removed the diamonds from their clothing earlier this morning and placed them back in the leather purse, which she'd kept. To revive their spirits and to return to London in decent health, she and he were in sore need of presentable attire. He required two people who could work quickly and well.

The job of choosing among those in the Lanes who were very skilled meant he asked a few tradesmen for referrals. Not finding anyone who could do the work within a day or two, he went into a pub for a pint of ale and fish chowder.

Three men, each one better dressed than the other, stood at the bar discussing the day's events. Garrick could easily overhear them.

"I can't publish *that* in the newspaper," growled a skinny young fellow.

"I tell you, he's here to peddle it all before that man walks into Paris," said another. "After that, there'll be no more supply!"

"Why did you put it in the gossip column that he's here?" another man asked the first.

"He told me to!" wailed the young man.

"Paid you well, didn't he?" sneered a gray-haired man with a long face and long, loose jowls.

"Aye. He's got me fast."

"Because," Loose Jowls drawled as he leaned close to his two companions, "he wants his flash men to know he's here so he can sell and run with the profits before we catch up with him. Face it." He poked the gossipy newspaperman in the chest with two fingers. "He used you, boy!"

"Don't give the bastard any more ink," warned the second man.

Loose Jowls grumbled. "Kirby's always had an angle. Never could trust him."

Garrick swallowed his mouthful of ale very carefully. Kirby was one of those whom Reg Courtenay had said was once a friend of Daniel's. Yet Daniel himself had named Kirby as one he could not trust.

Was Lord Kirby involved in smuggling or profiteering here in Brighton? Could this mean anything regarding Garrick's own stolen items?

Garrick casually turned more fully to memorize the looks of all three men. He drained his mug and motioned to the barkeep to allow him to pay.

⇒⇒⇒⇒⟨⟨⟨⟨

IN A WINDING lane far from the public house, Garrick found a bench outside a bakery and sat down in the sunshine to ponder what he'd heard. He replayed the conversation of the three men over and over. Then he opened the first of the two newspapers he'd purchased. A paper published in Brighton.

He inhaled, focusing. The young fellow, name unknown, had some connection to a local Brighton newspaper. Writing about Kirby's arrival in Brighton, he appeared to be a conspirator persuaded or paid by Kirby to stoke gossip. Kirby's name had certainly struck a chord. Of course, there might be more than one man named Kirby in this world. And none of the three had called him "Lord." But Brighton, like so many of the towns along the English coast, was known to not only tolerate smugglers, but welcome them. People of all classes were involved in illegal trade of goods. Even Nathan Rothschild was known to use special twelve-oared galleys of great speed, to smuggle gold bullion to France and bring back wine, silk, and perfume. Shopkeepers, innkeepers, and tradesmen all benefitted. Those who organized and covered the sale of the goods were often local gentry who took a profitable cut. Garrick could not recall where Lord Kirby's estate was situated, but he'd learn.

Then he found what he sought on page four of the *Sussex Advertiser*.

Among the few regular arrivals of the past week, we have to notice Sir W. Parnell, Bart; Right Hon. H. Sewell; Lady Smythe, and Mr. And Mrs. Frogmore.

Lord Kirby of Folkestone, we are pleased to report, arrived safely from Rouen to our shores through Le Havre, having escaped the growing panic among the French at the impending arrival of Napoleon Bonaparte to Paris. He recuperates from his harrowing journey at the Old Ship Hotel.

This evening Lady Smythe receives a select group of visitors to this fair town in the ballroom of the Old Ship Hotel. Eight of the clock.

RSVP to her at the Hotel.

AFTER BUYING TWO small chocolate cakes for Daisy in the bakery, Garrick hurried to find a modiste and tailor. That done, he hurried back to their hotel. He pushed Kirby's presence here in town and Lady Smythe's reception to the back of his mind. Daisy was his priority. She was tired from their escape from France and deserved a reprieve from the tribulations of the past few days. She and he would not have new clothes by this evening. Plus, expecting Lord Kirby to attend Lady Smythe's reception was a bad bet. Garrick stood a better chance of seeing the man by accident in the hotel dining room or the lobby. For now, Garrick had learned all he needed about the man's recent travel. When he returned to London, he would learn more.

Today, it was better Garrick reaffirm his intentions to take his new wife for a carefree walk in the sunshine along the Marine Parade and luncheon in a small café along the beach. He wanted to present his new wife with her husband, eager to be the man she married, her bridegroom devoted, for a few days, totally to her.

⇶⫘

WHEN HE ENTERED their suite, he saw her portfolio with her work on *Renard et Lapine* on the escritoire near the front bay windows. Her quill lay abandoned beside the pages.

He found his wife languishing in the small boudoir off their bedchamber in a lovely porcelain-coated tub. Around her curves, soapy bubbles concealed all those delights he'd viewed too infrequently these past few days. Her eyes were half closed, and she sipped a large cup of coffee. To the side of the bath, she had placed a table. Upon it, from the hotel kitchen, sat china, a tower of ham and cheese sandwiches, biscuits, one large coffee pot, and a smaller one of hot chocolate.

His stomach growled, but so did his cock. His wife, naked and wet, appealed to him more than mere sustenance ever could. But he wouldn't pounce on her. Not after all the deprivations she had endured since their marriage. He would never be a cad and rush her into bed. But by God, he wanted her. "That bath looks very inviting."

"It is." She sat forward, making the water rush over her round breasts, put her cup on the table, and beckoned him with a subtle blink of her large doe eyes. "Just what I needed. And what do you have, dear sir, in that little paper package?"

"Two chocolate cakes."

"Oh, you are a dear man!" She inhaled, a nymph inspired as she held out her slim, wet arm to him. "What else?"

He chuckled and handed over the sweets. "I got two newspapers. Learned what the dining room offers for the dinner menu.

Plus I arranged for a modiste and a tailor to visit later this afternoon." He removed his frock coat. The swirling water was more mouth-watering than any bath he'd ever contemplated.

"Oh?" She gave him a moue like a spoiled debutante. "I'll have to get out of here? Ugh. So soon, too! What time?"

"Three o'clock." He rolled up his shirt sleeves.

"I suppose that's enough time…" she said, and batted her lashes at him.

They might be married only weeks, but he knew her well enough to see that coy move as an act. But he took the bait and asked, "For what?"

She stuck out her chin and ran her pink tongue along her wide, luscious lips.

He swallowed his urge to grab her like a pirate. The tops of her pretty, plump breasts bobbed above the bubbles. He yearned to kiss each one. But he'd be nonchalant. Even if his cock was not.

He strolled nearer and nodded to her tray. "If I'd known you were ordering a feast for luncheon, sweetheart, I'd have returned sooner."

She crooked her fingers at him and urged him to lean down. "Come take what you like."

His heart tumbled over. Pride in her resilience and praise for her nobility of character swamped him. He put his lips to hers and savored her scrumptious surrender.

She arched up, one arm around his shoulder, one hand to his jaw. "I missed you. I need you. And you were gone ever so long."

Then she kissed him with an open mouth, dancing her tongue along his. This was his wife—playful, erotic, and aroused. He'd be a fool to temper her advances.

She tugged at his shirt. "You need a bath."

"I do," he murmured, his hands to the hard, begging points of her satin breasts.

"Take this off." She pulled at his shirt, and over his head it came. Only for her to tug at his flies. "And these, too."

How he got off his boots and his breeches would forever

remain a mystery. But at once, he stood near her and tried to urge her from the tub.

She would have none of it, and waggled her brows at the sight of his erection, large and ready. "You are in need, sir."

"How well you know," he said as he bent and sought a taste of the gossamer length of her throat.

Her nails dug into his bare arse as she prompted him forward. "Join me."

"We'll never fit."

"I think you fit quite well, sir."

And with a smile, he stepped inside, sank to his knees, and allowed himself to bring her up and catch the pleasure of her firm nipples in his mouth. Her urgent hands on his inner thighs, cupping him, brought him closer to all he needed.

He struggled to sit, his legs surrounding her, baring all her naked beauty to him.

She scooted up, her core to his cock, driving him mad with longing. She stroked him, praised his length, and, with a precision that surprised and astonished him, guided him home. Inside her, he lost himself in lush heaven. She groaned her delight, and he clasped her close, sinking deep inside her and giving her all he had for her.

She moved with him, ever more attuned to the rhythm of their lovemaking, and when she swooned, he found her little bud and stroked her until she throbbed and keened and burned for him.

Minutes later, thoroughly drained and decidedly in love with his wife, he rose from the tub when the urge to have her in a big, wide bed was hotter than the cooling water. Wet and slippery, he caught her up in his arms, and as she squealed in happy need, her arms clasped around him, he strode to their bed and laid her down.

Pushing back the wet tendrils of long blonde hair from her cheeks, he held her and kissed her lips in new and evermore intriguing pecks. He shaped her nipples to pretty points and toyed with the myriad folds between her shapely thighs. He would spend his entire life thrilling her, keeping her, hoping she might love him. With humility for all she'd done for him, he smiled down into her melting brown eyes. "Have I told you how I adore you, Mrs. Ruxton?"

"No." She giggled and wriggled against him. "Do tell," she urged as she sucked his lower lip into her mouth.

"You are naughty."

"But you like me." She dared him with an arched brow.

"You're persistent."

She gave him a shoulder. "Needy."

"Irresistible."

"As are you." She purred and hooked her legs around his hips. "Now do be quiet, sir."

"I cannot praise you any longer?" He sank forward, shocked he could be recovered so quickly to touch his cock to the entrance to her heat.

"No. You've work to do, sir. Be quiet and concentrate."

He snorted. And in the next moves that tempted her as much as him, he was once more buried inside her, where she sighed and cried. And he never wished to leave.

Chapter Nineteen

March 16, 1815

A FEW DAYS later, with new clothes, well fed and rested, they headed off to London in a hired traveling coach. Garrick suspected he may have glimpsed Kirby's tall, thin frame entering the ballroom the night of Lady Smythe's event. But they had not formally met during their stay at the hotel, and Garrick had no reasonable ruse to stay to try to establish a connection. He had searched the news sheets, looking for Kirby's name. But no further mention of him appeared. What Garrick needed to learn about the man was in London. From Courtenay. Perhaps from Thynne. And from Daniel.

The latest word on Napoleon was that he still advanced on Paris with more and more of the royalist army and French people acclaiming his return. The "usurper" was hailed as the "savior of France" once again. No one stood in his way.

AS DAISY TOOK her husband's hand that evening to alight from their coach at Chesterfield Street, she felt refreshed from their French challenges and ready to deal with the ones ahead. Garrick had sent word via mail coach of their imminent arrival tonight, and Nuttley greeted them at the front door with a huge smile.

"Welcome home, madam, sir." The old fellow was positively brimming with good cheer at the sight of them. "We are so happy you are with us safe and sound."

"Thank you, Nuttley." She admired his good spirits. She wished she might take the dear fellow with Garrick and her when they moved to their own house in a few weeks. Garrick had told her she was to begin her renovations of the house as soon as possible so that they might make their own home together quickly. She had agreed. Cora, the maid who had been so offensive, would not come with them. Nor would Daisy take her on again as her servant here in this house. "We are delighted to be back."

"We expect you had a harrowing time of it." Nuttley took their coats and hats. "We were very worried. Now that Napoleon marches north, we did not want either of you trapped."

Somehow those here had learned they had gone to France? The only ones who had known she and Garrick had gone to Dover were Miller—he would not have said a word—and Lord Courtenay. She did not think Garrick's friend would have told anyone.

"We weren't, Nuttley." Garrick caught her gaze as if to affirm her thoughts of how those in the house knew their destination. "My wife talked our way out of a few sticky situations and, with her ingenuity, we are here, whole."

"Sir Daniel feared you would be taken by the *gendarmes*."

Garrick cocked his head. "My uncle learned where we had gone, then?"

Daisy nodded at her husband's persistence on this matter.

"He did, sir. A friend of his called yesterday to say he'd heard you'd been to Rouen."

Daisy shot a glance at Garrick. *Who had visited?*

"Lord Kirby came to visit yesterday," Nuttley said matter-of-factly. "He told us he had heard you were in Rouen."

Kirby was the man Garrick had told her was mentioned by other men in Brighton. Kirby's recent retreat from Paris and Rouen via Le Havre had aroused Garrick's suspicions. Now there was this on top of the other fact, that Daniel no longer considered Kirby a true friend, and had told Garrick he might be the one who wished to hurt him. Yet Kirby had come to call on Daniel. Why?

"Interesting." Garrick appeared deadly calm as he looked at Nuttley. "I did not see him there."

"He said he was sorry he had missed meeting you both there, but he had to return to London on business."

"I should call upon him," Garrick said with a tight formality. "Has Mr. Thynne come to call on me?"

"Yes, sir. He came this morning. Said I should have him round first thing when you arrive home."

"Then do send one of the footmen and the coach to get him. Anyone else of note who called upon us?"

"Lord Courtenay left his card via his valet yesterday."

Daisy concluded Courtenay did not wish to leave any missive lest it be read or go astray in a house so besieged.

Garrick's brows drew together. "I shall pen a note in a few minutes. Do have another footman deliver it directly into Lord Courtenay's hands."

"I will, sir."

"Anything unusual in the watch? The security of the house?"

"Nothing, sir. Miller reports to me three times a day, sir. All is locked. No one is about, save the usual greengrocers in the mornings and the watch at night."

"Wonderful. I will meet with Miller in the morning. As for now, Mrs. Ruxton and I will go up and refresh ourselves. Then I will go in to see my uncle." Garrick offered her his arm.

She took it and climbed the stairs with him. Not speaking until their bedchamber door was closed behind them, she pulled Garrick into the center of the room. "Why do you suppose Kirby came here?"

"I will ask Daniel."

"Do you think he will tell you the truth?" Garrick had told her that Daniel muddied his previous answer about Kirby's relationship with him in ugly generalities.

"Whatever he says, I will use it." Garrick ran his hands over her shoulders and down her spine. She was stiff with concern, and he tried to massage away her tension. "Don't worry."

"I do. This Kirby sounds like a ne'er-do-well. I wonder what Mr. Thynne has to report, too. If he caught the men who attacked your uncle. And me."

"We'll get them, my darling. All of them. I will not rest until we do."

She curled close, her solace in this world only him. "I need you every day."

"And I you." He bestowed a glowing look of desire on her as he ran his fingers into her coiffure and took her pins away. "Every hour with you is more joy and comfort than I have ever thought to possess."

"I'm glad I can return to you what you give to me." She reached up and took his lips. As she pulled away, she shivered in want as well as fear for what he would learn with all his interviews. "Come back soon."

"I will." He hugged her with a fierce tenderness. "I will undress you."

"Only you. No need for a maid."

"We'll take our supper up here, together, alone and in peace."

GARRICK KNOCKED ON Daniel's chamber door and, without waiting for permission, entered.

"Where in hell have you been?" His uncle greeted him like a wasp's sudden sting.

"I am happy to see you too, Uncle." Garrick would be damned if he'd stoop to Daniel's rude level. In the twenty days he and Daisy had been gone, Daniel had grown years older, bloodlessly pale, frail, his sharp cheekbones defining a face of bitter hostility. "Daisy and I are very well. We did manage to escape the embargo by both countries and return to England in one piece."

"What did you learn about the stolen goods?"

Knowing Kirby had been here put the final bar to any trust Garrick had in his uncle. He'd share not one detail Daniel might find worthy of telling to anyone else. "Nothing."

"*What?*" Daniel coughed and, in his anger, choked on it once and again.

Garrick was quick to offer him his water glass. But he would not offer Daniel information leading to the location of the stolen items. "I talked with our man in Calais, and he had no insights as to the missing items."

"The trip was a waste?"

"Not entirely. We accomplished a lot for Daisy."

"What? How is *that* important? What did you do for her? Find those deeds, I guess. She bamboozled you into searching for them, did she? Ha." Daniel waved a shaking hand. "Whatever you did, or found, it means nothing for her now that Bony's back!"

"The little corporal is not in power yet."

"But he will be. Don't you think? I hear they praise him like Jesus entering Jerusalem." He had the gall to smile like a man who'd gotten away with murder. "A good thing, Bony back. Wouldn't you say?"

Garrick gave his uncle a shrug. "Why would I?"

"Better for us as a shipping company, right? Expand. Grow. This war is tiresome. Always was." Daniel fidgeted with the covers. "I always said it was best we leave off. Bring our men home. Put 'em on the sea, where we belong."

Wheels turned in Garrick's head. Daniel favored Bonaparte back. Why would he say that? He hadn't before. Why was that? Simple resignation to Bonaparte's return to the throne? Or a plan.

A hope. He'd divert Daniel, confuse him. "You think Daisy's quest to gain her domains back is in vain?"

"Of course it is! She was never going to get them."

Garrick considered his uncle, this stranger, anew. "But you were going to marry her to help her do it."

"Was I? Hmm. Yes. Well. You did that, didn't you? Bedded her, too, I wager. A nice piece. Was she good?"

Garrick swallowed bile. The man was repulsive. Yes, he was in dire health. Yes, he was in pain. But this—God help the man— was Daniel Ruxton's true self. Revealed in all his vile, self-centered glory. Garrick could summon pity for him, if not a drop of mercy. "I understand Lord Kirby came to call yesterday."

Daniel's pale eyes snapped with a sudden mix of defensive-ness and anger. "He did."

"Why?"

Daniel turned up his nose. "Came to gloat. Said he'd seen you in Brighton."

"Perhaps seen. Not met. Not talked." Garrick stepped nearer the bed. An odd fragrance struck his nostrils. "Why did he really come here?"

Daniel screwed up his face in a snarl. "I told you! To gloat that he'd seen you and you hadn't seen him. To tell me he'd been to France and had a lovely time. That he'd sailed up the Seine on a pleasure barge. Been to Paris and Rouen and on to Le Havre. Having a holiday. Trying to make me envious he can travel. Trying to make me jealous he escaped just as the French closed down all ships leaving the port. And you? Where in hell were you and your fancy wife?"

Garrick clenched his jaw. He would deal with his uncle at the right time. Now, he had Kirby's involvement to figure out. One possibility stood out. "Was Kirby ever invested in Ruxton & Company?"

Surprise weakened Daniel's *hauteur*. He glanced away and pursed his thin lips. Finally, he said, "Yes. Long ago."

Garrick recalled entries in the ledgers when he'd first gone to

Porto to take over the imports for the army into the peninsula. He picked one large payment. "In 1810 you paid a large sum to someone. You never would tell me who it was."

"You have a good memory."

"It's what you pay me for." But Garrick recalled two other payments to creditors whose identities Daniel had refused to divulge. "Was he an investor?"

"Yes. Damn you! Yes!"

"You paid him off?"

"I did. The bastard did not want to be involved with me any longer. I paid him. Then he decided he…"

"Decided what?" Garrick would not let this rest. "Why did he not want to be in business with you any longer?"

Daniel smacked his lips. "He changed his mind, I tell you!"

Garrick moved closer to the bed. That putrid smell repelled him. "You were making money. We were profitable. Why did he not want to be involved with you?"

"I told him you were in charge now and you would not like that I paid him so much."

Garrick snorted. "Well, that is the one thing you've said here tonight which strikes true. But the relationship did not end, did it? You made other payments. To those whom you would not identify to me. So, what happened? Did Kirby want to return to invest in the company?" That would make some sense, as the profits of Ruxton & Company rose with the increased shipping they did to supply Wellington in the peninsula.

Daniel lifted his chin, moved his remaining leg beneath the covers, and flinched in pain. "No."

"I see. So why pay him?"

Daniel picked at his covers. "Go away."

Dear heavens. A shocking wave rolled over Garrick. He remembered seeing one large payment from the household accounts in 1812. If Kirby were not invested, did not wish to be, but received large payments of money from Daniel personally, there was only one reason. "Did he blackmail you?"

"Get out! Get out!"

"Very well. Don't tell me. But I will know why he came to call here yesterday."

"I told you. He is an arse. He came here to sneer and preen and tell me he had sailed home from Paris and Rouen, and you and your pretty wife had to abscond in the middle of the night, disguised, like thieves."

How would he know? "Why would he care? I am nothing to him. Nor is Daisy."

"He hates me. I tell you."

"Because you cut off his ransoms."

Daniel seemed to shrink to half his size. "Yes."

Garrick inhaled. "And you always said after the accident that you could not remember who it was that pushed you to the street."

"I don't. I wish to Christ I did." Daniel fisted his hands and shook them at Garrick like a madman. "I would have him killed."

"Who would do that for you?"

He blinked. "What?"

"You heard me."

Garrick's uncle attempted to sit taller, but the effect was weak. Licking his dry, cracked lips, he stared down at the coverlet. "I have an associate in Seven Dials."

Garrick stood quite still, reflecting on the fact that he was not shocked at this news. "Used him often, have you?"

Daniel gritted his teeth and glared at him. "Twice. But you'll never get from me what I arranged."

"I don't want to know. No. But you'll give me your associate's name."

Daniel scowled. "Why?"

"I want to take out some insurance."

"He is nasty. Evil."

"His name?"

"O'Neill."

Dáire O'Neill. Dear God. The leader of one of the two gangs of

Seven Dials. Garrick's head buzzed with the improbable news that someone so infamous was employed by this man who was his flesh and blood.

Daniel raised a long, trembling finger at him. "He is a bugger, Garrick. Do not go near him."

"Oh, but I will, Uncle. If anyone in this house has one hair on their head harmed, I will see the villain pay. Dáire O'Neill is just the fellow to do it."

"You mustn't, Garrick." His uncle's words were rough with tears. "He will never let you go."

Implying that Daniel had paid that man ransom also. What a web of deceit.

"The price of satisfaction may not always bring one freedom, Daniel. But I will do what I must."

⫸⫷

HE RETURNED TO his bedroom, his peace, his wife. With a blind urgency, he closed his chamber door behind him and sought her out.

The Bow Street Runner Thynne could not come see him until tomorrow. But that was just as well. Tonight, this moment, roiled and appalled by what he now knew of his uncle and the past, Garrick needed only his beloved.

She sat at her dressing table in her silken banyan, transparent muslin corset, and chemise. She struggled, her hands above her head, to untangle a few pins from her hair. But at the sight of him, she halted and watched him in the mirror come to her.

He caught her wrists, bent over her, his gaze locking on hers in their reflection, and sank his nose into the lavender fragrances of her silken hair. He needed to drink her in, her clean essence, her special musk. She was perfection, his wife, his lover, his everything.

He spread kisses along the elegant length of her nape and the line of her shoulder, the dip of her collarbone. How he loved every inch of her. His lips savored her goodness, her rich curves. He ran his hands down her torso, over her lush breasts. At once, he slid off her banyan, and tugged and pulled away at her corset strings.

He needed her. Her never-ending agreement to allow him all of her giving body. Her readiness to defend him and fight for him. Her dulcet surrender to his desire for her, her match to his ardor as he craved for her every sigh and cry and keen. Inside her warm sheath, inside the comfort of her love, he wished always to abide.

He pushed away the corset, his mind reveling in the knowledge that, though she had not said the words, she loved him. The equal to his reverence for her.

"Come, my love," he whispered to her, and nipped her ear. "Let's make the most of the night and the hour and what we are together."

She swirled on the little bench, naked now, save for her white stockings on her lithe legs, held at the thigh by her two frilly pink garters. She rose, her brown eyes melting in her own need for him, and rubbed her hard nipples against his shirt and waistcoat. Her lips opened over his.

"I pray you'll need me always, my darling," she said against his mouth. "I will always want you."

He swept her up into his arms and strode with her to their bed. There he laid her down and rose on all fours above her. "The night is young. And you are all I will ever want to make my life sublime."

Then he proved it to her with each kiss, each lick, each sigh, each moan and every beat of his heart.

Chapter Twenty

March 17, 1815
London, England

EARLY THE NEXT morning, Daisy rolled over to see her husband emerge from his dressing room. "I'll be right down to have breakfast with you."

He walked over, buttoning his pale mint-green waistcoat, his eyes, that endearing color of the sea, shining into hers. "Don't rush, darling. I've a lot to do today and won't linger. Our Bow Street Runner Thynne should be here soon with his report. Afterward I'm calling on Lord Courtenay at Whitehall."

"I'd like to hear what Mr. Thynne has to report."

He kissed her forehead. "By all means, then, do come down."

"Will you tell him about the missing items we found near Rouen?"

"No, I doubt it useful to him. His charge was to discover who attacked you and Daniel."

She swung her legs over the edge of the bed and reached for her banyan. Garrick had told her nothing of his conversation last night with his uncle. Her husband had come to her right afterward, seeking the solace of her arms. She knew him well enough by now to recognize it for what it was, to welcome him—and treasure it. "Last night, did you tell Daniel about the stolen goods we found?"

Garrick paused and met her gaze. "No."

"You don't trust him, do you?"

"Less each day, I am sad to say."

"How is he?"

He scowled, his hands once more pausing in the act of dressing himself. "Not well. Worse, in fact."

She tied the sash of her robe around her waist and flipped her hair over her shoulder. She felt guilty that she had no desire to go to Daniel to visit in his bedroom and inquire about his health. With him, she felt exposed, raw, vulnerable. She would not go. "Did he tell you that?"

Garrick shook his head. "No. But I need to summon the physician to ask him the same thing. Daniel is thinner and paler. I am worried about him."

She reached out and took his hand to bring it to her lips for a kiss. "I'll send round this morning for the man to see Daniel. I thought to go to our house today and begin an inventory of what we need to properly move in. But now I think I will take the girls there with me, and afterward, we'll go for ices. They must be feeling penned in and need a good outing."

BREAKFAST WITH GARRICK was a quiet and somber meal. His brow was wrinkled with his thoughts upon the matters before him that day, and Daisy wrestled with her continuing reluctance to offer her solicitations for her husband's uncle.

She avoided the matter and, like Garrick, took up a newspaper to skim.

Most of the news had to do with Napoleon's continued advance north to Paris. Word this morning was that he headed a large army expected to arrive south of Paris at Fontainebleau within the next two days. Diplomats in Vienna were quitting that city and heading back to their home countries. Wellington, also at the Congress, prepared to leave for Brussels. There he would command a force nearly half what it had been in May at the time of the armistice and Napoleon's abdication. Now, because so many soldiers had been redeployed to the Americas or India, and others had resigned or sold out and headed home, Wellington would have one-third of his artillery men and half of his cavalry officers. Only forty-two cannon, and no shot to use in them. Alarm spread among the Allies, and supplying those remaining was of prime concern.

Daisy pushed away her paper and picked at her eggs and toast. Garrick and she had been able to escape to freedom, but millions once more would be victims of Napoleon's greed.

She ran a hand over her temple. Fretting was not helpful. She had to do something useful. She had to look to what was good in her life. And there sat her husband, the best part of her new life. Handsome, wise, ethical, Garrick Ruxton was the man God had been so benevolent to bestow upon her.

Last night in Garrick's embrace, she had exulted at her husband's devotion to her. His actions were those of a man focused only on one thing, her delights. As often before, he succeeded. Lost in him, his ardor, she had abandoned herself and found once more her love for him.

In that, she marveled every time. This morning, in the light of early day, she recalled all too clearly how she had been meant for his uncle. The man upstairs whom she could not bring herself to see even for a few minutes to be congenial. Unlike her usual self, she feared him. And her instincts, honed during the horrors of her childhood, warned her not to go near him. He did not so much repulse her—his very essence terrorized her.

She would concentrate her efforts on those in her life whom she could aid and enjoy. Daniel's two little girls were among them. Her husband, of all, was her primary concern. She loved him and could not live should harm come to him. The very air she breathed told her he walked into danger. More than he had in

Calais or Rouen. More than they had as they ran for the coast and a boat to bring them home. Home to England. Home, away from the other home she had hoped to reclaim.

Her heart skipped a beat. She pressed a hand to her chest. How it hurt to know she could not return. Once more, she was an outcast. Perhaps she might go back one day. If Napoleon died. If the rabble ever forgot the crimes done to them by those who had taken so much from them. If those among the mobs ever learned to differentiate between those who had been so abhorrent to them—and those, like her own family, who had not.

"What's wrong, my love?"

Garrick used the same endearment he had used last night this morning. Could she allow her soul to take flight at that? Could she hope he truly loved her?

She reached across the table for his hand and spoke of how she could address her emotions more easily. "I have a terrible feeling that you are in danger. I could not breathe if anything happened to you. You are my life now. All of it. Every hour, each minute, I wish to spend with you."

"Sweetheart," he said, and pulled her up and into his lap. In his embrace, she imbibed his strength and calm. "You must not fear for me. I am well."

"But these problems with the missing items. Now that we face the return to France of that man"—she swallowed a sob—"I want no one to blame you for anything that is missing."

"Listen to me." He raised her chin. His gaze caressed her. "I know Monsieur Michaud is on the job. He will receive my letters about the goods in the cottages along the river. Your man LeClerk and Corbin will deliver them to him. I trust them. I trust Michaud. He will fire those who stole our goods and redirect the items to our troops."

"But there were other items missing, aren't there?"

"In the past, yes."

"And so, it appears, you directed that."

"In some cases, yes. In others, I am not certain. I seek the answers to why that was. I will have them soon. All come together for me to see. And resolve. And I will, my darling." He traced a fingertip along the arch of one cheek. "I will, and we will be done. Then you and I will resume our lives. Take a real honeymoon trip. Refurbish our house."

"Our home." She hugged him. "I want to create that with you. I want it badly, and soon."

He brushed his lips on hers. "To be alone with you, love," he breathed. "My darling, that is my one ambition. After this nasty business is done, I devote myself to you and us and all we can become together."

She cupped his jaw and kissed him with an ambition to take him, keep him, celebrate him with all the love in her heart. Her tongue met his. She could kiss him like this forever.

A man cleared his throat, and she drew away from the promise of the kiss and the declaration on her lips that she loved her husband.

It was Nuttley in the doorway to the kitchen. "Ma'am. Sir. Mr. Thynne, the Bow Street Runner, has arrived."

GARRICK AND DAISY strode into the front parlor and greeted the man. Thynne, his demeanor all irritation and nerves, rose to greet them.

Pleasantries accomplished, Daisy invited him to sit, and Garrick asked for the latest on the man's investigations.

"You will not like my findings, Mr. Ruxton. I do not like them myself. I told the magistrate what I learned, and he's not a bit happy, either. Yes. Well, so. Here it is. Those men who attacked you, Mrs. Ruxton, were hired by a man who runs thieves and cutthroats. He commands a large group of ruffians, and he's got the pick of the best. Along with another. But he isn't our man here. This gang's the one that come for you, ma'am. We've got two in clampers down at Bow Street. Those two who were in that fracas at the bridge is what I'm talking about. The one's dead, as I told you before. And the other, he's gone. Don't know where yet. So that's the lot of them."

Garrick stood by the fireplace, his arms crossed as he took this in. "Of the four who attacked my wife, two are in gaol, one dead, and one on the run."

"That's right, sir."

"And the man whose fellows these are? Who is he?"

"Oh. Aye. There it is, sir. I cannot find any evidence to bring him before the magistrate. Clean, he is. Clean. Careful, this sort. Always keep their hands clean."

"And who is this careful fellow, Mr. Thynne?"

The man pursed his lips and flinched. "Jonathan Rivers."

Garrick's face went slack. "The Rivers of Seven Dials?"

"That's the one, sir. Hate to say it, but it's true. And there is no way, sir, no way he's telling me anything that'd mean I'd march him off to the clink. Er...to gaol."

"Why would Jonathan Rivers attack my wife?"

Thynne arched his long, narrow brows.

"Rivers had been paid to do so," Garrick said, answering his own question.

"Afraid so, sir. Admitted it, sir. No shame. Right to me, he said it."

"And it would be against his rules of engagement to reveal who had hired him to do it?"

"Right again, sir." Thynne shifted in his seat. "One thing we do know."

"What's that?" Garrick's gaze was dark green lightning.

"Rivers told me himself that he refused to do any more business with the person who hired him to attack people in this house—including you, Mrs. Ruxton."

Daisy was appalled at the audacity of the attack, the admission of guilt, then the change of heart. "And just why would that be, Mr. Thynne?"

"'Against the rules of good justice to attack women.' Rivers' words, not mine, ma'am."

Daisy shook her head. "Honor among thieves?"

"Aye, ma'am. There is a drop of it."

"And yet," Garrick said, "someone knows who hired Rivers."

Thynne snorted. "Who? One of his gang? No. No, sir. Rivers'd never tell."

"He'd never have to."

"What, sir? You mean another just like him?"

"There are only two, Thynne."

Two? Two scoundrels who ran gangs? Daisy frowned at her husband. *Who could that be?*

⟫⟩✦⟨⟪

ONLY AFTER THYNNE had been shown to the foyer by Nuttley did Daisy go to Garrick and ask what he meant by that last statement.

"Honor among thieves, my darling, may exist. But in varying drops of blood. And between foes, often no good blood exists."

"You mean a rivalry?"

"I do."

In Garrick's expression, she saw determination, and in his eyes, the dawning of a plan. Flummoxed, she put her hands to his crossed arms. "What do you mean to do?"

"Exploit the rivalry. Learn the secrets of their honor."

"You mustn't consort with criminals, Garrick."

"Consort? No. But talk, yes. It won't be the first time, my darling. These thugs have tried to hurt me, steal from me. I've not met Jonathan Rivers. But I have met his rival."

"No!" She put her arms around him. "Don't. Don't go to Rivers or his rival. That kind of man is dangerous. I won't lose you to anyone so…so ugly."

Garrick cupped her cheeks. "My darling, listen to me. These creatures attacked you. I will learn who, and why they dared. Go to the new house. Take the girls. Have ices. Enjoy yourselves. This madness is about to end."

Then he kissed her with the mighty determination of a man on a mission.

And left her standing in the parlor, praying for his safety.

Chapter Twenty-One

Garrick found Courtenay at White's.

Eyeing Reg in the morning room far from the public display of those seated near the bow window, Garrick noted his friend in a heated discussion with the MP from Yarmouth. After ordering coffee service for two from one of the footmen, Garrick chose a large lounge chair in the opposite secluded corner.

Minutes later, Reg greeted him with constrained manner, albeit with a fond glimmer of welcome in his eyes. "Good to see you home."

"Thank you. Wonderful to be here."

"And your wife? Well, I do hope."

"Yes. Very. Thank heavens. She was my saving grace."

Reg inhaled, relief evident in his sagging shoulders. "Word is that you both ran for your lives."

"Heard that from those in Brighton, did you?" Garrick thought the *ton* there the most likely source.

Reg spread his hands out. "Gossip. The newspapers. Servants. All contribute."

"Someday we will have more reliable forms of communication."

Reg gave a barking laugh. "I do hope you're right. What we wouldn't give for an accurate picture of where the little corporal walks this morning."

"Close enough to Paris and yet too close. The French are confused. They don't know whom to support. Royalty, whom they despised before, and do with good reason again, or the return of the man who has buried the men in their families in distant lands and ruined their farms." Garrick went silent as one of the club's staff approached with the coffee. "Will you have a cup?" he asked his friend.

"Thank you, no. I must get back. We have much to do."

Garrick waited until the footman finished pouring and walked from earshot. "I have news."

"I am relieved. So do I. Our supply lines are in fine shape the past few days. Also, I have noticed our lines from Calais into Brussels are secure. What's more, the numbers of all items are exact. Did you do that?"

Garrick took a drink. It was hot and bracing. Exactly what he needed. "I did."

"I won't ask how."

"It's a long story I will tell you one day."

Reg leaned forward. "Can you guarantee this viability is going to continue?"

"To the best of my knowledge, yes."

Reg shook his head. "I need more assurance than that."

"I'm certain you do."

"What will it take for you to promise me, us, the government, that no more items will disappear?"

"A bit more time for me to conclude this matter. Not long. Today. Tomorrow perhaps all will be resolved. But first I must reacquaint myself with an old friend."

Reg went still. Garrick had told him of his brief and binding relationship with the Irishman many favored but few wished to acknowledge. "What sort of friend?"

"You know, Reg. You know."

Reg's eyes went wide with concern. "Why him?"

"I say the man knows more than you or me about matters that occur beneath the nose of many a man or woman in this city."

Reg scoffed. "He *dares* more, too."

"And is so aptly named."

"I don't like it, Garrick. O'Neill is dangerous."

Garrick took a sip of his coffee and accepted all the negative reasons he should not seek out the man in Seven Dials. "I assure you, he is quite essential. Afterward I call on one person who is responsible and confront another who began it all."

"And they will stop the thefts? Just like that?" His friend was skeptical.

"When I expose them for their treason?" Garrick felt the bile rise in his throat. "Oh, yes."

Reg sat back, frustration in his stiff demeanor. "I want to know who they are."

"You will. I promise you that. And now," Garrick said as he rose to his feet, "I leave you to do just that."

"Wait!" Reg got up. "Shouldn't I come with you?"

"Not a good idea, Reg."

"You need more than a few strong words to get these traitors to admit their treachery."

"I do have that." Garrick smiled, the pain of it in his guts, foul and sharp.

"What *do* you have?"

"Logic."

To that, his friend shook his head and opened his mouth to argue.

But Garrick shot him a quelling look.

Then he left, headed for the butler in the hall, not telling Reg about the pistol he had dropped in his inside greatcoat pocket.

DÁIRE O'NEILL, SO said those who dared to describe him, was as spectral as the legendary giants who had once walked the green valleys of Ireland. Most in Britain had never heard of him nor seen him. But to hear from him was not what anyone who wished to live long wanted. And to be shown to his presence was not an experience one soon forgot.

Towering over most men at over six feet, built like an ox with hands that could span a man's throat, fast as the swift wolfhounds he kept at his side, Dáire could also be a man or woman's best friend…or his deadly enemy. He'd gained his prowess boxing, his fortune betting against wild odds, and his fame seizing from lesser foes wealth they never should have stolen from others. In fourteen years as one of the two most powerful men in London's underworld, he possessed money, influence, and knowledge that those in Whitehall and Carlton House envied.

He ran his kingdom of thieves and smugglers as tightly as a Royal Navy captain ran his sailors. He was renowned for his refusal to run brothels and employ children, and many at first assumed Dáire to be soft. "A right cove" was not the phrase he favored, but in his dealings with friend or foe, he earned it. For he had rules of engagement for those jobs he took. Ethics for those he employed. To break his laws meant one did not enjoy his favor again. Ever. Because he never forgot a violation. Never forgave an error. Never countenanced a foe.

Dáire had a list of those who were his enemies. At the top was his rival, Jonathan Rivers.

Six years ago Garrick had called upon Dáire O'Neill and asked a favor. Few did. Garrick had little choice. Accused of killing one of his laborers on the docks, Garrick could find no proof otherwise. He had no help from Bow Street. The Runner, Mr. Thynne, had done his job as well as he could. But he could not prove Garrick innocent. Garrick's Uncle Daniel had not believed he killed Foley, but he'd been unable to persuade the magistrate to determine his nephew innocent. Garrick had gone to O'Neill to ask for help identifying the murderer. The Irishman had agreed to investigate, but asked for a favor in return. Garrick had provided the information O'Neill sought about one of Garrick's men who had disappeared after he attacked and raped one of O'Neill's sisters. He had learned the man had bought passage to the Indies. But he had never discovered who had really killed Foley.

"I owe you that in return." Years ago, he had said that to Garrick. He had risen from behind his broad mahogany desk in a lavishly appointed office in a building that appeared from the outside to be a decrepit bit of rotting wood. "You came to me in need. I failed. Therefore, I am your servant. Name the day."

Today was that day. Garrick's need was that great. He knocked upon the broad oak door with peeling forest-green paint. One of O'Neill's body men stood beside him. Tall as Garrick. Burly as his leader. Surly as one could predict was vital to survival in the underbelly of London's back streets.

"Says 'e's to see our Dáire," the watchdog told the troll who slid open the door that scraped the expensive, polished tile beneath.

A good once-over from the misshapen gnome and Garrick was admitted. Stopped just inside, he put his arms up as another brute who was O'Neill's Cerberus ran his hands over every inch of his body. For that rude groping, Garrick was granted a grunt and a nod toward the richly red-carpeted stairs.

Cerberus led the way up the stairs. He knocked, thrust open the door, barked out Garrick's name, and stood aside at O'Neill's agreement to give him the time of day.

Garrick was met at the threshold by the barks of two gray, giant wolfhounds. He knew enough to stand still and let them sniff their fill.

"Many years since I've seen you," the Irishman greeted him with a toothy smile. With a staying hand to make his wooly dogs sit, he came around his huge desk to put out his hand. His Black Irish hair was a mass of tousled curls. He wore a black frock coat finely tailored to the breadth of his shoulders, a frothy cravat around his thick throat, and fawn breeches that fell over his muscular frame like a second skin. "Six years. You've grown."

Garrick accepted his handshake. "So have you."

"Older."

Garrick laughed. "Richer." A dark painting that had to be a Caravaggio hung upon the far wall.

"Ha! Wiser, I hope. Are you?"

"Aye. In some respects. Not others."

"Do sit." O'Neill indicated one of the big, polished wooden chairs before his desk. "Whiskey?"

"Please." One did not drink anything but good Irish spirits between these walls. *John Power & Son*, Garrick could see by the label, was to be his reward today. And two large tumblers of it, O'Neill poured.

"Yer health, Ruxton! Congratulations are in order to you." O'Neill raised his own glass brimming with amber liquid. "I understand your bride is not only beautiful, but a princess from the wrong side of a Bourbon blanket."

Truth was more important in this house than diplomacy. Garrick nodded and drank. "A few generations between that blanket and my wife." He put down his glass. "Thank you. The good wishes, the whiskey, and your welcome are all appreciated."

His host took a drink. "I was hoping you'd come to see me."

That had Garrick unwinding in his chair. "I have a few mysteries about what has happened lately in my business and my family."

"And you hope I might have answers?"

"I do indeed."

"The first?"

"Jonathan Rivers accepted a commission recently."

O'Neill's black eyes met Garrick's, heavy with anger. "To put down those in Chesterfield Street."

The crudeness of the term to kill animals socked Garrick in the stomach. But one did not show weakness in this house.

O'Neill growled. "A dire business. Rivers failed. The right smarmy bastard." He got up from his chair, grabbed his tumbler, and strode to his serving bar. He poured more whiskey for himself, then whirled to walk over and top up Garrick's glass. "Failed not just once with your uncle, but then again, thank God, with your wife."

"I come here knowing who is responsible. I need you to confirm it."

"Hell, Ruxton. You'll soil my house with that traitor's name."

"I have only circumstances and logic to tell me who my target is. I come to you for help."

"Better drink up then, Ruxton. I hate scum who have no loyalty to country. Who attack innocent women. Who cannot do their own dirty work but hire others to take the noose for them."

"I need you to tell me who hired Rivers to do these crimes."

"Will you get Bow Street after them?"

And the prince regent. Whitehall, too. "I will. For the one. As for the other… He is dying."

"Gangrene?"

"Yes."

"Your physician confirmed it for me yesterday."

Garrick was not surprised. "No one escapes your net."

"Make no mistake. That man is not one of mine. I called him to treat one of my men who got caught in a fishing net the other day, and has a fever and the ague now." O'Neill sat on the edge of his desk. "I want the first traitorous bastard to know how I despise what he's done. I want him to hang. So I ask you a favor."

Garrick tarried. Agreement could cost him his own honor. "What is it?"

"Allow me to give you the services of one of my friends."

"Who?"

"A judge."

A man in O'Neill's pocket. "I came here today hoping for solid evidence from you that he has ordered army goods stolen and attempted to destroy Wellington's efforts."

"I don't have that. Only rumors of it." O'Neill smacked his lips. "But I have evidence he killed your Adam Foley."

Garrick let that news warm his blood. "Enough for a charge

of murder, then."

"Ah, but as an earl, he can avoid that noose. You know it. So do I. But I tell you, Ruxton, there is more he's done. He has stolen many a maidenhead as well as blackmailed their weeping fathers. He needs to be eliminated—and shamed."

"I'd prefer to do it without your judge."

O'Neill slapped a hand to his knee. "Ever the right answer. What can I do with you?"

"Confirm his name."

O'Neill gave it.

Garrick nodded. *As I thought.* "One question for you before I go."

"Ask anything. I still owe you."

"Did you ever do any work for my Uncle Daniel?"

"Never."

Daniel had lied. Again.

DAISY ALIGHTED FROM the carriage Garrick had rented for daily use of those in the family. The one she'd ridden in the night of the attack was still being repaired, and the wheelwright was not certain if he could repair it so that it would be safe to use henceforth.

She waited on the stone walkway in front of the house that was to be hers and Garrick's as Elizabeth and Susana climbed down. Miller, Daisy's ever-present bodyguard, was right behind the children.

"Oh, it is grand, isn't it, ma'am?" Elizabeth, the older, enthused as she gazed at the four-story townhouse.

The younger nudged her sister. "Aunt Daisy now, silly. Uncle Garrick's wife."

Daisy stroked her fingers down the younger girl's long braid. "Susana is just getting used to me, aren't you, dear?" They both would do so easily, she and Garrick agreed. He'd told her this morning that he had figured out that his uncle would not live too much longer. He wished to ask the physician and the surgeon who'd amputated their predictions. Without knowing how quickly gangrene spread through Daniel's body, both of them resolved to be prepared for his passing and taking guardianship of both Daniel's daughters.

The older girl pouted. "I wanted you to be our mother."

"I know, Elizabeth. But we can be almost as close as aunt and niece. Better yet, we'll become good friends! What do you think?"

"Maybe." She eyed the house. "Can we go in? Will there be bedrooms enough for us to visit?"

"We'll make sure of it," Daisy said as she fished the key from her reticule. "Knock down a few walls. Do what we must. It's our house, isn't it? Come along now. We'll go inside."

And oh, it appealed to Daisy. Her own house. Her home. Hers and Garrick's. The house outside was a creamy stucco, with black lacquer shutters and big, broad windows. Four bays of them. The entrance hall was small but serviceable. The butler's closet was behind the straight staircase, but to the right of the foyer lay the main salon. The room, lit only by sunlight, promised to be bright and useful for guests. Lots of guests. The dining room behind was just as grand. All the walls needed painting, the plasterwork repairing, the floors sanding and waxing. Every room required new furniture, drapes, and sconces. Downstairs, a kitchen with a glass-domed ceiling and huge fireplace made Daisy smile. A butler's wine cellar and servants' hall led to a kitchen garden. The servants' sleeping quarters would do well for a housekeeper, the butler, and, at the back, the cook. Upstairs, beyond the master suite and boudoir, were three more bed-rooms. One might easily become a nursery. On the top floor, four large bedrooms would do for maids and footmen.

The house was more than Daisy had ever imagined to become hers. Far from her original home so many miles away. Greater than any of her aspirations was the charming lure that, in this house, she would live with the man she adored.

The hope Garrick might love her, too, danced in her head as she surveyed the house. What did one do if one loved alone? Could there be friendship and camaraderie? Lust? Passion? Yet no love? She dared not contemplate a negative answer. It would kill all this euphoria that filled her, as everything she'd ever wanted seemed to belong to her now.

Miller followed behind her and the girls. Quiet, contemplative, he looked at every aspect of the rooms with a slow examination that unnerved her.

She had survived the horrendous run from Molyneaux to Honfleur and did not quite feel as anxious as she did now. Watching Miller, reminding herself what Garrick proposed to do today, whom he'd see, had her reaching for her pistol in her reticule. Patting its smooth barrel, she tried to absorb its promise of safety.

"Shall we go have our ices now?" She turned to the girls, purposely putting on a happy air.

She had to get home.

As the afternoon progressed, a dark cloud had relentlessly come to hang over her. Her knowledge of what Garrick did today shrouded her, obscuring her happiness with the house, the girls, the day.

Her instincts for disaster were at work. She would not ignore them.

Chapter Twenty-Two

GARRICK DISMOUNTED FROM his horse and tied the reins to the iron rail. Irritated that he'd not found Lord Kirby at home or at White's, as the man's butler told him he would be, he was in a fouler mood when Nuttley did not open the door. Nor did a footman come out to tend to his horse.

Anger gave way to curiosity. And alarm.

Up on his mount at once, he urged his horse down the street and around the next street. From the corner of his eye, he noted no one appeared at the windows, and Nuttley did not belatedly come to open the front door.

What was amiss here?

He cantered to the mews, threw the reins to his stable boy, and asked for his head groom. A quick instruction to the man and he set off at a run to the alley at the back of home.

With the stealth of a cat, he snuck toward the shed where the servants placed their tools and paused to recollect which servants were where. At this time of day, his housekeeper and cook were busy in the larder and the dining room. The footmen were cleaning the family's shoes and boots in the servants' hall. The scullery maid was in the far nook off the kitchen, cleaning dishes from everyone's breakfast and luncheon. Cora, the maid whom Daniel had wished to spy on Daisy, should be upstairs dusting the furniture. The gardener who cared for all the vegetable plots in back of this row of townhouses was nowhere to be seen. Not unusual, that. Yet Garrick's senses were on alert. Glancing up at the dark windows of his house, he saw no one inside seemed to be alive.

Wary, he ran from the shed past the garden to the kitchen door. He winced, opening the wooden portal with nary a squeak. He closed it and stood like a statue, listening. Listening. Straining…and hearing not a sound.

Why not?

But then, above him, someone growled an order. A man with a gravelly bass voice sought silence. But a pot or a vase crashed to a wooden floor. So. Not in the salon, then, where a carpet spread from one wall nearly to another. Not in the dining room, though carpet was laid there, too. But in a room higher up.

Daniel's bedroom, where they'd rolled up the rugs so that cleaning up after him and nursing him would be more efficient.

As he had now for weeks, Garrick had his pistol with him. He put one foot and then another to the servants' plain wooden staircase. The old wood—he applauded his foresight—had been replaced last year on his orders. The planks bore his weight with nary a sound.

He climbed the two stories with speed and ease. Pushing open the thickly padded servants' door to the level of family bedrooms, he took the hall on silent footfalls. At each step closer to Daniel's bedchamber, the silence grew more unnatural. Eerie.

Garrick stood a moment, licked his lips, fingered the metal weapon in his hand, and whirled for the door to his uncle's rooms.

He was inside in a moment.

"Welcome!" said a fat little fellow with a toothy grin and his own pistol in his hand. "Happy to see you, Ruxton."

The barrel of another pistol bored into his back.

"Thank you, Cora." Lord Kirby, Angus Charles Moreland, gave Garrick a sanctimonious grin. "Do give her your gun, sir. Then come in. Sit! Enjoy our visit! Your uncle and I were just getting started."

Daniel was sitting up so straight against his voluminous cushions that Garrick wondered where he summoned the strength. But fear and hate could do strange things to a body. His uncle, his pale green eyes glassy, stared at him. "Kirby arrived about ten minutes ago."

Garrick's gaze swept the room. In addition to the fleshy creature that Lord Kirby was, two more men stood at the far side of his uncle's bed. Both were so similar in fair, red-haired coloring with middling height and weight that they appeared to be twins. They also dressed alike in black frock coats and trousers. However, only one leaned upon an ivory-handled walking stick.

The man Daniel had described as his attacker.

"And that fellow there?" Garrick asked, his manner as cool as his outrage was hot. "The man who pushed you to the street."

"He is," Kirby said with a bit of humor in his words. "Artful fellow, aren't you, Higby?"

The man narrowed his beady eyes to an evil line. "Aye, Kirby. Right good that word 'bout me. Artful!"

"If you're here to get more money from my uncle, Kirby, you and your friends may leave now. I'll give you nothing."

"Seems like you have no say in that, now do you?" Kirby strolled nearer and cast up his round little face into Garrick's. "I'm here with more metal and more men than you. Eh?"

Garrick flexed. "And a woman, too." He stepped to one side to regard the maid who still had her pistol pointed at his stomach. "Clever of you to ingratiate yourself with my uncle and collect your money and your orders from old Kirby here."

"Enough talk!" Kirby dashed a hand out and wiggled his pistol.

"Careful with that, man," Garrick said. "You don't want to shoot yourself."

Kirby stuck his fat neck out and sneered. "I am a careful man, little nephew."

"Not very much so when I saw you in Brighton."

"Ba! Nothing!"

"And I have proof you ordered my goods stolen from my warehouse in Rouen."

"You've no such thing!" he yelped.

But Garrick saw the fear he might indeed possess such a thing widen the man's watery blue eyes. "You can't kill me and cover all this up, Kirby."

"Oh, but we'll do a good job. That's why I have my boys with me."

"Oh. Right. And her, too." Garrick arched his brows and scoffed. "Does he have you here, Cora, to wash away his mess? What a great man."

Cora's lips thinned.

"Enough of you, Ruxton! A draft. I want a draft on your bank. For ten thousand pounds. Let's go—shall go we down the hall to your office to get it?"

DAISY SAT IN the carriage examining the closed front door. Where was Nuttley? A footman? Anyone?

Was Garrick in there?

Nom de Dieu!

She scanned the windows and reached across to grasp her bodyguard's wrist. "Miller, take the girls to the stables."

"Ma'am. You should not go in there."

"We both will, Miller. You take the girls now. Go, my dears. Go, please, like good girls. Stay there until I—or Uncle Garrick or Miller or…or Nuttley—come for you. Promise me."

The little girls cowered into her side.

"Don't go," said Elizabeth.

"I'm afraid." Susana sniffed.

"We will all be just fine, but you must go with Miller now." Daisy eyed him.

He waffled. "Aye, but this is not proper—"

"This is my husband, my family, *our* household, Miller. I go in just as you do." *No one threatens my family.* She slid her pistol from her reticule just enough to show him and to not alarm the girls. "You come in the back door. Check the basement and the staff. I go in the front. We meet…as we can."

"But ma'am—" He clamped her hand on her pistol.

"Do not worry, Miller. My papa taught me necessity demands superb skill."

"But you…?"

"Can shoot a tattoo on your forehead, sir."

"I see." He backed into the squabs. "Go, then."

She alighted, stepped nonchalantly up the steps, and opened the front door. On Nuttley's hall table sat a calling card. Lord Kirby, Sixth Earl of whatever-it-was. The card sat haphazardly on the white marble tabletop, having missed the silver salver. *So thrown there.* The polished oaken door to Nuttley's little night-watchman's closet stood ajar. No coats hung on hangers. *So we have Lord Kirby, sixth of his line, in the house, and the poor fellow passed through with his winter greatcoat still around his shoulders. Not done.*

Daisy tutted and felt her pistol. *I should like to help him remove it.*

She set down her reticule, shrugged from her wool pelisse, and praised her seamstress for the pockets in her gown.

She stood to one side of the stairs, a blind spot to those upstairs and on this floor. Then she listened to the music of the house.

The clocks. The large casement on the landing upstairs. The small but noisy ormolu in the main salon. Somewhere upstairs, a fireplace log fell in a grate. Footsteps emerged from Daniel's bedchamber and traversed the hall past the stairs and walked onward to…where?

"I'm not going to do this, Kirby." Garrick was chastising their visiting interloper.

"You will," declared a man whose voice she did not recognize.

But she followed the sound of their steps and knew where they went. Into Garrick's office. At the end of the hall.

From the other end, from Daniel's bedchamber, came bits of conversation.

Her eye caught on the servants' door to this floor as it inched open. Miller ducked his head around, and she lifted hers in acknowledgement.

He nodded. He pointed downstairs to the servants' quarters and cupped each wrist in turn.

She tipped her head. Who was tied? Her servants?

He scissored his fingers, smiled at her, then fisted his hands.

Ah. Their foes were tied up. *Good. Time to move on.*

She pointed upstairs, once to Daniel's chamber, once in the direction of Garrick's office. She pointed for him to go to Daniel and, with a hand to her heart, indicated she would go to the office.

Miller nodded, then bent over, and for the big man that he was, he ran as if he were a little bunny. She'd laugh later, but for now, she took the stairs, quiet as a mouse.

Upstairs, she and Miller took advantage of secluding themselves in two niches. Meant to showcase lovely Ming vases, the hollows in the walls served well for the two of them to catch their breaths, nod to each other, and then walk silently in opposite directions.

The door to Garrick's office stood wide open. Clearly this Kirby thought he had the run of the house.

Le fou.

"I don't understand, Kirby," Garrick said. "You must have a hollow leg. From my books, I could see that my uncle paid you plenty over the years. God knows how much before I started to manage things in Porto. And you could no longer siphon off goods from our shipment. Tell me, really." He snorted. "How much money can a man need?"

She whirled into the doorway. Kirby had his back to her.

Garrick sat at his desk, his hands on his ledger.

"Just write the paper for me, Ruxton. Ten thousand."

Blackmail. This Kirby never stopped. *Idiot.*

He pointed his own little pistol at her husband. "I don't need the money, Ruxton. I never needed it so much as I wished your uncle had continued with his ruse to foil Wellington's army. But the fool got cold feet. After I did away with Adam Foley and Daniel got scared you'd hang for murder, he sent you to Porto and fouled my plans again. I had to find new men to take the goods and hide them! Six long years of finding new men to steal the army supplies. You were ever my nemesis."

Kirby had killed Garrick's man and blamed Garrick.

This man needed to be stopped.

And so Daisy stepped forward, stuck her barrel into his ribs, and purred like a kitten. "Do put down your weapon, Kirby."

He spun, and she shot him in the foot.

He glared at her, screamed, and hopped around—a jiggling bit of custard, he was so chubby. But he also had the audacity to call her quite a few really insulting names.

She waved her weapon at him. "You insult me in English, sir. Thank goodness for you! If you had used French, *ahh…*worse for you. But if you don't stop screaming, I can shoot the other foot." She smiled at him.

Garrick, in the interim, had fished his own nasty-looking pistol from his desk drawer and strolled toward her, a huge grin on his face. "He's done, sweetheart."

But the man shouted and screamed and stumbled toward the chair, cradling his ruined boot and damaged foot. "Done! Done! She shot me!"

"Oh, do be quiet, sir." She allowed Garrick to kiss her temple. "My husband and I have more work to do."

WITH A HAND to the back of Kirby's frock coat, Garrick frog-marched the whimpering man down the hall to Daniel's room.

Daisy smiled at the scene before her. Miller sat, pistol out, pointed at Kirby's two male minions and sour-faced Cora beside them. They were backed to the far wall as Garrick dropped Kirby like a stone into the large chair nearest Daniel's head.

Just then, another of Garrick's recently hired footmen charged into the room and came to a halt. "Ye've got 'em all!"

"Downstairs?" Miller asked him, his gaze still trained on the two bully boys at the far wall.

"All's in order. Them two, on the floor, tied. What can I do here?" the footman asked Garrick.

"Take one of those two at a time down to the foyer. Tie one to the iron banister. The other to the marble table leg. Then send one of our men to Bow Street for Thynne. Another to Whitehall for Lord Courtenay. Tell them they need to come at once."

Off he went, nudging one man before him toward the stairs.

Daisy stepped aside so that they could leave.

Garrick continued. "So now, a few of you have a few things to clarify."

"You get me a surgeon!" Kirby yelled, lifting his bloody foot.

"In due time," Garrick said, and gave him a tepid smile.

"Now! Damn it! Now!"

Running footsteps up the stairs had Daisy training her pistol on the doorway. But she sagged in relief at the sight of tall, thin Mr. Thynne.

The Runner rounded the doorway, hands up at her pointed weapon. "I've come with news. So what's all this?"

Garrick beamed at him. "You're back! Good. Just in time. We're having a confession party."

"All your pistols seem to tell that story, sir." The gangly man offered a winning smile, then crossed his arms. "I've got good news, but not as good as yours, I see. Do proceed, sir."

Garrick nodded. "First, do tell us who killed Adam Foley. Kirby?"

Daniel swept a hand toward Kirby. "He did. Foley refused to siphon goods. Kirby had to kill him. Convenient that he blamed it on you, Garrick. You were there. No one else was about. He even got his puppet Gordonston to say he saw you do it. Created more problems for me."

For you? Daisy was livid. Garrick was the one who bore the brunt of that. For six long years.

Her husband absorbed that confession with a calm that tore her heart out. But he went on. "And Daniel sent me to Porto to avoid my going to the hangman."

"Yes!" Kirby yelled. "You went to Porto and fouled my plans again. I had to find new men to take the goods and hide them. Six long years of making it happen! You were my pain."

"Indeed I was. So then, do tell us why, Daniel, Kirby received large sums of money from you."

Daniel glared at his nephew.

"No?"

Daniel sniffed. "I am a dying man. Why do you need to have me say it?"

"Because you will bear your own guilt. Why did you pay him?"

"He wanted money from me for his silence." Daniel dropped his gaze to stare at his covers. "He knew what I'd done. He knew why."

"You," Kirby seethed, "you bastard. You were the one who had the idea. I went along because back then it was a good idea."

"And that idea was what, Daniel?" Garrick asked.

"I would be prime minister! I would! I was worthy! I was farsighted. I should be the one to lead the country."

"How could you possibly do that, Daniel? Tell us, do." Garrick set his jaw.

"Destroy Wellington. Deprive him of supplies. Make him weak. Defeat would mean the end of the damn Tory government. I'd join the Whigs, and we'd make a peace. A lasting peace."

Garrick shook his head. "And earn more profits from the expansion of shipping? Eh, Daniel? That's what you thought an end to the wars would bring?"

"Of course it would! Bonaparte would have the land. We'd have the sea. He and I would work together. Rule the world!"

Daisy gasped. She remembered what Daniel had written to her about his ambitions. "'One day,' you wrote, 'I will be as powerful as the king here and as important as the French king in your country.'"

"Yes! Damn you!" he bellowed at her. "And you were to be *my* wife! *Mine!* Not his! *What can he do for you, Marguerite?* Eh? If you were my wife, I would be prime minister and you would be the equal of Josephine and that ugly Austrian whore Bonaparte married."

Her gun still pointed at Daniel, she sidled near him. "And you thought if you had a wife who was French, one who was a princess of the blood, that, too, would be to your advantage."

"Why not?" He spat at her. "Why not?"

Kirby snorted. "Big ambitions. But you were a washerwoman about the whole mess. You never could find good men to steal a decent number of goods. I did that. I improved your silly scheme. Even if you could never rob enough from Wellington's supplies to defeat him, I could!"

Daniel sneered. "You have not the brilliance. You are good enough only to steal in little dribs and drabs. You fool."

"Fool enough to almost kill you, wasn't I?" Kirby winced and bemoaned his ruined foot.

"Your man downstairs, Kirby," Garrick said, "the one with the ivory walking stick, he'll confess it was your idea to push Daniel into the street."

Daisy shivered at the scene that conjured.

"I bloody well paid him enough to never say a word!" Kirby blurted.

"But do you think he'll hang by himself," Garrick continued, "if he'll never be able to use the money you paid him for the service? Really, Kirby. I am shocked at your childish belief that men like that have any standards."

Kirby hung his head. "I want a surgeon. Morphine, at least!"

Mr. Thynne, who had stood listening attentively this whole time, tapped his fingers to his lips. "I don't think that's a good idea for you. Kirby is your name?"

"*Why not?* Who the hell are you?"

"Runner, sir. Runner."

"Get me something for this!" Kirby gestured like a madman to his foot.

"Later. But for now," Thynne said, his skinny brows knitted tight, "pain gives us the truth. Wouldn't you say?"

"I will kill you, Runner."

"Doubt it, sir. I do. Now. Let me understand this." He pointed at Kirby. "You joined with Sir Daniel"—he pointed at him in turn—"in a scheme to take supplies from the army so they suffered defeat. It worked and then it didn't. Kirby, you blackmailed Sir Daniel, and planned a murder, and all of you blamed all this on Mr. Garrick Ruxton."

Neither of the accused did more than stare at Thynne and shake their heads.

"I see. No argument from you, then. Well!" The Runner rubbed his hands together in what Daisy would have called glee. "Murder is a charge I will definitely see prosecuted. Treason is one I refer to king and country."

Chapter Twenty-Three

LATE THAT NIGHT, order had finally come to the house. Elizabeth and Susana were quiet, as yet unaware of the challenges their father faced. They were at peace, sleeping in their beds. All the servants, including the unruffled Nuttley, had taken to their own beds long ago. Garrick had ordered a feast brought from a local hotel dining room, and all of them had eaten well in the servants' dining hall and gone to bed early. Miller and his men had declared themselves the heroes of the day and joined together to go out to a nearby public house to hoist a few.

Thynne had consulted with Lord Courtenay, who had not arrived in time to hear the numerous confessions, but accepted Thynne's summary. He had agreed that Thynne should take Kirby into custody, but that he would return in the morning to the gaol with the prime minister's orders of confinement on the charge of treason.

Daniel remained in his bed. Irascible, testy, admitting to so many crimes, he was uncontrollable. He could harm himself. Both his physician and his surgeon advised removing all morphine from Daniel's presence. If he took it, it would hasten the inevitable. He would die soon of the poison that was in his own blood.

Garrick and Daisy vowed to each other they would keep the charge of treason from his daughters' knowledge for as long as they could. Forever, if possible.

They retired to their chambers as the ormolu clock struck eight that evening.

Garrick undressed her with an ease born of the many times he'd done it since their wedding. She, too, did her service to him in minutes.

"Brandy?" he asked her, his bottle in his hand after she refused to climb into bed and claimed nerves as her problem.

She walked the floor in their bedroom and agreed to a glass.

"Come sit with me," he said when both of them had a snifter in hand. He led her to the chaise longue, and there, with her resting against him in his warm embrace, she found at last some peace.

She put her glass on the small table and nestled close. "Do you think the scandal will destroy the shipping company?"

"No." He stroked his fingers down the length of her hair along her shoulder. "Well, I say that, but I am not certain. Who knows?"

"Everyone will know your innocence," she said, and raised her head to peer at him.

His smile was quick and faint. "I hope so."

"It would not be just to ruin you. Not after all this that you have suffered. Not after all your uncle has put you through."

To that, her husband said nothing.

"Thynne will stand up for you." The Runner had found one man from the group that attacked her that night in the carriage. The fellow had told the Runners that Rivers hired them, and it was Kirby who had hired Rivers. "Courtenay believes in you, too."

"He always did. Both of them always did, actually. Thynne could just never find any proof to vindicate me."

"Now we have it." She reached up and kissed his lips.

"Now we can live like everyone else."

She smiled at him with a growing joy. "Open our house. Have friends to dine. Maybe have a child."

His green eyes alight with kindness and certain sadness, he traced a fingertip down the arch of her cheek. "I long to kiss you every day, every hour, without fear there may be no more hours or no more days."

She sought to bring lights of desire to his countenance. "We will have many."

"Will we?" he asked with desperation in his voice.

She grew chilled. "Why wouldn't we?"

"The Allies will fight, and this time, there will be no stopping until Napoleon is gone from their doorstep. No island will be far enough for his exile."

She blinked, confused they suddenly spoke of Napoleon.

He cupped her cheek. "He will be gone, my darling. You can go home. It will be yours again. All of it."

"Ours!"

"You are the one of royal blood. I am but an Englishman of no title or wealth or import."

She grew frightened. Was he forsaking her? No. No! That could not be. "You are everything to me."

"I am the man you married out of necessity."

"What? No! You are the man I married because I wanted you. From the first moment you appeared to me. An angel in my midst. Like magic, you were there. And I knew!"

"Love at first sight?" His gaze poured over her in silent desire she saw and understood.

"Yes, yes, it was. It is." She pressed her hand to his heart. "You were my archangel come to aid me. Offering me friendship and help. Succor and…"

She would not ascribe love to him if he did not claim it himself. How foolish would that be? Yet she had. She had seen it in his face, in his deeds, in his words. In that she was not mistaken.

"Why did you marry me?" she asked—goading him, yes. But terrified as she had never been at anything else in her life, save his answer.

"Why would I want you? Ah, my darling. Aside from lovely

you—tall and regal and truthful and vulnerable—there was what you told me when I asked you why you would take an advertisement for a husband."

She shook her head. Nothing was in it, save fear he was telling her he cared not one whit for her. And she would run. Leave. Never return. Never love again. Anyone. She clutched his banyan. "What did I say?"

A fond look overtook his handsome face. "You were crushed you would not marry a husband. Crushed. And I had done it to you. Denied you." He touched a finger to the tears upon her cheek. Tears she did not know she'd wept. "You looked at me as if I were a mirage and said, 'I am alone. I have no one. I could remake my life, and your uncle sounded like a man who had given love and received it. Nothing finer could any man or woman wish for than to give and receive love. And I, for once in my life, wished it for myself.'"

He stared at her. "I knew then that you spoke words I too wished to declare. For once in my life, I wished love for myself." He pushed strands of her hair behind her ear. "I knew then I could love you. And, my darling, I do. I love you with all my heart."

She rejoiced. She kissed him fast and hard. "I knew it days ago, weeks ago."

"And you love me." In his eyes stood the truth that carried her to heaven.

"I do. It came to me as you did. Sweet and full of promise. I was honored to know you, proud to be yours. I love you, Garrick. I love you." She kissed his lips again, this time with the tenderness he bestowed on her.

"I love you, my darling, but now you must listen to me." He cupped her cheek. "Where you are concerned, I am selfish. I want you forever. I want you until I die. I want you fierce and strong and funny. But you have this other life, the one you had before me, and I think you need it. Will reclaim it. Must have it. The possibility to possess it all will come again. And I will take you to

France, and we will appear before the judges with your deeds and your bright perseverance. And you will win back the chateau and the land and all you lost. You deserve it. And I will not stand in your way."

"What are you saying?"

"If you want that and wish to enjoy it by yourself, I will never stand in your way. I want you to have all you wish for. I love you. Your strength, your dedication to me, to everyone. I love you. And no chateau, no land, no bit of earth could mean more to me than you."

She was all rage and sorrow. "I don't understand."

"If you wish to live in France, I will go with you if you wish it."

"I do!"

"But I cannot guarantee I will thrive there. I know much of France, but, my love, it is not my home. And soon, I will have charge of the business here. I cannot run it easily from a chateau in the countryside. And I need to operate the business for income, for the men who depend on their income through me. But also for my own sense of accomplishment."

"Oh, I do see that. All of it. I understand." She kissed his cheek. "I wanted the chateau and the land given my family. Wanted it badly. And I would do much to regain it. Even advertise for a husband to help me get it back. I never thought beyond the acquisition. Never planned what animals to nurture or crops to grow. I wanted it out of pride and family connection. I wanted it out of revenge and triumph. But as I looked at it all, the terrain, the house, the stables, all of it was strange to me. Not the visions I had of it in my mind. A child's mind.

"But I am no longer a child. I have had to put away those childish visions and keep the memories fond and fresh. But I grew up here in England. It was foreign to me. Only a refuge. Never my home. But one afternoon, I met you. And you showed me the kindness of a stranger, the concern of a man I could admire. So when you asked me to marry you, I accepted with hope in my heart that my instincts about you were correct. They were. They are. I love you, Garrick. And wherever you are, there is my heart, my hope, my desire for all we can be together. My home is where you are. No bit of earth, no building, can ever mean more to me than the hours and days and years I spend with you."

Tears brimmed in his eyes. He hugged her close, his lips to her crown. He trembled then lifted her face to him. "I have never loved another as I do you. No one compares to you. No one loves as you do. No one else will I ever need. I have loved you from that first moment in the parlor. You were so earnest, so demanding, and so lost. I loved you then. I love you now. Allow me, please, my darling, to love you each day we are given. Each crisis we bear together. Each gift we are given. Each challenge we face and endure and overcome. I love you. Will you stay with me and be my love here and anywhere we are together?"

She threw her arms around him. "Anywhere you are is where I love you."

"Always. With every beat of my heart. Each breath I take. I love you."

Epilogue

July 3, 1815

"THE MEN HAVE finished painting the guest bedrooms, ma'am." Nuttley was atwitter with all his responsibilities in Garrick and Daisy's new home. They'd decided they would sell the Chesterfield Street house. They had no need of it. Nor did they want it. Most of the staff there came with them to their new abode. All save Cora, who had been duped and used by men. Daisy had sent her to a service with a spare and reserved reference.

"Ma'am?" Nuttley urged her with a tremulous grin. She had been lost in her reverie again. "Would you care to come approve their work now?"

She rose from the small kitchen table in the family breakfast room and patted the heads of her charges, Elizabeth and Susana. Garrick and she had decided the other day that the girls would address her as "aunt" the same way they regarded Garrick as their uncle. "You finish this puzzle, will you?"

"And when you're done, you will return and we'll play cards?" Susana asked. Games were her favorite pastime, and since her father's death in April, she'd found peace in them as never before.

"I will."

Daisy followed Nuttley up the main stairs to the third floor. The house that Garrick had inherited was a fine bit of Georgian architecture. But it needed the refreshment of paint to the walls and sanding of floors, new furniture and drapes. For one month now, workmen had come each day to improve the house. Though all of them were in mourning for Daniel, Garrick had ordered the renovation of the house to begin. They had taken no honeymoon. The girls needed them to provide a stable environment and help them heal from the death of their beloved father. They would never tarnish his image in the girls' eyes. One did not do that to children.

All of the renovations were expensive, but, thank goodness, Garrick and she could afford it. She had sold many of the diamonds and invested the money to renovate the Molyneaux chateau and aid the farm, if and when she ever returned to France. That restoration would take much time. As for now, she and Garrick assessed what they might do from afar, because they would not go to France soon. Perhaps not for a year or two. As for her other assets, Daisy had also sold her aunt's parure of rubies and diamonds to a reputable jeweler for a good price and gave Garrick her one hundred and two pounds that she'd inherited. That money, Garrick told her, went into a trust for their first daughter.

She smiled now at that idea, a hand to her belly, as she took the stairs up. For soon she would tell Garrick what she knew to be true. She'd missed her past two months. She loved to make him smile.

She paused at the landing and looked down upon the finished walls and the marble-tiled foyer. A lovely home to live in for decades, this would be.

She turned on a grin and went up.

The first room they'd finished was the family breakfast room downstairs in a bright green and yellow. The bedrooms for themselves and the two girls came next. Then the salon. Cabinetmakers were busy building chairs and tables, chaises and sofas for all of it. Even Garrick's library and office would wait its turn for new furniture and paint. Eventually, perhaps next year, the craftsmen would be commissioned to finish a long dining room table so that Garrick and she could have dinner parties.

They would have many. The news of Daniel and Kirby's treason had shocked all the kingdom. At first, conjecture and rumor asked questions of Garrick's involvement. Even that he had married a Frenchwoman, a princess of royal blood, contributed to the speculation that Garrick had been involved. But declarations by Bow Street and by Whitehall, with the insistence of Lord Courtenay, won the day. Garrick was received well in public, at White's and in his business dealings. Ruxton & Company thrived. Even to the point that they transported precious cargo of gold to the Continent to help pay the expenses of the Allies' military.

Garrick automatically assumed the title of Sir Ruxton, and he was now Ninth Baronet BeauClaire of Ashford. Daisy found it odd to be addressed as Lady Ruxton. For so long, she had felt afloat, dispossessed of her family, her heritage. Taking the honorific with her husband, however, was thrilling. She vowed to do the name proud. For Elizabeth and Susana. For her husband. For herself.

Daisy had done nothing regarding her deeds to her lands. The past few months had been chaotic in France. Napoleon had arrived in Paris and summoned an army that was so debilitated it did not survive the dedication of the Allies and the determination of Wellington. Garrick's shipments of goods, delivered in the right numbers and on time, had contributed to the victory at Waterloo. The little corporal had run back to Paris afterward and abdicated once again. Two days ago, the British government ordered him banished to a distant island in the Atlantic. There, he would not so easily escape again.

She could return to France once more. The king on the throne was her distant cousin. She could go to Normandy and Paris to claim all that was hers. But she had so much to do here.

Her new home. A home built of love and respect. A home filled with comfort and peace.

She turned into the guest bedroom and smiled at the two workmen who stood aside for her to view the pale lavender of the walls.

"What do you think, my love?"

Garrick walked in behind her and wrapped his arms around her waist. He was not shy or ever reluctant to exhibit his affection for her in public. Nor was she. Love was rare. Respect, too, just as worthy to be displayed to others.

She spun into his embrace. "I do love the color. What do you think?"

"I like it. I like the fact that you chose these rooms to receive the southerly breezes."

"Do you really? Why is that?"

"Well, let me see." He gazed up at the ceiling, thinking. "Those breezes are gentle and kind."

"For guests, a good thing."

"Exactly."

"You don't think I should have used this room as my writing room?" They had debated that, but had chosen a small nook off their master boudoir for the purpose. She was working on completion of *Renard et Lapine*. Had even visited with Germaine Hammond, who was the publisher of the *Fleet-of-Heart Chronicle*, to ask if the lady might branch out in her business and publish books.

"No. If you get ideas in the middle of the day, you can easily retire to your little room and dash off your next thought."

She cupped his handsome jaw and tipped her head in question. "You think I will have occasion to work in the middle of the day?" She never had before.

"I believe you will." He dropped a kiss into her palm and eyed her purposely. "Won't you, my darling?"

She caught the sparkle in his seagrass gaze. "You rascal! Are you telling me you know?"

"What do I know, my love? That you are the sugar in my tea? The light in my step? The very beat of my heart?"

She chuckled. "You astonish me."

"A good thing, I'd say. I have to keep up with you, Lady Ruxton. My incomparable wife. Who is about to have our first child."

"One of many."

"I hold you to it, my love."

"They will have the honor and privilege to enjoy the finest man in the kingdom as their father."

"And the delight of having the most magnificent woman in the world as their mother." He swept back a strand of hair from her cheek. "Whom I adore, and will until the end of time."

Fleet-of-Heart Chronicle
Serving London and environs

NUMBER 10—Volume VII. Monday, July 3, 1815 Price~Sixpence Halfpenny
Published Mondays and Fridays

WANTED: Matrimony!

Frustrated in your search for domestic tranquility?

Search no more!

Place your advert with the *Fleet-of-Heart Chronicle*!

News sheet now totally devoted to marital bliss.

Find happiness in a thrice!

Affordable!

Exclusive. Confidential.

The strictest honour observed!

A Lady of education and morals seeks a third husband!

A Lady, aged thirty-two, having no children, although the widow of a second husband, possessing sixty thousand francs in ready money, wishes to marry a third time—and quickly so! She hopes for a kindly bachelor

between ages thirty-five and forty. He should have a sizable income, valued at between ninety and one hundred thousand francs. She has talents, education, and morals and wishes her spouse to possess same.

Responses to G. Hammond, Publisher, 140 Fleet St., London with all due speed as the lady wishes to wed within the month!

A bachelor, aged fifty-five, an agreeable and healthy person of handsome stature, with brown hair and eyes, mouth of good size and perfect white teeth, and fond of the pleasures which life permits, wishes to marry a lady of good birth and happy disposition between ages eighteen and twenty-five. She need not possess a trade, only beauty. He has a respectable practice within his village of clerk to the local magistrate and undertaker to the local coroner.

Responses to G. Hammond, Publisher, 140 Fleet Street, London, to be forwarded to him in Canterbury.

About the Author

Cerise DeLand loves to write about dashing heroes and the sassy women they adore. Whether she's penning historical romances or contemporaries, she has received praise for her poetic elegance and accuracy of detail.

An award-winning author of more than 50 novels, she's been published since 1991 by Pocket Books, St. Martin's Press, Kensington and independent presses. Her books have been monthly selections of the Doubleday Book Club and the Mystery Guild. Plus she's won nominations and awards for Best Historical of the Year, Best Regency and scores of rave reviews from *Romantic Times, Affair de Coeur, Publisher's Weekly* and more.

To research, she's dived into the oldest texts and dustiest library shelves. She's also traveled abroad, trusty notebook and pen in hand, to visit the chateaux and country homes she loves to people with her own imaginary characters.

And at home every day? She loves to cook, hates to dust, goes swimming at least once a week and tries (desperately) to grow vegetables in her arid backyard in south Texas!